TWISTED TRUTHS

Stories from the Irish

Selected by Brian Ó Conchubhair

Foreword by Colm Tóibín

Cló Iar-Chonnacht
Indreabhán
Conamara

First Published 2011

Stories © Cló Iar-Chonnacht/the authors, 2011
Foreword © Colm Tóibín, 2011
Introduction © Brian Ó Conchubhair, 2011

Publisher: Cló Iar-Chonnacht, Indreabhán, Co. na Gaillimhe.
        Tel: 091–593307   Fax: 091–593362   e-mail: cic@iol.ie

Printing: Brunswick Press, Dublin.

ISBN 978-1–905560–71–4

Editor: Alan Hayes
Typesetting: Arlen House
Cover artwork: Pauline Bewick
detail from 'Ballet Dancer and Orchestra', (2010), watercolour/acrylic, 142cm x 71cm

Cló Iar-Chonnacht receives financial assistance from The Arts Council.

CONTENTS

Colm Tóibín

In the summer of 1901, while staying at Coole Park, W. B. Yeats had a dream. He told Lady Gregory that his dream was:

> almost as distinct as a vision, of a cottage where there was well-being and firelight and talk of a marriage, and into the midst of that cottage there came an old woman in a long cloak

who was:

> Ireland herself, that Cathleen ni Houlihan for whom so many songs have been sung, and about whom so many stories have been told and for whose sake so many have gone to their death.

Yeats and Lady Gregory set to work. When the play was performed in Dublin in 1902, with Maud Gonne in the role of Cathleen, Yeats claimed sole authorship, as he did during the Playboy riots in 1907, as he did again later when he wondered if 'that play of mine sent out/ Certain men the English shot'.

The typescript of the play is among Lady Gregory's papers in the Berg Collection at the New York Public Library. On the first page, she wrote in pencil 'All this mine alone' and on one of the last pages: 'This with WBY'. In a diary entry in 1925 she complained that Yeats's refusal to acknowledge her as the co-author was 'rather hard on me'. When her family urged her to insist in public that she was the co-author, she said that she could not take from Yeats 'any part of what had proved, after all, his one real popular success.'

Yeats wrote the transformation scene, and the chant of the old woman at the end; such scenes came naturally to him, since his mind moved easily among metaphors and symbols. But he could not write naturalistic dialogue, he could not write ordinary peasant speech, or set a domestic scene. The play, as created by both authors, had an extraordinary power over the audience, and helped set the tone for a strand of Irish writing in the twentieth century.

This idea of a tone which was so uncertain that it needed two imaginations to create, a style which mixed the plain and the real with fantasy and the possibility of transformation, was not invented by Yeats and Lady Gregory alone; nor was it something which belonged only to Ireland either. They wrote that play at a time when doubleness was all the rage, when, for example, a number of writers in London, none of them English, set about creating powerful stories in which the personality itself seemed open to rupture and division. These were the years, as Karl Miller wrote in his book, *Doubles*, when 'a hunger for pseudonyms, masks, new identities, new conceptions of human nature, declared itself.'

One of the writers was Robert Louis Stevenson whose *The Strange Case of Dr Jekyll and Mr Hyde* appeared in 1886. Thus Dr Jekyll could announce with full conviction: 'This, too, was myself' as he became 'a stranger in his own house'. Jekyll:

> learned to recognise the thorough and primitive duality of man; I saw that, of the two natures that contended in the field of my consciousness, even if I could rightly be said to be either, it was only because I was radically both.

So, too, a few years later Oscar Wilde set to work on the creation of his character Dorian Gray. Every man, W. B. Yeats pointed out in these same years, has 'some one scene, some one adventure, some one picture that is the image of his secret life.' In 1909, Joseph Conrad wrote his story 'The Secret Sharer', in which the captain of a ship is confronted with his precise double. 'It was, in the night, as though I had been faced by my own reflection in the depths of a sombre and immense mirror.' Conrad's narrator's refers to the interloper as 'my second self'. In August 1891, as he stayed at the Marine Hotel in Kingstown in Ireland, Henry James had the idea for his story 'The Private Life' in which the sociable writer in the drawing room could at the same moment be found alone with his other self in his study. In those years the writer was either two people, or he was nobody.

The doubleness was not merely thematic, but it was also stylistic. Stevenson, Wilde, Conrad and James set about forging a style in English prose which operated as a kind of mask for them. They took available systems – the adventure story, for example, or the costume drama, or the romance – and they set about playing with them, almost mocking them at times, or adding an elaborate layer of technical skill to them. None of them took the style they inherited at its word. Although they were deeply alert to what could be done with realism, it would be hard to call any of them a realist. They were engaged in a game with style and tone, and they did it the honour of playing it with immense skill and seriousness.

Thus when Synge, for example, wrote his great openings, the reader knew to move with caution; this territory was mined. When he wrote the first sentence to his book *The Aran Islands*: 'I am in Aranmore, sitting over a turf fire, listening to a murmur of Gaelic that is rising from a little public-house under my room', for example, it is clear that the simplicity is masking, or perhaps even evoking, a great complexity. And when Joyce wrote:

> Once upon a time and a very good time it was there was a moocow coming along the road and this moocow that was coming down along the road met a nicens little boy named baby tuckoo ...

the reader knew to be very careful.

In the case of Synge and Joyce, the very idea of narrative itself was under pressure. The function of form and tone was thus to register the pressure as much as tell the story. In *Ulysses*, Joyce would cause the novel to parody not only the story, and the idea of form and tone, but allow it to mock the very pressure itself. In an early radio play, 'All That Fall', Samuel Beckett has Mrs Rooney say, in response to her husband's accusation that she sounds like she is talking a dead language: 'Well, it will be dead in time, just like our own dear Gaelic, there is that to be said.'

For writers in Europe now, who write in Irish, or Catalan, or Basque, or Galician, the pressure to respond to Mrs Rooney is very great. It is equal perhaps to the pressure which exists within storytelling itself. Story, character and event have to do battle now with the most highly wrought narrative procedures. Every writer is alert to the idea that there is a lack of full conviction, a sort of deadness, in any fictional form; this is enabling and nourishing on one hand as it makes its way playfully into style, but it also is demanding, as it is so filled with echoes and so open to parody and indeed to fantasy.

These questions and pressures live in Irish writing from as early as the eighteenth century. It was not merely a question that two languages did battle, but also two versions of reality. Thus the tone in language which could make laws and regulations, could speak in Parliament and produce rhyming couplets seemed to have no connection to another tone of voice which allowed in chaos, madness, excess, mayhem and violence. Elizabeth Bowen insisted that the tone of Irish literature was invented or re-created by Swift. 'With Swift began the voice,' she wrote in her own hybrid voice.

For the two hundred and fifty years after Swift, the idea of linear time, say, in fiction, or words merely meaning what they said, or objects having an exact and precise value, or characters having a coherent agency, would be under constant pressure in Ireland in the literature written in Irish as much as the literature produced in English, or, in the case of Beckett, in French. So what you look for is the voice beneath the voice, the supernatural hovering over the natural, the shimmering rhythm in the ordinary sentence, the strange connection between the domestic story and its roots in myth and folktale, and the idea of time as something to be played with, rather than accepted as a rule. Thus history is a comedy from which we are trying to awake, as in Dara Ó Conaola's story 'Sorely Pressed' in which Daniel O'Connell enters the present, as he does in Alan Titley's 'The Judgement' as much as do figures from Portuguese history in the fiction of António Lobo Antunes.

Thus it seems natural also that the Killiney in Seán MacMathúna's 'The Queen of Killiney' is both a real place and has supernatural elements, and that his protagonist is a real man, but his body has functions which seem surreal. Swift would have recognised him, as indeed would Somerville and Ross have recognised the landscape, for the Irish landscape they evoked in even their most Anglo-Irish stories was filled with fairy forts and places with magical properties. So too both Swift and Flann O'Brien would recognise the sheer hilarious excess of MacMathúna's 'The Doomsday Club', and Swift would have relished the savage indignation in the tone and indeed the content of Mícheál Ó Ruairc's 'Cannibals', a contemporary version of 'A Modest Proposal'. This idea of the story as a site to explore not only areas of darkness within the self, but as a way to offer a dystopian vision, or a version of an alternative universe, is at the centre of Micheál Ó Conghaile's 'The Stolen Answer-Bag.' In Ó Conghaile's 'Whatever I Liked', the protagonist rails not against injustice, or the hurt done to him, but uses his objection to the very idea of life itself, indeed procreation, as his motive for murder. In his other stories notions of identity and the space it inhabits, both public and private, are playfully questioned and dramatised.

So, too, the argument between the protagonist and his mother-in-law in 'The Atheist', is filled with an undertow of first and last things, and has echoes of a folktale. Those same echoes reverberate with even greater force in Angela Bourke's dark and powerful story 'The Dark Island', but there are other sounds in the story too, sounds that move from the mythical into the modern, without allowing the two to lose sight of each other. 'The Dark Island' is one of the best examples we have of a story which allows a contemporary story to be given greater depth and seriousness as the elements of a folktale are allowed to nourish it.

There is an early paragraph in Éilís Ní Dhuibhne's 'Rushes' which is filled with that nourishing battle between scene-setting and something else, something more mysterious and rhythmically interesting in which the object becomes an image. The protagonist has come to a cottage 'like little Red Riding Hood' with her son:

> Within these things: light and shade. A turf fire. Mícheál and 'Peig Sayers', the cat, on one side of the hearth. Pádraig and Jim – my husband – on the other. An oil lamp on the table. Three faces gleaming in the twilight. Three glasses of whiskey also gleaming. Yellow, brown, gold, black. Dutch interior.

There is another sentence later in the same story which seems merely to do its work, to signify something almost precise and exact. It makes a difference, maybe, the knowledge that the sentence was translated, that it lived for a time in another language and then, as it was changed, some consideration had gone into it. Whatever happened, it contains here that shimmering aura which lifts language out of itself, allows it to enter the nervous system as much as the mind. The sentence is: 'Suddenly all the gardens are filled with the green spikes of the daffodils, pushing up from the winter earth.' This sentence has a strange beauty, its contours filled with a mysterious grace. It manages to be double in its effect – it conveys a meaning which moves the story on, but it also conveys a hidden emotion which gives the story its power.

In none of these stories is the known world taken for granted, is a recognisable society taken on its own terms. Thus fiction insists on its own authority, and its world is constructed with new rules. No one can take time or space for granted, and the body itself, as in Deirdre Brennan's 'The Banana Banshee' is a fictional space, open to suggestion. In Daithí Ó Muiri's 'Great and Small', nature itself, the smallest objects, are given human proportions, human feelings and the voice narrating sways between the real and surreal, as though both were equal to each other. The social world here is limited and circumscribed; there are many solitary and strange individuals in these stories such as the collector in Gabriel Rosenstock's 'The Khrushchev Shoe' or the man in the toilet in Micheál Ó Conghaile's 'The Closeted Pensioner'.

In some of the stories, the concept of story itself is mocked and played with from the start. The second paragraph of Séamas Mac Annaidh's 'The Three Clichés' begins:

You're going to enjoy this one, for believe it or believe it not, this is a true full-blooded controversial metafictional short story, or to put it another way, this is a work of art that is totally contrived, artificial, deliberately assembled; it's pompous, self-conscious and minimalist and is about absolutely nothing, but itself.

The reader will have noted the irony around the word 'true'. The title of Fionntán de Brún's story is 'How the Author Died' and it begins by establishing that 'clocks and watches cease to have any use.'

In all of these stories there is a strangeness around domestic life, domestic space. Space itself is moved out of the ordinary. Therefore, when Dáithí Sproule's 'There is Someone Else Living Here' opens with a couple watching television in a quiet house in a quiet street, it is clear that the drama will not arise from the domestic, but from space being disrupted. So too with civil space which will, in Alan Titley's 'The Judgement' not be filled by citizens, but by angels. And if there are angels, then there will also appear 'a motley collection of emaciated corpses, rotting bodies, skeletons, skiffs, cadavers and carcasses'.

What each writer in this book is dealing with, then, is freedom rather than restriction; they are seeking hybrids rather than pure traditions; they are at play in their fiction as much as they are at work. The language they use may have noble and ancient roots, but it is how the roots were broken and how the weeds grew around which interest the writers. In an essay, 'The Divided Mind', the poet Thomas Kinsella pondered on what it meant to be an Irish writer and write in English: 'I believe that silence, on the whole, is the real condition of Irish literature in the nineteenth century ... Beyond the nineteenth century there is a great cultural blur.' He wondered if there was a virtue for literature, for poetry, in 'the continuity of a tradition.' He believed there was not. 'But for the present,' he wrote:

> it seems that every writer has to make the imaginative grasp at identity for himself; and if he can find no means in his inheritance to suit him, he will have to start from scratch.

This book is an ambiguous display of the virtues of that starting by writers also alert to the echoes of earlier tradition, and the freedom such fusion offers, the story it tells.

THE TWISTING OF TRADITION:
THE POSTMODERN IRISH-LANGUAGE SHORT STORY

Brian Ó Conchubhair

> 'Things that the Irish not only never said,
> but also could not by any possibility say'
> – *Ristéard de Hindeberg*

The coupling of postmodernism and Irish-language folklore may at first glance seem as incongruous as many of the stories in this anthology. Admittedly many of these pieces fail to offer a traditional story: they are narrated by incoherent and unreliable individuals who, while blessed with vivid imaginations, seem smugly content to ignore standard conventions of plot, character and linear progression and intent on frustrating and confusing readers. Despite their contemporary temporal settings and locations, these stories are nonetheless marked by the energy, imagination and verve of traditional Irish folklore and folktales.

The collection and dissemination of folklore as an antidote to cultural effeteness is a defining motif of numerous European revivals. The culture of the Volk, understood initially by German cultural theorists to be the timeless repository of indigenous wisdom and insight, was honed and sanctified over generations. Personified in tales, songs, rhymes, riddles, proverbs, arts and crafts, this folk culture, in both style and spirit, contained the very essence of the nation and, consequently, the key to national regeneration and resurgence. This vernacular culture and its amorphous spirit provided a matrix for nationalist intellectuals to mould and shape as they steered their listless nations toward cultural rebirth and renewal. The Volk, whether conceptualised as 'romantic savages', 'last of the tribe', 'oral intellectuals' or 'exotic others' provided a radical alternative to the dominant social and cultural paradigm: for cultural nationalists folk culture offered not only an alternative to colonial culture but the basis for a social and moral revolution. In Ireland they offered primitivists such as J. M. Synge and W. B. Yeats the essence of a pre-Christian Celtic pagan past; for Irish Catholic intellectual leaders such as D. P. Moran and Pádraig Ua Duinnín, a fundamental antidote to pernicious Protestant materialism, urbanism and secularism; for cultural provocateurs such as Micheál Mac Liammóir, an alternative to prevailing orthodoxies.

The incorporation of folklore into the Irish canon not only empowered those previously disenfranchised – the rural and often unlettered informants and active tradition bearers – but also offered potential renewal to an ancient, but stilted, literary tradition. In addition, it provided accessible reading material in idiomatically rich vernacular Irish, material in short supply among the expanding network of Gaelic League branches and classes that populated the Ireland of the late nineteenth and early twentieth centuries. Irish revivalists' efforts to adapt folklore and folk motifs and integrate them within the modern short story form are for the most part unsatisfactory. The content deemed most likely to interest and inspire native speakers was that contained in existing folktales already in oral circulation in the Irish-speaking districts or *Gaeltachtaí*; hence it was these very stories that collectors targeted, edited, published and redistributed as reading material. The regurgitation and circularity of this approach failed to encourage, or reward, literary innovation or artistic experimentation. The tension between those authors who sought to reinvent the past through retrofitting folktales and re-parcelling antiquarianism, and those who sought to embrace mainstream European modernism is well attested in Irish-language critical discourse (O'Leary 1994, 2004, 2011). The resulting hybrid genre – part folktale, part modern short story – floats in a liminal area between transcribed oral tales and maladroit modern short stories, belonging clearly to neither genre but striving valiantly to honour both traditions (Ní Dhonnchadha 1981). Obliged to be indigenous and idiomatic on the one hand, yet eager to be innovative and in vogue on the other, they failed to satisfy either linguistic purists or cultural innovators. Despite some notable and important exceptions naturalistic and nationalistic impulses swamp all other traces and influences. The almost ubiquitous semi-mythical glorification of the *Gaeltacht*, the apotheosis of its inhabitants' heroic grandeur, the exaltation of their uncontaminated language and the bombastic bromides about their melodious speech and moral values were, it seemed, at odds with genuine literary achievement (Ó Torna 2005).

Writing, editing and critiquing oral texts – stories and tales – creates a tension given the inherent contradictions and paradoxical nature of the competing styles and aesthetics. In their efforts to capture and set down folktales in permanent print form, the patriotic linguistic-nationalists and grammarians failed to recognise that a text's meaning can, and often does, transcend the tyranny of print and grammar. In their haste to salvage as much precious folklore as possible from the looming vortex, they were blind to the very malleable and nuanced aesthetic underpinning and invigorating these highly evolved and artistic folktales. The permanence of print culture, where the written record serves as faithful preserver of a singular, empirical 'truth' is constantly at odds with orality's mutability and flexible essence. The characteristics of print logic – multiplicity, systematization, and fixity – stand in stark contrast to oral discourse where a 'speaker's meaning is preserved in the mind of the listener: the actual words, syntax, and intonation are ephemeral, they are rapidly exchanged for those interpreted meanings which can be preserved' (Hildyard & Olson 1982). The tension so evident in stories and criticism during the Free State period revolves around the contested roles of realism, supernaturalism, irrationalism, fantasy and non-rational folk belief – fairies, curses, charms, traditional practices and beliefs, taboos, stigmas, ill-fortune, fate, omens – in an Ireland rapidly, if somewhat reluctantly, embracing modernity. Despite the significant achievements of writers such as Pádraic Ó Conaire, folklore masquerading as modern literature was still commonplace in Irish-language literary discourse in the 1930s and 1940s. It would remain thus until the emergence of Myles na Gopaleen and Máirtín Ó Cadhain in prose and Máirtín Ó Direáin and Seán Ó Ríordáin in poetry in the post-World War II era. As a generative framework for understanding human behaviour with its own discourse, the eventual rejection of folklore/folk wisdom as a legitimate basis for contemporary modern literature in favour of a modernist aesthetic and style may be construed as a fundamental shift from one ideological framework to another. The transition may have been torturously slow, uneven and faltering, but Ó Cadhain's post World War II writing represented the undeniable (re)emergence of literary modernism in Irish-language literary discourse. Literary modernism had firmly arrived in Irish.

If modernism replaced folklore as the dominant literary and aesthetic style, its reign, however, was relatively short lived. The emergence of non-realism as a dominant style in Irish-language discourse marked the 1980s (Ní Annracháin 1994). These non-realistic developments – introversion, self-obsession, morose humour and tendencies toward the fantastic – were linked to the fate of Irish as a minority language in an English-speaking world and the growing perceived threat of cultural homogenisation with Ireland's recent membership of the European Economic Community (later European Union). Literary critics considered such developments a consequence of authors' inability to create successful realist urban fiction, further proof of the symbiotic link between the language and its rural peasant roots and incompatibility with the forces of modernity (Mac Giolla Léith 1991; Nic Eoin 2005). Such interpretations are tempting: partly because of the marginal linguistic state of Irish and partly because of its identification with countercultural protest. This reading interprets such manifestations as a reflection of the ambiguous and marginalised cultural and sociocultural state of the language and its speakers in modern Ireland.

Yet, the reality may be far different. Rather than representing a reluctance or resistance to deal with urban reality, these stories may represent not only a proactive engagement and willing embrace of a postmodernist style and sensibility, but a partial return to a folkloric aesthetic (Ní Annracháin 1999). The compression of time, distance and space by advances in electronic communications, the urbanisation, and later globalisation, of Ireland, and the ease and fluidity of socio-economic relations created a crisis of representation and identity, not only among Irish speakers, but globally. Traditional grand narratives and metanarratives, so long the cornerstone of our common knowledge, are disgraced, discredited or disregarded. This disenchantment with the dominant narratives of the past and the failure to replace them with new grand narratives has led to a focus on micro narratives, but the major questions and concerns remain as stories by MacMathúna and Titley in this anthology demonstrate. The paradox of this postmodern position is that having scrutinised all doctrines and principles with an intense skepticism, it ultimately demonstrates its own flaws, as Ní Dhuibhne, MacMathúna and Titley make abundantly clear. Dismissing religion or even assassinating God, as Titley envisions, does not solve the problems of human existence. It simply shifts the responsibility and reassigns the burden. Problems and dilemmas do not disappear, but re-emerge. Neither the Enlightenment nor modernism have provided satisfactory answers to the age-old questions that folklore attempted to engage.

To appreciate these stories' artistry, technique and style may call for an aesthetic appreciation similar to that of the nineteenth-century unlettered peasant rather than the 'educated' modern citizen. Postmodern stories are never comforting and rarely tasteful in the traditional sense. Indeed they are the very antithesis of those stories which presented a wholesome image of Ireland, the saintly *Gaeltacht* and homely Irish speakers – underprivileged in material terms, but wealthy in vernacular culture – pious and brave, patriotic and blissful. These stories will not appeal to those comfortable or complacent about Irish culture as they challenge many of the sacred cows and eschew standard interpretations. Readers familiar with postmodernism will recognise its standard stylistic motifs: difference (Brennan, Ní Dhuibhne), duplication (Sproule, Rosenstock), the use of hyper-reality (Bourke, Ó Conaola, Ó Conghaile, Ó Muirí) to undermine and destabilise identities), historical progress (Titley), and epistemic certainty (de Brún, Ó Ruairc). These stories create space and awareness of multiple meanings, ambiguities and contradictions as well as a mischievous and playful approach to non-standard language to critique, probe, question and challenge. As behoves postmodern literature in general, these stories rely heavily on fragmentation, paradox, unreliable narrators and pastiche to critique the Enlightenment idea implicit in modernism and the notion of an absolute truth. Faced with an Ireland that has become increasing fragmented – socially, linguistically, politically and economically – and where the hierarchical and stratified social order has gradually collapsed in the light of scandals, tribunals and controversies, these stories attempt to come to grips not only with the role of the Irish language and of Irish-language speakers, but with the human experience. In doing so they achieve a universal voice and an appeal that extends beyond the language of their creation and speaks to a wider, plurilingual audience. The world presented in these stories is dominated by the ephemeral, the discontinuous and the chaotic – experiences all too familiar not only to Irish speakers in the Anglo-American globalised cultural and linguistic world, but to marginalised groups and individuals globally, regardless of language, heritage, ethnicity or colour.

These stories are post-local and international in appeal and, other than their embrace of Irish folklore as a springboard, are neither local nor provincial. Playfully and indulgently, they challenge us to face the immediate issues of their time, the incessant need to answer questions about who we are and what and why we believe. Inherent in these stories is a deep seated distrust and antipathy toward authority, especially in any totalising form. Existing in a non-rational world, inhabited by unreliable narrators with competing and contradictory versions of events, these stories eschew easy choices and binary oppositions and fixed categories. The use of pastiche, collage (Mac Annaidh) and the blending of high and low culture, native and foreign elements, pure and impure fundamentals, English and Irish languages (Ní Dhuibhne, Titley) and even the use of transliteration and hybrid forms of language contribute to the enhanced interrogation at multiple levels of the very notion of a single, definable, defendable truth. There are ultimately, these stories suggest, multiple competing truths, manifold levels of contradictory meaning, and no single satisfactory answer; rather there are multiple versions, contending realities and contradictory truths: truths that we may twist, bend and shape to give meaning, solace and hope to ourselves and others as occasions and circumstances demand.

The authors here are *Gaeltacht* and *Galltacht* born, tradition bearers, heritage speakers and language-learners, but all share a common vision. That vision finds its context not in the ghetto of minority languages and minor literatures, but in the global literary phenomenon of postmodernism. Rather than consider the preference for employing such narrative strategies as demonstrating literary isolationism or irrelevancy, it may be viewed as a conscious choice to seek communion and common ground with global writers in coming to terms with contemporary existence in a world – dominated by reality television, media spin, trivial tweeting and instant gratification – where prevailing belief systems no longer hold sway, and nostalgia for the past is insufficient. These stories acknowledge an understanding of reality as a construct, a mutually agreed and sanctioned construct, but for each construction we can offer our own particular and personal realities and twisted truths.

The postmodern Irish-language short story may appear irreducibly unrelated to the cultural artifact produced by the early Revivalists. But its tension with the metanarrative, its rejection of dominant discourse, realism, and rationalism, and its embrace of impurities and contamination are not so much a radical self-authentication as a return to basics. This trend should be recognised in a broader context and acknowledged less as an abandonment of established, albeit relatively new, aesthetics than a reconnection with earlier pre-Revival aesthetics values. The fun and the fantastic, the weird and the wonderful, the magic and the miraculous are in vogue once again in contemporary Irish-language literature, just as they were a long, long time ago in a far distant place.

Hildyard, A. & Olson, D. 1982. 'On the comprehension and memory of oral vs. written discourse', in Deborah Tannen (ed.) *Spoken & Written Language*. Norwood, New Jersey: Ablex.

Mac Giolla Léith, Caoimhín. 1991. '"Cuma faoin scéal": Gné d'Úrscéalaíocht na Gaeilge', *Léachtaí Cholm Cille* XXI, 6–26.

Ní Annracháin, Máire. 1994. 'An tSuibiacht Abú, an tSuibiacht Amú', in Seosamh Ó Murchú, Micheál Ó Cearúil & Antain Mag Shamhráin (eds.) *Oghma* 6, 11–22.

Ní Annracháin, Máire. 1999. 'Litríocht na Gaeilge i dtreo na mílaoise', in Micheál Ó Cearúil (ed.) *An Aimsir Óg*, 14–25.

Nic Eoin, Máirín. 2005. *Trén bhFearann Breac: An Díláithriú cultúir agus Nualitríocht na Gaeilge*. Baile Átha Cliath: Cois Life. 406–36.

Ní Dhonnchadha, Aisling. 1981. *An Gearrscéal sa Ghaeilge*. Baile Átha Cliath: An Clóchomhar Tta.

O'Leary, Philip. 1994. *The Prose Literature of the Gaelic Revival 1881–1921: Ideology and Innovation*. Pennsylvania: The Pennsylvania State University Press.

O'Leary, Philip. 2010. *Irish Interior: Keeping Faith with the Past in Gaelic Prose, 1921–1939*. Dublin: UCD Press.

O'Leary, Philip. 2011. *Writing Beyond the Revival: Facing the Future in Gaelic Prose, 1940–1951*. Dublin: UCD Press.

Ó Torna, Caitríona. 2005. *Cruthú na Gaeltachta 1893–1922*. Baile Átha Cliath: Cois Life.

TWISTED TRUTHS

THE QUEEN OF KILLINEY

Seán MacMathúna

Dinny Long, TD, was too wise to get married and too young to recognise the pain of loneliness. At forty-four, his name was as familiar to his constituents as was their brand of cornflakes, Land Rover, or cure for scour in cattle. He had an intense feeling for geography. He lived within thirty yards of his constituency boundary, and he knew that if he lived any closer, his constituents would accuse him of trying to escape. He lived close enough to Dublin to visit his mistress twice a week and far away enough to be safe from the marauding hordes of scavengers when the country had a debt of forty billion and the dole would be stopped.

He was busy; but sometimes busy became hectic and hectic became insane. Then he withdrew to Bowlawling House, Georgian Residence, c.300 acres plus eight loose boxes – home. And his housekeeper, Kitty, who could charm away callers as well as she could jug a hare. But they still pursued him up the gravel drive, on foot, bikes, mercs and now and again an oddity on a horse.

'Mercs are the worst, they walk down on you,' said Kitty.

They almost did, pushing past her, saying firmly, 'Tell Mr Long it's only a minute.'

It never was. It was an eternity of 'Swing this for me and I'll canvass for you' or, worse, 'Swing this for me for I canvassed for you'. It was all a litany of supplication that dulled his mind, and which he barely acknowledged by nodding at the pauses. Humanity had become transparent. In an ironic moment he had the idea of getting a badge with 'Support your local swinger' written on it, but Sambo said no, it would only draw them on. When things really got bad, Dinny sought out the damp quiet of the cellars in Bowlawling. They were filled with the remnants of former occupants. In such moments he leafed through old diaries, fingered books spotted with mould, and, closing his eyes, drew their antique fragrance deep within him. If ever he were free he would bottle the smell of old books and hawk it through the world to lost romantics. And photographs. A woman, a parasol, in the doorway of Bowlawling, smiling, all washed in the sepia of eternity. Scrawled on the back with surging flourish 'Remember Ballskarney! Love for ever, Rodney.' In such moments he would press the object to his heart and whisper 'Maybe I do love humanity after all.'

But out of the cellars he had to come, into the bright insanity of day. And that meant Sambo. Dinny walked into the clinic in Rathgrew. Sambo had his kinky snakeskin boots on the desk.

'Howdy, Pal, just havin' me some shuteye. Git off your feet and have a seat.'

'Sambo,' said Dinny, standing in the middle of the clinic, 'this place is looking more and more like the OK Corral.'

Sambo drew on a large Havana and blew a smoke-ring towards the ceiling. 'Gawd damn, Dinny, you're real ornery, guess it's gonna be one o' them days.'

Dinny eyed the walls of the clinic – a paradox of posters advertising Sambo Reilly as a Bronco Buster, a cowpoke, a gambler on a Mississippi sternwheeler, a laster of nine seconds on a Texas Longhorn, all set against the posters of the pro-life campaign. Nowhere did the name Dinny Long appear; more and more Sambo was taking over the clinic.

This suited Dinny. 'Sambo, I don't mind you wearing a stetson because you have a face only a mother could love. It adds a bit of class, the cigar some flavour, but the spurs I object to. You're my election agent, secretary, fender-offer of *Gaeilgeoirí*. I need you but you're trying to escape into a western. Spurs out.'

Sambo didn't move. He pulled the brim of his stetson down to the half-moons of his eyes and lay back farther on the swivel.

'Folks agettin' kinda nasty about mah face. Waal, ah guess there must be sumpin to it – guy rode into town yistahday, said I got a face like a corduroy trousers – gal way down Tucson way tells me ah got a face like an unmade bed.' Slowly he eased his boots onto the ground and removed the spurs. 'Dollar ninety-five – Maceys – only plastic.'

Sambo filled him in on the goings-on. Dinny was president, secretary, patron, committee member of so many bodies that he needed help. Sambo told him what funerals should be attended, weddings, christenings. But above all, he'd have to go down to the Rathgrew Community School, where he was chairman of the Board of Management. Detta Hearne, the Principal, needed him fast. 'The old gal's in a flap.'

And then the Amendment Campaign. Dinny eyed a number of placards that Sambo had made with markers. There was no double 'M' in amendment. It didn't matter, said Sambo, folks didn't care whether he was illiterate or not, they were all raring to vote against abortion. It was important that Dinny be associated with that response. The whole constituency was ninety-five percent Catholic farmers. But Dinny looked after everybody – Catholic, Protestant and

Atheist. The Atheist's name was Tom Ruddy and he snarled about God, Ethiopia and the price of drink.

Dinny felt dynamic and grabbed a hammer and nails and began to nail placards to the battens. Suddenly he stopped and said, 'Sambo, this is the way Christianity started.'

'How, Boss?'

'With a hammer and nails.' He paused in thought for a moment and then continued to hammer. Manual labour of the monotonous kind eased his mind.

'Boss, waddya think o' this abortion business?'

Dinny paused again. 'Sambo, my father told me once – in this politics business you don't think, you interpret. If I start thinking, I'm out of a job in the morning.'

Sambo wanted to know what he meant. Dinny was a thinker. Things stuck in his throat, especially in the Dáil. But they always vanished, not into thin air, but into his thin blood. Thinner and thinner.

The typewriter clicked; it was time to leave. Sambo had recently discovered its magic. Any moment the questions would start – spell this, spell that, a nicotined finger waiting for the answers. Dinny needed Sambo's flamboyance to flood him with votes and that was all. But sometimes Sambo went too far. If he was caught personating again, Dinny would have to give him a dressing down. Anyone in the constituency would know that face boiled in porridge.

Click, click. Dinny headed for the door. 'I'm going to need you Sunday night at the concert, bound to be a *Gaeilgeoir* problem.' Dinny didn't hate Irish. He even had one sentence – *Vótáil Donncha Ó Longaigh, Uimh. 1*. He knew that in Irish all the four-lettered words were three-lettered – fifteen in German – and that there were only three ways to have Irish. One, to be born into it; two, to pretend to have it; three, to have a ventriloquist. As he wasn't a hypocrite he rejected the second, but sometimes toyed with the third. Sambo had a way of putting a pint into a *Gaeilgeoir's* hand, and a way of talking pure cowpoke without subjunctives that stilled all linguistic differences. On his way out, he picked from a shelf a copy of the Irish Constitution, *Bunreacht na hÉireann*, and stuffed it into his pocket. Seeing as they were going to amend the Constitution, he might as well read the damn thing.

Down at the community school, Detta Hearne ruled with an iron fist. Her office was decorated with posters of babies and tiny tots, all proclaiming the sanctity of life. On the wall behind her was a huge replica of a voting paper. 'VOTE X TÁ/YES TO PROTECT LIFE'. She explained rapidly that he would be chairing the appointments board – and that there was a certain young lady part-time on the staff who had a good chance of getting the job. Detta wanted her stopped; out. She had recently been to England. Her health had improved immensely since that visit. Did Dinny understand? He nodded. She was also a member of the following organisations: Well-Woman's Centre, AIM, Women's Right to Choose, Rape Crisis Centre, Women's Political Association and the AFMFW. 'No way is she wanted here. She is trouble with a big T.' It was important that it happen today, because the girl was not beyond using influence.

Dinny tried to argue, but it was no use. Who else would be on the Board? Old political friends – Joe Heaslip, Cecil Falvey, Tadhg MacCarthy. And Seosamh Ó Mianáin. He was just one of the staff. She'd take care of him. She ranted on about the Fight, the Glory. Dinny found himself twisting *Bunreacht na hÉireann* in his hands. She was going to have a great school. There were the Brothers up the road and the convent down the road, and by God she'd drive both of them to the wall yet. Her lips snipped the words like scissors.

Dinny did what he was told. It was easy. The girl in question was in temperament identical to Detta. She had enough fire in her soul to set any school ablaze. She'd get a job somewhere else, he felt, as he crossed her name off the list.

Afterwards, as he walked the gravel with Tadhg Mac to the car, their footsteps sounding like chewing horses, Tadhg said, 'Did you get the irony? If the girl aborts – no job. If she has the baby – still no job.'

At the door of his car Dinny paused. 'The structure of society is a flimsy thing – it is vulnerable, a stand must be made.' He fell into the seat.

Things lingered on – wrong things in his mind. It was time for Jenny. Jenny was his favourite person, a roan Irish hunter who never answered him back. Although, once she had thrown him on the lawn, and the Chief standing on the steps of Bowlawling. He had raged at her, 'Jenny, you thundering fart, you whore out of the rag and bone yard, may you never foal again.' But the Chief had said it was all right, he fell off his horse too. Today, he allowed her to take him all the way across the fields to Faarness Wood. He threw himself upon the ground, listening to Jenny champ stray grass among the shadows. He watched the trees release the clouds one by one, by one. He searched his pockets for *Bunreacht na hÉireann*. He must have left it in the school.

Dinny loved Dublin, the freedom of a city where you could drink a pint without having your hand pumped by someone on the take, get a hamburger without being set upon by swingsters. He avoided the Stroke Triangle, between Mount Street, Stephen's Green and Dublin Castle, like the plague. Even Sambo agreed: 'Only Billy the Kid would go in there and come out with his hat on.' Sometimes when the whip was on, he had to go to the Dáil. He disliked it. He had made his maiden speech there a long time ago, on sewerage schemes. He had worn a blue pinstripe mohair suit with a rose in his buttonhole. Sealy, the political correspondent, who made TDs crawl all the way to Slea Head, had seen some irony in this and dubbed him 'Dinny the Swank'. It had stuck. His opponent in Rathgrew, Jack Halloran, who, according to polls, was narrowing the gap between them, had dubbed him 'Swing-along Dinny'. It was Jack Halloran that Dinny feared. Jack had beaten him to the Rathlickey disaster, where forty pigs were drowned. Jack Halloran was shown in *The Post*, standing, hat off, beside the trailer of dead pigs, a solemn look on his face. 'Halloran is as slow as the second coming of Christ,' was Sambo's verdict, however.

The freedom of Neasa's flat always overwhelmed Dinny. It was home not just because he paid for it; it was a safe house in good or bad times. And Neasa a beauty – he only went for beautiful women. She was also vivacious.

'Do you like me in this, should I wear pink – will the blue go with this? How about black? Are we going to the Dáil restaurant? Will Jamsey be there, and Finnegan? They're great crack. How's Sambo, I have cigars for him. Who's this Kitty? Why is she always gone when I go down? I could do Kitty's job better. I'm great with people.'

Dinny told her that with a face like hers, she'd only draw them on. She should see Kitty's face. Would he like to have dinner or did he want to go to bed now? She had chilli with red and green peppers – she had wine. He wasn't drinking. The blinds killed the sunshine and turned her bed to rose. He didn't just love her, he needed her. Only he knew that. And he'd have to marry her. Only she knew that.

He crossed Killiney Hill to his brother, Paddy, parish priest of Tigraskin. They were in his sitting room.

'Why can't you have a brandy, just one?'

Dinny wouldn't. 'This place reminds me of my clinic – no sign of God in it.' He glanced around the room, strewn with spears, flints, skulls and photographs of digs.

'This room is for me, brother, and as for God, God is everywhere. No need to remind him,' said Paddy, cupping his brandy in his hands.

'You'd have made a great politician,' said Dinny.

'There's very little difference,' was the reply. And then, 'Come up to Killiney Hill with me before it gets dark.'

'You still rootin' up there?'

Paddy said he was. He had discovered something. His eyes twinkled. But it had to be before it got dark.

They stood in the wood of Killiney Hill. It was a tangle of light and leafy shadows. Paddy stood in a glade and pointed out the three large stones. They were boundaries.

'Of what?' asked Dinny.

'Come,' said Paddy, 'look!' He pressed a spade into the turf and levered it back to reveal a widening crack.

Dinny peered in. 'What is it, a bone some dog buried?'

'No, it's an infant's skull.'

Dinny felt a shiver pass through him, going somewhere fast. Paddy told him it was a *cillíneach*, a graveyard for unbaptised infants and aborted foetuses. In Irish they said 'as lonely as a *cillíneach*'. No man could go in at night. Women were free. The dead had their power and the underprivileged dead the greatest power of all.

'To the people who live near here, Killiney Hill is but some rocks, some trees and a place for the dog to piss – they holiday in Spain, work in the city and drink in Dalkey – the media has swamped their souls – but the magic of Killiney waits – woe to those who tread on the magic of Killiney.'

The shadows were getting too long. They would have to go.

Back in the sitting room they talked some more. 'You talk like a pagan,' said Dinny.

'God loves pagans too,' replied Paddy.

'Superstition is wrong, it doubts the love of God,' said Dinny.

'You'd have made a good priest,' said Paddy.

They talked into the night. Dinny decided to walk over the hill to Neasa's flat. The night was dark. Late closers had cleared. The night was still. He could barely make out the path through the trees. Then he lost it and stumbled on. Suddenly he was in the glade. He stood at the boundary and looked in. He did not believe. He walked into the middle. Nothing, just the moon and all the stars. He pressed on until he saw a light through the trees. It was some kind of hotel. The moon shone on its sign-board: 'The Queen of Killiney. Open to Non-Residents'. He had never heard of it. Curiosity made him mount the steps. He stopped and listened. Something was wrong. He couldn't hear the city traffic. He pushed the door and entered a bar foyer. It was tasteful. 'Just like I'd design it myself,' he muttered.

'Were you talking to me?' said a voice full of laughter. In the shadow he saw a woman. As she moved into the light, he thought there was something familiar about her. But when she came up close, he knew.

'Incredible!' he said. 'You're the spitting image of Jean Simmons.'

She stopped in front of him, her eyes glassy with pleasure. 'Is that good or bad?' she asked, wetting her lips.

'The best,' he said. 'She was always my favourite actress, even more than Ursula Andress.'

'What was *she* like?' she asked, with fluttering eyelashes.

He looked into eyes that were the colour of faded jeans. She blushed slightly under his gaze, dropped her eyes, raised them again quizically, brushed a lock of hair and smiled.

'Ursula Andress is magnetic in an animal kind of way – sullen, demanding.'

'Go on,' said the girl.

'She radiates desire but never peace. She'd need a lion-tamer or weight-lifter or something.'

'I know what you mean,' she said, 'I'm not like that.'

'Not in a million years,' he said, looking into her sky-blue wells.

He thought of Jean Simmons, gorgeously frail, helpless and alone, always waiting to be rescued. Dependent beautiful Jean who couldn't buy a drink for herself or cross the road. If he were married to her, he would gladly spend his life buttering her bread and peeling her potatoes.

Suddenly he was aware that he was still staring into her eyes. He thought of Neasa and excused himself. 'I've got to go.'

She looked at him with disappointment, her fingers twisting the comer of her blouse. 'Please don't go yet. Stay and have a drink. It's lonely here, the hotel hasn't opened yet.'

'By Christ, I will have a drink – a big brandy and fast,' he heard himself saying. The girl radiated so much well-being that he felt himself recharging.

She brought a huge drink to the fireplace and, taking his arm, led him to a chair. Her hand excited him so much she could have pushed him off a cliff. She placed a pillow behind his head, and this made his toes open and shut. He began to relax so much he could hear the hiss. She sat beside him on a footstool. He looked down at her dress and could have sworn it was the one she wore in *The Big Country*.

'Do you go to films?' he asked.

No, she said, she was an orphan and knew nobody. Her name was Macha. It was lonely on the hill at night. She leaned over and whispered into his ear that twigs snapping in the scrub frightened her at night.

The glow of her breath in his ear and the proximity of her mouth made springs go twang within him. He looked down at the curve of her firm thigh, very much at home in her *Big Country* dress. When he had finished his drink and she asked him to see her as far as her door, which was down at the end of a long corridor, it seemed natural to say yes.

At the door she paused and said, 'Come in a minute.'

All he noticed was the black bedsheets trimmed in scarlet, colours he had once seen on his cousin's panties and which remained in his mind as symbols of carnality. But there was no need for symbols, for the real thing was in his arms and the ancient heritage of man ruled.

One morning a month later, Dinny Long got sick in the clinic. Sambo said, 'Boss, you been hittin' the booze again.'

Dinny looked as frail as a shadow in a bottle. He just shook his head at Sambo and said, 'Christ.'

After a week of his getting sick, Sambo was convinced it wasn't booze. 'You gotta see Doc Holliday, Dinny, fast.'

Seamus Cridden listened to the symptoms: forty-four years old, sick, would like to be young again. 'Male menopause – classic symptoms,' said Seamus. He prescribed a tracksuit and a tonic and to send Kitty up to him. As he departed, Seamus called after him, 'If it isn't that, you're pregnant!' His laughter followed Dinny all the way to the car.

He looked fine in his plum tracksuit, except for the middle-age spread the doctor had mentioned. Once while jogging in Killiney, he searched for The Queen of Killiney. Nothing but briars, heather and rocks. He stood at the Obelisk looking out to sea, his eyes clouded, seagulls drifting through his dreams.

One night he awoke. He called for Kitty. 'Have we any blackberry jam in the house?'

'No, but we have gooseberry, lemon curd and pear flan.'

'I want some blackberry jam and I want it now.' Kitty put on her coat and went looking for blackberry jam. Nothing surprised her.

Dinny asked Paddy about the hotel. 'No such hotel – Heights, Castle and Court, but no Queen.'

'Even in the past?'

'Negative. You look in poor shape, you should see a doctor.'

'Has there ever been a Queen of Killiney in this dark world and wide?' he wailed.

'No sir, never been – I'm the historian – you sure you won't have a drink? No, never been a place like that. Only Queen of Killiney I ever heard about was Macha.'

Dinny Long bundled himself out of the sofa and stood bolt upright so fast that Paddy was taken aback.

'You either take a drink or I call a doctor.' He poured the drink carefully and passed it to Dinny. 'Fella called Léinín, sixth century. Had five daughters: Druigan, Euigen, Luicill, Riomthach and Macha – five saints, feast day sixth of March. They built the old church in Killiney which still stands – hence the name Killiney, which means the church of the daughters of Léinín. The awful people who live around here never spare a thought for those girls. Macha was beautiful and called the Queen.'

'Did she look like Jean Simmons?'

Paddy smiled. 'You should drink more often. See, you're getting your sense of humour back. No, we haven't a snap of her. All I know is she's the patron saint of stillborn, unbaptised and aborted children.' He looked at his brother, a frail thing in the embrace of a wing chair. He was pale and remote.

'Do you believe in magic?' Dinny asked.

'God is magic.'

'I thought magic was the dark end of the spectrum.'

'God created the spectrum.'

'But –'

Dinny pulled the cord over his bed. He had never done it before. Kitty came in in a nightdress.

'Any peaches in the house?' he asked. 'I'm dying for a spoon of peaches.'

'No,' she said, 'but you never ate the blackberry jam. Will you have a spoonful of that?'

He grew fatter and depressed. One morning as he was shaving, something kicked him in the belly. He dropped the razor and backed all the way into the shower. He placed his hand on his stomach; then it kicked again. 'Crucified Jesus! Kitty, come up here fast!' he roared. She came tearing in. 'Jesus, I'm terrified, something is moving in my stomach.'

She made him sit on the bath and ran her hand expertly over the swelling. 'Get down on your knees and throw your head back.' He did so, and all the while, the hand on his stomach. She made him go on all fours, take a deep breath and hold it. He did. Shortly, she told him to get up.

'What's wrong with me?' he whined.

'It's only the baby,' she said.

For a long time he stared at her, and then he began to fall like a tree. She caught him in time and dragged him to his bed. When he was tucked in he began to wail. 'I'm a man – how could I have a baby?'

She fussed around the room. 'Look,' she said, 'I was midwife in this parish for twenty years. That's what they all said. "How could I be pregnant?" From the way it's sitting, I'd say it's a girl.'

'I love God,' said Dinny. 'Why would he do this to me? If it's a baby, how do we get it out?'

Kitty was hanging his clothes in the wardrobe. 'No problem getting it out. What I'd like to know is how did it get in? Do you want those peaches? The place below is filling up with stuff. Do you want them?'

'No. But I want the bottle of Redbreast, and I want it fast.'

'No drink, bad for the baby, no pills, aspros or tobacco.'

Suddenly he sat up. 'You wouldn't tell Sambo or Seamus Cridden? If word gets out, I'm ruined. I can make you rich. I'm in the agri business. I have shares in pubs and hotels from here to Helvick Head. Sure you won't tell anyone?'

'Nobody would believe it,' she said as she closed the door quietly.

He took to his bed, refused to go out, refused visitors. Word got out that he was dying. His opponent Jack Halloran called the whole thing 'Long D's journey into night' in *The Post*. The throng at the door kept Kitty going all day. Every second hour he called her up to make sure that it wasn't a phantom, air, something he ate, or a baby. When she pronounced it a baby, he wailed and thumped the pillows. On the way downstairs, she'd mutter about having two babies on her hands. All this fuss over a perfect pregnancy.

Kitty brought him every medical book she could find. He spent days going over the reproductive system. The whole thing was a mess. From the fallopian tubes to the vulva was a crazy plumbing system of nooks and crannies. He thanked the Lord he was a man. Then he remembered the baby and he sank into the pillows.

Kitty tuck her head in the door. 'Do you want those apricots?'

Paddy brought the bishop, who put his hand on the bulge.

'Liver,' he said. 'French liver, gets very big, seen it in Avignon.'

Dinny shook his head. 'Tell him, Paddy.'

Paddy said he didn't drink at all.

'Not a drop, at all, at all,' said the bishop. 'That's bad, makes a man mean and cranky. Then it's gluttony.'

'No, I hardly eat anything, not even blackberry jam or bloody apricots.'

Paddy told the bishop it was true, that he had become quite ascetic.

'He's dying so,' said the bishop. 'Would you like to go to St Clement's?'

Dinny shook his head vigorously. 'St Clement's is for the living dead,' he snarled.

'The living dead should be damn glad they're alive,' retorted the bishop. He gave Dinny his blessing and moved on to the next tragedy in the queue.

The Chief came to visit Dinny. Sambo waited outside the door, while they whispered inside. 'Sambo won't work for anybody 'cept you,' said the Chief, trying to persuade Dinny to change his mind.

'Then let Sambo work for himself – he'll do it hands down,' said Dinny.

The Chief gulped, looked at the door and thought aloud, 'Jesus, Sambo?'

Dinny felt himself laughing, but the baby stirred. Sambo would head the poll. His maiden speech would be a eulogy on Jesse James. Buswell's would stock his favourite cigars.

'Who can I turn to for help, Kitty?' he begged.

'Try these,' and she dropped some women's magazines on a tray. Knitting patterns: 'Is your husband jealous of your baby?', 'Knit your own babygro', 'Diet for Mums'.

Neasa came. Dinny sank into the blankets. 'Don't come near me, stay five yards away from me.' Neasa stood three yards away.

'Is it one of these transmitted diseases?'

'No,' said Dinny, 'just contagious. Stay away from me.'

It was Neasa's visit that did it. The courage and immorality of desperation brought him in a taxi to the Liberties in Dublin. He knocked at a house in Protestant Row. An old woman answered. 'I've got business for you,' said Dinny, as he pushed his way in, ' a girl in trouble.'

'If it's that kind of trouble, forget it, after what they did to that poor nurse.'

Dinny remembered. They had hanged her.

'This girl is rich.'

The woman hesitated. 'How rich?'

'Three thousand pounds.'

'For that kind of money, we'd do an elephant. I'll send for Mena.'

'Who's Mena?'

'Mena's for special tricks. Have your girl here at seven o'clock tonight.'

He spent the day around Camden Street, Wexford Street and in the back streets off St Patrick's Cathedral. He noted the shabbiness of the houses – the poverty of the people – and yet their happiness. He was no longer a man. Nor a woman. He was a hunted animal. Yet he was discovering himself, discovering humanity.

He was at the door at 7 pm sharp.

'Where's the girl?'.

'She'll be along – she's shy.' Cold sweat was breaking out on his forehead. 'I want to see the place first.'

They took him into a room in which there was a large tub in the middle of the floor. Beside it was a large electric boiler, bubbling. He eyed it suspiciously. On the table was a large bottle of CDC gin. He looked from the bath to the gin. He had read *Saturday Night and Sunday Morning*. And the revulsion returned.

'How much gin?' he asked.

'The lot,' they said. 'That way boiling water might move it.'

He hated gin. 'What's the sawdust on the floor for?'

Mena came forward to the table and opened a large box. She took out a needle as big and curved as a coat hanger. She held it up, gleaming in the light.

'How?' he asked.

'How do you think?' she said.

He felt his sphincter muscle close like a door in a storm. Quickly he dug into his pockets and pulled out a fistful of notes and flung them onto the table.

'She changed her mind,' he said leaving quickly and escaping into the clamour of Dublin's streets.

All night he spent walking the back streets off the Quays – Lotts, Great Strand Street, Liffey Street – there nobody knew him. The depressed and defeated found comfort in back streets. At twelve o'clock, black Liffey waters swelling from Ringsend, many, many mouthfuls. A ship, a man, somebody's newspaper flapping at his feet, unlit stores. Three more inches to eternity. He couldn't swim – it would be fast. But if his body washed up in Sandymount – the autopsy would find the child. Christ, he'd be in the *Guinness Book of Records*. His relatives would curse his name. He staggered back into a dockside doorway. If only he were a woman, he would gladly drown himself, herself.

'You OK?' It was an elderly Garda.

'Yeah, just looking for a parishioner of mine.' He passed himself off as a priest effortlessly. 'A girl.'

'She on the make – sailors?'

'No, just pregnant.'

'They all go to England now 'cept the very young and frightened.' He stamped his feet against the chill. 'Time was we hauled out three a week from Alexandra Basin – poor little drowned rags of things.' He stamped his feet again and left.

He took the boat to Liverpool. It took some time with directories before he found the expensive private clinic, east of the city, that he knew would do. He slunk in for the appointment like a thieving dog.

The room was opulent, more like a film set for a period drama, and the consultant's cultured mildness matched the scene. He wasn't in the least perturbed that the patient was male. Such genetic quirks were quite fascinating, but, of course, it would cost double. Or would he like to have the child perhaps, and put it up for adoption? And give it a name. Most Irish girls called them either Patrick or Mary. Dinny took fright at the suggestion. Such a thing would damage his career. And then he remembered he didn't have a career. He was finished with all that sordidness.

'I'm afraid I shall have to ask you to proceed with the, the –'

'Abortion?'

'The operation.'

'Yes, there's a great comfort in words.'

They offered him a local anaesthetic, but he asked to be knocked out, as it was a caesarean. When he awoke, there was a group of white-coated surgeons all around his bed.

'Is it over?' he croaked.

'Yes,' they said.

'Is it –?'

'Dead?' said one.

'Alive?' said another.

'No, it is not alive,' said somebody.

He felt a lump in his throat. The enormity of it all got to him. He felt loss.

'Who'd want to be a woman?'

'In Ireland,' they added.

'Was it a boy or a girl?'

They looked at him for a long time in silence. Then one of them beckoned to a nurse. She came forward, pushing a trolley to the bedside. This sent him under the bedclothes in terror. But they insisted that he look. He raised his head and looked at the trolley for a long time. It was a copy of the Irish Constitution, greatly enlarged. The doctors pointed to the words on the cover – *Bunreacht na hÉireann* – and asked what it meant.

'It is meaningless,' he answered in a far-away voice.

Translated by the author.

THE QUIZMASTERS

Seán MacMathúna

I lived in an old house by the river. Except for the swish of the water and the rafters which creaked in the cold, it was a silent house. At night things moved in the weeds. In winter I stood to my ankles in the cooling snow and gazed in wonder at the beauty of my house. In summer farmers gathered with implements to cut the things that had chanced to grow, releasing their sweet quick on the dry air. They planked their misshapen faces on the fence. 'Let us kill your weeds for you,' they implored, waving billhooks and sickles in the air. I smiled with contempt at them.

I sat in my house and listened to the thistles knock at my window in a breeze, reminding me that I do not meddle, that I do no violence to this earth. This creed left my house in disarray, but it is better to live in squalor with a philosophy than to be tidy and in pain.

I worked in a funny place: the Quiz School of St Patcheen. The Quizmasters were all funny too. If they saw me laugh they shook their fists in anger and scolded me. 'Shirker, layabout, get some work done.' One doesn't laugh in a funny school. There were also 325 brats in my school.

Brutus Iscariot was the headmaster; some said he was an escaped priest. He was very involved in the community. Every morning he put a 'Do Not Disturb' sign on his door and shinned down the drainpipe at the back of the school. I waited for him there one morning to discuss with him the matter of my money, which was in arrears. He came down with a thump, surprised.

'Oh, it's you, you feckless lazybones. When are you going to stop swinging the lead, pull up your socks, get off your ass and get down to the nitty gritty?'

'I've sent for some new quizzes,' I said. Then I paused for words. Should I call my money a stipend, gratuity, or honorarium? It was always in Latin, all part of the insult. 'What about my pay?' I blurted out.

He gave me the humourless smile of the escaped priest. 'Why do Quizmasters think so much about their pay, and so little about their reward?' and he squinted slyly up to heaven. Then he was gone in a flash down the boreen to say mass or open a dog show.

The Quizmasters never stayed out sick. Every morning they presented themselves for duty with crushing repetition. Nor did they ever interfere with the running of the school, except once in their lives: that's the day the Great Inspector himself came to visit. They say the angel of death is so busy in schools that he wears a mortar board; but he is efficient and kind to teachers. One great farewell thump in the chest, chalky hands grasp the air, before your brave pedagogue keels over to achieve the Great Horizontal. There he lies fallen until discovered by charwomen. But if the brats in their desks liked the Quizmaster, one usually went to Brutus and shouted, 'Another cardiac arrest in room Five A.' The brats were well used to the discipline of Quizmasters' funerals and their behaviour was good, for they would rather follow a

Quizmaster to his grave than follow him down the grey road of the third declension.

It is easy to fill a Quizmaster's position. Take Cerberus, for instance. He was originally trained for the jail next door to St Patcheen's, but he came in the wrong gate. Brutus immediately banished him to the classroom. They say old Cerberus never knew the difference. At night he wandered through the corridors communicating with doors and locks. Brutus got most of his teachers like that, anybody who came to the door, plumbers, gravediggers, and Jehovah's Witnesses. The butcher's boy was terrified of Brutus. His latest plan was to hang the sausages on the door-knocker and run. It was also because of Brutus' little habit that no inspectors would visit the school.

All the Quizmasters had long shadows but Rigormortis beat them all. He was very thin and carried a shadow twenty-three feet long. I know because I measured it one day when he wasn't looking. When he came in in the morning his shadow was in front of him spying out the corridor, but in the evening he had to drag it all the way out into the twilight. The other Quizmasters said that Rigormortis' shadow wasn't his own but belonged to something that had died. It was bad luck to step on it. He never approached the staff-shed in the yard but took his lunch by himself in the stone corridor. There he sat erect among the Ogham stones, his bony fingers filching bread from a paper bag, masticating each bite thirty times. He was proud of his thirty mastications and resulting good health. Rigormortis had no nickname, for Rigormortis could be likened to nothing, but things could be likened to Rigormortis like Celtic crosses and Ogham stones.

Size is very important; people don't realise that. I'm always measuring things. Interruptus, the first day he came to the Quiz School on his tricycle, was all of four and a half feet. He was unusually energetic; tall Quizmasters had to be wary of him or they were chinned in the crotch. One day when we were in the queue for our free pencils and rubbers, I noticed that Interruptus, who was in front of me, came up only to the bottom button of my waistcoat. When I explained to him that he was diminishing and would shortly have to be replaced, he disagreed with me. After that Interruptus cut me dead but took to wearing large hats. Nobody likes the truth.

Neither did Sufferinjaysus. Nobody ever spoke to Sufferinjaysus when they met him in the corridors, they just grunted in sympathy. He quizzed in a room with the curtains continually drawn. Two fires heated two generations of sweaty adolescent BO and Vick. Sufferinjaysus was concerned about his health. He stood in the room with his back to the fire and tossed Euclidian cuts to the brats. We borrowed fag-ends from each other; but when I heard his Local Defence Force boots drag in the corridor I had to be wary; to this day I think he owes me three. He was at his best in a pub when he enthused about body-building courses, and laughter, and sunshine in his childhood. But he was not graceful. I always say that those who are neither graceful nor elegant should be belted with porter bottles on the back of the head.

Vercingetorix was the greatest enigma of all. He was the Latin Quizmaster and was so calm and composed at all times that I was suspicious. He never did anything wrong like being sick, laughing or having a cardiac arrest. But his brothers told me his secret. Every Friday Vercingetorix covered the dining room table with copybooks to be corrected. The brothers, all six of them, bachelors, played poker by the fire. Suddenly something would happen to Vercingetorix's mind. For a split second in his week sanity took over. He would arise from the table trembling, looking strangely at the copybooks. 'I'm not a Quizmaster; I couldn't be one,' he'd say in revulsion.

'Yes you are,' the brothers would reply in unison.

'Well I deserve a good walloping so.'

Immediately the brothers would rush upon him, fetching him clouts and wallops until they brought him to the ground; while on the ground the oldest brother, who was a dwarf and had to wait his turn, would kick him in the crotch. Vercingetorix would then pass out with a delighted groan. After a while he'd pick himself up, the calmest man in Academia.

Ah, but Miss Parnassus, dear, darling Miss Parnassus. She is a born Quizmistress, quite literally. When she was seven days old her parents put chalk into her hand, and her dear little fist closed on it so tightly they couldn't feed her for days. I'm in love with Miss Parnassus. I was always asking her for chalk so that I could touch her, my little finger tarrying in her chalky palm. What a treat I say! She has a little hair on the tip of her nose that I would dearly like to play with. I was always pressing my rulers on her. I never gave rulers to anyone else. As a result I had lots and lots of them in my press, rulers of every kind, mind you. But she didn't seem to need them. I need them myself for measuring.

One day I told Miss Parnassus that I had a little house by the river in the country. She didn't seem interested. But because she is a born Quizmistress I knew she would relent when I told her about my invention for correcting essays. We went out on a spring day and walked in pedagogical communion by the river banks, she remarking on how gaily the little verbs twittered in their conjugations, while I pointed out the tidy nests the nouns built in their declensions.

My little house stood out proud from its greenery. Her face began to harden as she picked her way through my weeds. She almost balked at the briars at the front door. I took my Miss Parnassus into my house, a real live woman in my house. I almost felt weak. I hastened to her needs, dusting chairs for her, putting on the kettle, rinsing a cup for her and cushing the flies out the window. She stood in the middle of the floor, her eyes narrowing at the disarray of my parlour. I sat at her feet and gaped up at her, my eyes imploring some kindness.

'Why don't you kill those filthy weeds?' she asked. I lectured her on labels, pointing out that weeds were careless flowers, that the word weed was divisive and suggestive of a rank (no pun) that did not exist, that I preferred the word 'plant' for all green things.

'Well, why don't you clean up this?' she said, sweeping her hand in contempt at my little disarray. I looked about me and said that the things in my environment could depend on me not to destroy them. While the iron was hot I showed her my invention. From a purple box I took out four rubber stamps. On each was written, respectively, 'Very good', Very bad', 'Not so good', 'Not so bad.'

I grabbed a bundle of copies that had been in the corner for years and attacked them with the rubber stamps, each correction raising a cloud of dust.

'This is revolutionary,' I said with excitement and Miss Parnassus began to cough. In no time at all I dispatched forty of the wretched things back into the corner. But poor Miss Parnassus, she was still coughing and her eyes were red. She said she had flu and had to go. I escorted her tenderly to the door.

The next day I went to Miss Parnassus' room and with a big smile asked her for chalk. She said she had none. I retreated in consternation to my own roomful of brats. There I did a lot of thinking. I decided that if I were to be successful I would have to rearrange my furnishings, do some dusting perhaps.

That evening I wandered through the rooms of my house, noting the soiled shirts, the coffee stains, the cigarette ash, old shoes and dirty socks, beds that had never been made, broken delph and mildew. It was no use, I could not raise my hand against them.

So it went for days, reflecting, contemplating, vacillating, round and round my head went in agonizing circularity.

It happened on Friday. As soon as I opened the door I smelt it: floor polish. I opened my eyes wide at the shining hall. I inched my way in, in dread. All the floors shone like plates, walls scrubbed down, furniture polished and arranged in a pleasing fashion, neat rows of shining delph on the dresser, and the bathroom smelt of flowers. But I nearly lost my mind when I saw the bed. White starched sheets, pillows puffed out with pride, eiderdown arranged artistically. I took one jump and landed in the middle of it, yelping with joy, burying my face in the white coolness of the sheets. It was like an iced cake and I could have eaten it. I jumped and frolicked and tossed my pyjamas in the air. It brought me back to my childhood and the smell of the bread in the oven. Suddenly I got up and looked about me. Then I pranced around the house examining doors and windows. Everything was intact.

I have a host of good friends who would only be too willing to do all this in lieu of the many kindnesses which it is my nature to perform, but after a second glance I realised that this had been done by a woman. Bang went the friends theory. It was of course Miss Parnassus. Yes, I decided, this was performed out of love.

Next day I didn't ask her for any chalk. It is always better to let these things happen naturally. I stayed in my room smiling knowingly and listening for her dainty walk in the corridor. The brats were sniggering, they were quick to catch on to something. I don't mind, in love one can be tolerant. I even promised them new quizzes.

A few days later she had been there again. There were two laundry bags in the bathroom with labels attached to them, 'Coloureds', 'Whites.' In the kitchen delph was laid out for a meal. I was very pleased with her work, and I yelped with lonesome glee. I went on my now accustomed pilgrimage through the room, sniffing, and feeling, and peering at myself in mirrors. Then I noticed my whiskey. With great misgivings I extracted a ruler from my pocket and measured. I was right, there were about four half-ones missing. I slept very poorly that night for I would not be pleased with a tippling woman for a wife.

On the following Monday I rushed home on my bicycle without even bothering to fasten the clips on my trousers. More whiskey was gone and some food. I didn't mind about the food. Then I saw a note on the mantelpiece, 'Use the ashtrays please'. She was so right in a way. I was proud of the house, I was pleased with her work, but the whiskey was another matter. I decided to go to her the following day and have it out with her.

But alas, next day old Semper Virens, the Irish Quizmaster, achieved the Great Horizontal in the middle of the past subjunctive.

He had been sitting so long in his oaken rostrum that bark encased his knees. It had been decided that should he take root he should be cut down and made into rulers, a commodity in sore supply in my school. But no plans were ready. As they took old Semper Virens out through the hall in his coffin, Brutus Iscariot was livid with rage.

'Jesus Christ, what a day to get a hea- ... a cardiac arrest. Six weeks to the Leaving Certificate; where will it all end?' Only Semper Virens knew. Brutus had to give us all a half day and both brats and Quizmasters ran for the gate in high glee.

I went early to the house and that's how I discovered it all. There was a man in my kitchen with an apron on; he was washing dishes by the sink and hummed idly to himself. He didn't even look up.

'Who on earth are you and what are you doing in my house?' I was outraged. He had an unusual calmness about him which I found cheeky. His eyes were cold and expressionless. He never answered, just continued to hum in an empty fashion.

'Where did you get the key to come into my house?' I said, not without anger.

'I didn't come in,' he said, 'I was here always.'

'Now, now,' I said, 'I'll have none of that, not in my house.' I was quite firm, a quality I have learned from my profession.

'Come,' he said peremptorily. I followed him out to the hallway. 'Look,' he said and he pointed up at the attic trap door. It was open, and I gazed up at the square darkness.

'I never saw that before. You came down from there you say?'

'Yes, I have been there always, it's quite a nice place really.'

I found a stepladder and climbed up. I stuck my head into that inky blackness and I immediately felt a strange calm.

'I can't see anything,' I said. 'It's very dark.'

'You don't have to see anything, that's why I'm up there. It's also quiet and peaceful and nobody bothers you.'

'I suppose you're right. Is it dry?'

'As dry as a haystack. There's great shelter up there. There's wood, felt, and slate between you and the weather.'

'How do you spend your time up there?'

'In thought.'

'You're right too. I'm worn out from thought myself, but it's great isn't it?'

I came down and we went to the kitchen. I filled out whiskey for myself as I usually do in company. I think he looked rather perturbed about the whiskey, or maybe it was my feet.

'I'd appreciate it if you wouldn't put your feet on the table.'

I did as he said.

I'd like you to know that you're doing a grand job here, and I'm very grateful.'

'You needn't be grateful but be careful.' And he danced off around the house, flicking pictures and ornaments with a rag.

'You have a nice house,' he called from the hallway.

'We both have,' I shouted back, but I heard the attic trap door bang. I was alone again. I walked around my little palace a few times, as proud as an archdeacon. It was as clean as the chalice. I made tea and called up to him but he didn't answer. I have noticed that people of great depth are like that. I drank my tea and watched my purple thistles dance in the breeze. Company is a great thing.

Next day I went into Miss Parnassus' room. She charmed me with a gorgeous blush. She spoke crossly to me but I know that a good Quizmistress must be cross. I pressed some rulers on her but she refused. Then I spoke to her out of the side of my mouth about a certain house, telling her (and I winked at her) that it was a palace. The brats began to snigger and Miss Parnassus began to write on the blackboard. I shrugged at the brats and left the room.

I sat alone in the kitchen. After a while the man from the rafters alighted. He examined the house and I am proud to say it was perfect. While he helped himself to my whiskey I complained about Miss Parnassus.

'Have patience, man, you'll see her in this house yet.' He said it with such conviction that it fired my soul. I was getting fond of a man who could give such good advice.

For days I sat in my quizroom listening for her dainty walk in the corridor, knowing that each step brought her closer to me.

'What kind of work do you do?' he said one day to me. I explained about the Quiz School. But he wanted details. I explained about the importance of working at a higher level than the brats. He immediately stood on an old orange case.

'Like this?'

I nodded. Then I explained about the quiz book in the Quizmaster's hand, and the quizzes.

'What sort of quizzes?'

'Oh,' I said, 'the usual thing: who made the world. Depths of rivers, tombstones and anything generally about long ago.' He wanted to know what one did if they didn't answer.

'Correct them,' I said.

'How?'

'Roar,' I answered. The man from the rafters roared suddenly and gave me quite a fright.

'Is that all?' he asked. I mentioned the importance of learning to balance copybooks on the carrier of one's bicycle, of having at least three good jokes and of the folly of joining a pension scheme.

'Sure any old fool could do that,' he said. I hung my head with shame for I knew he spoke the truth, but my loyalty to the profession would not allow me to admit it.

On another occasion he said to me when he had alighted beside me, 'It grieves me to see a man of your potential and undoubted talents slaving your life away day in, day out.'

The truth of the statement shocked me. I got up on unsteady feet and grasped his hand. 'You are a true friend.' His hand was cold.

'Isn't it time you took a day off?'

'It certainly is, but what excuse could I have?'

'Sick.'

'Can't go sick. It's not permitted.'

'How about a heart attack?'

'You may only have one cardiac arrest. He who has the second one is never forgiven.'

We were silent for some time. Suddenly he slapped his hands together.

'I have it: you stay here and I will go in your place.' It was a brilliant idea but it was dangerous.

'They'd be quick to catch on to something like that where I work. You'd be recognised.'

'How would I? They don't know me. Anyway, I'm good with disguises.' I was uncomfortable.

'I'd be missed, I think.'

'Maybe not, try it. Just think of it, you could take a week given over to thought. Furthermore, I invite you to go the attic and really contemplate.'

That did it.

'Really, you wouldn't mind?'

'Certainly not, you are more than welcome.'

I was dying for a go at the attic; for too long I had been observing the man from the rafters and marvelling at what an attic could do for a man. With a mixture of foreboding and excitement I agreed, and we went to bed.

The sun was hardly up when the commotion in the kitchen awakened me; I trotted out in my bare feet. There he was on his knees with my rubber stamps, giving the copybooks hell.

'What's going on?'

'Correcting.'

'They've been there for years, some of those guys are dead.'

'It doesn't matter,' he said, 'their parents might like a souvenir. Anyway, the place has to be cleared.'

I looked down at the battered, dog-eared copies, stained with beer and coffee on the outside, and inside a cemetery of useless information.

At eight-thirty he tottered to the door with copies and piled them on the carrier of my bike. As he was about to mount he called out to me, 'By the way, what's your name?'

'Anthropos, Mr Anthropos,' I shouted back as I watched him sway away to work. I had misgivings, but I felt exhilarated at the prospect of the attic.

I stuck my head through the square darkness of the trap and entered upon the black peace of freedom from the flesh. I lay on his rug and felt the fears and regrets and terrors of work rise off my bones as a fine dust and float away into the unknown abyss of the attic. I developed a theory about attics and the wonderful way that wood, felt and slate protected a body from the hostile vibrations that beset ordinary rooms.

The door-bang signalled me to emerge from that sweet well of release and to enter the world of foolish men again. I shoved my head down to welcome the man back, but he was so busy with armfuls of copies that he didn't notice me. I alighted full of wonder at the world again and I followed him into the room.

'Well, how did the day go?' I said as I picked up a fistful of copies and flung them into the corner as is my wont. The man from the rafters grew very flustered at this and ran to the corner to retrieve them. He restacked them again. The copies were new and had freshly inked work on them.

'Got to keep the place tidy,' he said.

'Anybody say anything to you today?'

'No.'

'Anybody remark anything peculiar?'

'No. Have you not made tea yet?' He was disgruntled. He was so right to mention it.

During tea we had a conversation.

'Did Brutus Iscariot see you?'

'Yes.'

'I had a bloody great spiritual day in the attic.'

'Good, that's the place to be, the attic.'

'I feel marvellous after it, never had to lift my hand all day.'

'There you are, not a tap to do and all day to do it.'

'Oh, yes, and the peace of it all.'

We had a great conversation like that. I like the bit of company. He offered me the attic for the night. I gladly accepted.

When he came in the following evening, he still bustled about with more copies.

'What's this, I say,' he said, 'no beds made and no tea.' While I did the necessary housework he corrected furiously with my invention.

By sheer chance I happened to see one of the copies. 'Good Lord,' I said, 'what are you doing with Rigormortis' copies here?'

I'm just giving my friend Mr Rigormortis a helping hand,' he answered in a threatening manner.

I went through more of them. 'And Sufferinjaysus and Interruptus? Well I declare, their copies processed by my invention. I'm not at all pleased.'

He looked at me with that cool cheeky look of his. 'Rest assured that both Quiz School and Quizmasters are indebted to you for your invention.' This had a mollifying effect on me.

That night I had an attic dream; I dreamt that cold porridge was being flung into my eyes. And all the next day uneasy thoughts began to press in on my meditation. I stopped him at the door that evening and checked through his copybooks. My suspicions were correct: he had got to Miss Parnassus. I took his wretched copies and scattered them evenly throughout the house.

'Double-crosser,' I roared at him. 'And I thought you were my friend.' I shook the stepladder in anger. I know I look very terrible in a rage. He crept quietly up into the attic and I pulled the stepladder away.

'And stay up there from now on. I'm going to work tomorrow.'

He stuck his head down and looked dissatisfied. 'But I must go to work tomorrow or I will be accused of being sick.' I couldn't argue with a man whose face was upside-down.

I was up early, feet washed, shoes polished and all that. I was very pleased as I went into the staff-shed that morning; I like to assert myself. All Quizmasters were along the wall as usual. Brutus Iscariot detached himself from the noticeboard and came over to me.

'Well, my good man, and what can I do for you?'

'Nothing, I'm going to take my class.'

'You must be mistaken, you are not known here.'

'I'm Anthropos.' There was a dryness in my mouth.

'Where is Mr Anthropos this morning?' he addressed the Quizmasters.

They all surrounded me, their long shadows falling all around me like the spokes of a wheel.

'He must be sick, he's working too hard,' said Sufferinjaysus.

'Yes, I agree,' yelped Miss Parnassus.

'I'm Anthropos,' I said with the wail of a man betrayed.

'Liar, imposter, actor,' they roared as they pointed their chalky fingers at me. I backed away from these monsters and fled down the steps. I fled along the lanes through the countryside in terror for I felt the shadow of Rigormortis in my rear.

I rushed in the open doorway of my house so fast that I was up the stepladder and encapsulated in my attic by the man in the rafters before I realised where I was.

'And stay up there,' he shouted after me. 'I'm late already as it is,' and he trotted off to work. I was so jaded from my experience that I never said a word. It took a whole day of meditation for me to regain my composure.

Towards evening as I levitated around the rafters, I heard the screech of metal on stone. Someone was edging a scythe, backwards and forwards went the motion, its sound filling the attic with foreboding. Then I listened in horror to the dry shearing of its blade as it set my plants in a swathe, scattering the green force of their lives on the evening air. I lay back and felt my courage ebb further with each vicious swipe.

He had company in the house. I like company, but this was a woman. I heard their low talk and sudden laughter. The nudges, the knowing winks and the slyness, I could imagine. I groped around the rafters until I found a chink. I put my eye to it. Red hot pokers stabbed my brain; Miss Parnassus was on the sofa. But that wasn't all; flesh, white flesh, the whiteness of sheltered modesty there in carnal display. Oh, the filth of it and the poison of such sinful undertakings. Just anger swept out from my soul and terrible was the sound of my grinding teeth. I'm a terror in rage. Like Samson I gripped the rafters and could have brought the house down upon their lusting bodies were it not that Mr Anthropos wants no noise from the attic. I lay back and had to listen to their delight while they shared each other's privacy until my sleep released me.

Last night I knocked on the trapdoor. After a while he unlocked it and stuck his head up.

'Could I have a drink of water please, sir, it's dry up here.'

He considered this for some time.

'Will you want to make your wee-wee after it?'

'Oh, no, sir, that only happens after two drinks of water.'

'Very well,' and he fetched me a nice cool drink.

'I'm rather pleased with your housework, although I would suggest greater effort in the culinary area,' he said.

'Right, sir. You just leave that to me,' I said. 'By the way, sir, when do we have a little chat again? I rather like a little chat.'

He paused to think. 'After tea tomorrow then, if everything is in order.'

I thanked him and he locked the trapdoor.

Mr Anthropos is like that, straight if you are straight with him. I help a little now and then but in the attic I am king. Up here I never have to lift a hand, and himself waits on me hand and foot. Up here I have great peace, as I listen to the woodworm burrow the dry seconds of their lives away.

Translated by the author.

The Doomsday Club

Seán MacMathúna

It was so quiet in the Doomsday Club that you could hear the spiders spin their webs. Quiet because hope had been banished, and hope brings noise, and only in despair is there unqualified peace. We had investigated the outside world only to discover that hope also caused wars whereas despair ended them. The world was upside down – virtue was the enemy of man.

And so we enshrined in the club constitution the qualifications of membership. Only people of a despairing, melancholy and negative disposition could become members. Those who were dedicated to desperation were barred, for any kind of dedication in a world that was doomed was a contradiction.

However, an analysis of the early membership showed a disturbing trend. The club was filling up with Irish speakers. It appeared that in matters of pure negation, they have no equal. With them as a bonus came other admirable human qualities such as spite, jealousy, envy, sloth, pride, bitchery and begrudgery. To fall in line with the Futility Clause which is the cornerstone of our constitution, we agreed to join them and speak only the Irish language which is so doomed that each morning we have to check that it is still there. Soon we were all convinced that the Celtic way of doom was more poetic.

Nobody was in charge of the Doomsday Club, for that would be an overture of neatness, a recognition that order had a place in our dying world. Futility and despair were things of beauty that gave the necessary cohesion to our group. It would also be suicidal for anyone to contemplate leadership for we would batten on his strength like leeches, we would hate him into sickness, hurt him into shame, hound him to an early death. Woe to the head that would raise itself above the crowd. For sustenance we had our dream, the dream of Celtic supremacy over the nations of the earth. We had examined the dreams of others and decided that ours was the safest, for never would our dream be touched by the sordidness of this world.

None of us were native speakers of Irish, but once we did have one as a member. He continually bewailed our poor grasp of cliché and corrected our grammar. We expelled him under the Perfection Clause. And so we practised our bad Irish, drank beer and generally sat around, waiting for the trumpet blast that would tear the skies apart, doom us all and get it over with.

The first indication we had of the Second Coming was in the strange behaviour of one of our members. Críostóir Ó Maoil Íosa was a man who drank pints faster than Irish was dying, which left him continuously intoxicated. However, he began to develop Christ-like qualities such as beating us all to the round of drinks. Kindness was against the rules, but the way we looked at it that was his problem.

He also took to wearing a beard and developing those eyes that followed you around the room, like those of the picture of the Sacred Heart. When he finally appeared in a flowing white robe we knew that something was afoot. Finally he simply indicated to us all that he would like to apply for planning permission for one crucifixion. We were not allowed by the rules to show our delight. Delight is only allowed at the funerals of colleagues. On being asked his reasons he explained that he didn't think his name in Irish, Christopher the Follower of Jesus, was a coincidence. We knew there was no such thing. And he was also an Irish speaker. Why should God choose an Irish speaker for the Second Coming, we asked. He replied that God had a hangup about linguistic scenarios, having chosen the Aramaic Gaeltacht for his First Coming. (The beauty about the Doomsday Club is that one doesn't have to be logical.) The Irish language was moribund and its speakers degenerate, it had eighteen different words for telescope, it had resisted many attempts to standardise it while each new dictionary confounded all that went before. Its speakers were so devious that they had devised no exact word for 'yes' or 'no.' The result was a permanent commitment to uncertainty. And there was no word for 'have' in the language. The 'have', 'yes' and 'no' problem gave rise to the ridiculous situation where one could not translate the words of the immortal song 'Yes, we have no bananas'. Was it any wonder he said that he had taken up the study of Manx, Cornish, and Old Irish, three languages that were safely dead.

We commended his bitchery but pointed out that we were still not happy with his answer. Desperation leaked out of his eyes and pulled and tugged at the muscles of his face (he had the kind of face that one would dearly love to crucify). He finally gasped that if man were created in God's likeness then there was a possibility that God had a sense of humour. This was satisfactory but then we came to the tricky bit: we informed him that in the matter of sacrifice, especially self-sacrifice, a benefit usually accrued to the survivors and that the bestowal of benefits was contrary to the spirit of the constitution. He said he was disappointed in us and that his only motivation was the sheer and utter waste of it all. We were so pleased that we immediately granted him full planning permission for one crucifixion. We appointed a crucifixion committee to assist him in his undertaking and wished him every success. The agreed day was the following Good Friday. As an afterthought we asked him if he believed in God. He drew himself up to his full height and replied with dignity, 'I am God.' We were quite pleased, an Irish-speaking God and high time too. We celebrated by getting him to buy us all a round of drinks.

At the first meeting of the crucifixion committee, Críostóir, who will henceforth be called the Subject, stood on the stage, slowly releasing the aura of martyr, evangelical light, a good hundred watts, radiating from his eyes. He requested that the writer, de Brún, be allowed to script the whole affair, but cautioned him to avoid the sentimentality of the original. Mac Cartagáin, who was an engineer, was elected stage manager. The latter, being a person of some dynamism, proceeded immediately to measure the Subject's vital statistics in order to get the dimensions of the cross right. There was spontaneous applause and many offers of hammers and nails. But the Subject indicated that even though his life up to this had been a stunning failure (failure was obligatory for us all), he felt that one request for uniqueness should be granted to him: namely to have the distinction of being the only person ever crucified on a Celtic cross. The hammers-and-nails set were disappointed with this news because Celtic crosses are made of stone. They argued with him, pointing out that Celtic crosses were small and he might find them too confining. But the Subject said confinement had been the Celtic lot and to go in such a manner would be more poetic.

After a while Mac Cartagáin said he knew where he could get a cement cross. The Subject thanked him and asked him if he could make it three because he felt he might like a little support. This was going to be great, three crucifixions, we had forgotten the thieves. Somebody pointed out that we didn't have any thieves in the club. Mac Cartagáin said that he could hire a couple of Irish-speaking actors – not only unemployed, but also out of work. There wasn't much point in crucifying them because already the disposal of bodies was a problem high on his list. At the mention of bodies the evangelical light wavered a little in the Subject's eyes.

How, someone asked, was the Subject to be nailed to a cement cross? That was no problem said the stage manager. He then explained to us the workings of the Hilti gun nail-driver, which, with the aid of an explosive cartridge, could drive a steel bolt into the cement. The Subject would not feel a thing, he felt. The Subject looked quite concerned. Somebody mentioned that it would be one hell of a job getting the Subject off the cross, what with the Hilti nails and all. But Mac Cartagáin said that was a bridge we would cross in good time. Críostóir began to look a little forlorn at this stage and he asked what preparations had been made for his scourging at the pillar. The script writer came forward and said he had written it out of the script. He didn't mind a little crucifixion, but he was totally against blood sports. Still and all, the Subject said, he felt entitled to some ceremony. As an overture to this we offered Iníon Ní Chuíosaigh, the only female member, the part of Veronica, i.e. to wipe the face of the Subject. Her answer was unprintable, which we took as a refusal. At this point the Subject began to complain and said, granted we couldn't have too much ceremony but there should be some flourish, something exotic, romantic even, something eloquent of the Celtic story. We told him that the Celtic story was the most tawdry record in the annals of Homo Sapiens, that from the Celtic Dawn to the Celtic Twilight was such a sordid picture of treachery, slyness and rascality, that the Celts deserved to become extinct – and that only in the official Club Celtic Dream was there preserved some modicum of dignity. Celts lived in misery during the day, went to bed at night with defeat and only in the morning did the prospect of failure give them the will to persevere.

A Campbell from the Isles offered to play the bagpipes during the highlights of the occasion. The Subject thought about it and said he'd like a lament. We offered him a choice of 350 laments for the 350 battles we had lost and five laments for the one we won. We finally settled on 'Phil the Fluter's Ball' much to the annoyance of the Subject. The stage manager said that talk about battles had reminded him that we needed a spear. Somebody said he could steal one from the railings of an old Protestant Church. We weren't mad about the idea because we wanted to keep religion out of it. There was much discussion among the technically minded about how best to sharpen this spear for the purpose in hand. It was at this time that we noticed that the Subject's evangelical light had dwindled to a leak from his left eye, and within his white robe his proud bearing had begun to droop somewhat. He was asked if he wanted to go through with the being offered vinegar on a sponge bit. Somebody suggested that it should be stout seeing as it would be his last taste ever. This latter helpful remark and the stage manager's secret plan (no point in bothering the Subject) for the disposal of the body, which involved a JCB, combined to give Críostóir Ó Maoil Íosa's face a look of deep disappointment – unreasonably we thought in the circumstances. The proceedings were concluded.

On Good Friday the Standing Committee for Linguistic Coordination was in full swing in the club. We were endeavouring to translate 'Yes, we have no bananas' into terms that would be in keeping with the genius of the language. We decided to take the bull by the horns and hijack the verb *habeo* from the Latin which means 'I have', thus bestowing on the Irish language a new concept of ownership.

It went like this: *Habaim, Habann Tú, Habann Sé,* et cetera. We agreed that *Habann tú banana?* sounded bad enough, but *Sea, ní habaimid aon bhananaí* was so dreadful that it should be adopted as standard straightaway.

At this stage Iníon Ní interrupted. She said crucifixions were a waste of men, and that she was waiting for no 'resurrection'. There was immediate consternation – there was no planning permission for a resurrection.

De Brún, the script writer, said it was a terrible crucifixion with everyone departing from the script, especially the Subject. When the latter had announced that he intended to resurrect, the script writer had given him a warning. But he insisted, saying that he intended to do it the following Tuesday. Everybody pleaded with him to resurrect on a bank holiday or on a weekend, but not on a Tuesday which was a workday. But he had been adamant. He said he was in bad shape and, try as he might, he knew he wouldn't make it till Tuesday. Everyone was so annoyed that they proceeded to dispatch him immediately. His last words were that when he arose he would make an important announcement for all humanity which he wanted published in all the local papers.

This resurrection thing was a bad business. A live member we had some control over, but a deceased member could say anything, for we had lots of secrets – real compromising stuff. Then we discussed the event of his resurrection and asked for suggestions as to the possibility of his rehabilitation within the club. Everybody was against it, saying he'd be cut up pretty bad and an embarrassment to us all. Furthermore the Achievement Clause ruled out his being taken back. Mac Cartagáin said it was ridiculous to seriously consider his resurrection, because he had with his JCB dug a large hole in the hill and rolled a massive granite boulder over it. He'd never move that stone, he said. Still, just in case, we decided to attend the affair on Tuesday.

All day on Tuesday we waited on the little hill, watching the mountain fog swirl about the lonely crosses – and of course the stone – we really watched that stone. We watched it so hard that it swelled and heaved and bulged. But it was our eyes that did all the heaving.

We had a plan. If he were to roll aside the stone and arise, we were going to make a big long welcoming speech, present him with a translation of 'Yes, we have no bananas' in *Book of Kells*-style Celtic script, and then, as there were thirty-five of us, we were going to persuade him to remain in his new dimension. So, we waited.

Twilight descended until the rock blended with the hillside – there was no resurrection. Gratefully we eased ourselves towards the club. Just then a member brought our attention to some graffiti on the main cross. It was written in Old Irish and in old script. One of our many academics read it out: *gimigam fol cech nech*. He translated it as 'everything is a banana'. There was no doubt about it, this was the Subject's message to humanity. We were so much in awe of its searing beauty that we almost went to our knees. In four little words it summed up all Mankind wanted to know about mystery. This was no ordinary-revealed secret, but a weapon that, if set loose upon the wretched thought and philosophy of today, would wreak havoc among the minds of men and bring about the realisation of the Great Celtic Dream. But we are fond of our secrets and fonder still of our dreams and he who knows our secrets would surely tread on our dreams. And so we enacted that these precious words were classified and would be allowed only mingle in the minds of Oisín and Ó Maoil Íosa and all the countless heroes of the Gael till time and time were done.

Translated by the author.

THE ATHEIST

Seán MacMathúna

The day after she was buried the cork blew off her elderberry wine. It was only then he knew she was dead and that he would never see her again. The bird had not flown. She hadn't even been snatched. She had been torn through the bars of the cage, leaving some blood and a fine down lingering in the air. It was this fine down that drifted through his mind now, eternally heavy, deathlessly cold. He stood in a bay window somewhere on planet earth, which was but a stone twirling in the sunbeams, and he wanted to shout out her name loud enough for it to ring out for all time, he wanted the whole universe to know how much he loved her. But he didn't. For he knew he might as well talk to a rocking horse. He watched the curtains being sucked out into the garden by the gale. He looked up at the sky. Nothing except cloud chasing cloud, and somewhere above them the moon and all the stars. All dead. There were no other worlds. There were no more dimensions. There was merely what is. No could be's, should be's, might be's, maybe's. Just the reality of the indicative, and the nightmare of subjunctives. There was merely Time and if you were in it, you were of it. And at any given time there was only one microsecond and we were all, all five billion of us, biting on it together. And as we bit, each one of us journeyed towards our eternity and the road flying from under us.

He cursed intelligence, culture, education and insight. These things had deprived him of the comfort of a God, and the solace of a happy eternity united with loved ones. But in a way he was proud that he felt like this, for such loneliness was dearly bought and paid for in Ireland. She would have felt the same if it had been he who had died, for she too was a lonely disbeliever.

He had envied the others at the graveside, the weeping relatives and friends, as the sods thumped down on her coffin. Their show of emotion went with their religion. He remained erect, whitefaced, and fierce throughout it all. Dry-eyed atheism. If she could hear he would beg her forgiveness for the awful funeral and tell her that it wasn't his fault. They, that is both his and her relatives, wouldn't hear of cremation. Her brothers would attack him. It was taken out of his hands and was a traditional funeral: priests, splashing of holy water, full requiem mass. Some woman sang 'Lacrimosa Dies Illa', she would have liked that. But the rest of it was sordid, and the display of religiosity and piety, especially from her side of the family, was sickening. How had so fine a mind as hers escaped from that dunghill called the extended family? Yes, forgive him all the bowing and scraping. For the last few days he was as a man tumbling through another's dream. But what was the point in talking to her, for he knew that a few seconds after the head-on collision on the Killshaskin Road the billion, billion cells of information that was Emer Riley, flickered out one by one, all the poetry, laughter, plans, music, memories of her father, taste of blackberries, smell of fuchsia in the Gaeltacht, joy of dawn, the know-how for making plum puddings stay alight, the feeling of cool windowpanes with the rain streaming on the outside, the warmth of a kiss from the man she loved – all gone like last year's snow. And he had paid the priest. It was ironic that the only contact she ever had with priests since she became an independent teenager was at her death. Fr O'Herlihy had gently suggested that now he might reconsider his ways and start coming to church. He gave him a most emphatic no. As she would have done. It was a bitter cross to carry – to carry in Ireland – the cross of Godlessness. But carry it he would through dungeon, fire and sword.

Suddenly the movement in the scullery brought him back to reality. The symphony of rattles, bangings, tinklings, rubbings, scrapings, and poundings that was titled 'Life must go on' carried all over the house. Then silence. Then the footsteps of Julia, her mother, slow and heavy up the hallway, then the pause, then the rattle, the knob and the creak of the door. He didn't turn but he felt eyes peering at him, as if someone had parted the curtains in another world and gazed at the miracle of a man standing alone in his own bay window.

'You can't go on like this.' The voice was taut but quiet, telling of the effort of resignation. 'You'll have to eat, even a little.'

He didn't turn, nor did he reply. He felt totally indifferent to her and to his own bad manners. She coughed, then paused before saying, 'If you don't eat we'll be running another body into the ground. 'Tis what she would have liked: that you should eat something, even a small bit.'

She was only here a few days he thought and already she knew that to mention her was the way to get him to act. He teetered for a moment then sighed and turned and said almost inaudibly, 'Whatever you say.' They went to the kitchen. The meal she had prepared was prawn provençale. It had always been their favourite meal together. Now, to eat it without her seemed thoughtless. He would have preferred something more neutral like a hamburger. He ate a forkful and nibbled at a piece of bread.

She sat opposite him and watched him eat. Then, as if she felt it was the right time, she said quietly, 'I know how you feel about the mass cards. It is a pity, but that's the way it is. Remember it's love and sorrow that makes people go to pay a priest for a mass card. You'll have to read them, there are two hundred and twenty in all. They are mostly from people who couldn't attend the funeral. They will have to be answered. I've a list of the people who sent wreaths. They must all be acknowledged.'

He went on chewing. He found himself wondering why they had been so attracted to each other. It had he thought been their agreement on so many things. That and her face. It was full of sensuality and energy, very impressive. She had been a rebel. God had been one of the early casualties. They had spent many of their first meetings sharing their hatred of Catholicism. They had a huge long litany which was almost inexhaustible: scapulars, rosaries, confessions, communions, indulgences, prohibitions, aspirations, sins, masses, bowings, bells, candles, scrapings, *mea culpas, mea maxima culpas*, mortal sins, hell, priests, nuns, holy hours, processions, shamrocks, holy wells, churchings, god boxes, three Hail Marys for Holy purity, the rhythm method, et cetera. Where religion had come from had engaged endless hours of speculation. He always quoted the chapter and verse of atheism: it was fear that first made gods in the world, and the religion that followed was nothing but submission to mystery. It was the sum of scruples that impeded the free exercise of our faculties. She always gave as an example the belief in the west of Ireland about acne. If you had acne, watch for a falling star. As the star fell, wipe your face. All eruptions would vanish. If they didn't, it was because you were not quick enough.

Julia's voice came from another world. 'Flanagan is cutting a stone, it will be black pearl granite. It's dear but it's the least we can do for the girl. I didn't like the limestone. Flanagan has a machine in from America that can cut a picture of the crucifixion on the granite, all on its own, for an extra hundred pounds. It would have taken an old stonemason a month to do it and he wouldn't do it half as good.'

He stopped chewing and looked at her. Her eyes were polished from recent crying. Any minute she could start again. She was brave and it had been her only daughter. He leaned towards her and said gently but firmly, 'No crucifixions, no crosses, just her name: Emer Riley, nineteen fifty-three to nineteen eighty-five, and the words

"Sunset and evening star,
And one clear call for me!
And may there be no moaning of the bar,
When I put out to sea."'

She looked down at the ground and fought off the tears. 'What in the honour of God does that mean? What bar? Whose bar?'

He told her they were favourite lines of Emer's from Tennyson.

'And who around here is going to know that, for God's sake?'

'I will and that's enough,' he said.

She got up from the table and busied herself about the sink. Idleness she knew brought the wrong kind of emotion. He felt that there was quite a lot of unnecessary splashing. She stopped and looked out into the garden above the counter.

'It was a shameful thing that both of you never darkened the door of a church.'

'What would we go in for?'

'To pray for your immortal souls of course.'

'We might as well play hornpipes to a couple of signposts.'

'It was a mistake not to. She knows it now.'

'How dare you say that about her. How dare you,' he shouted in anger. Terrifying images from his childhood suddenly erupted in his mind. The face of a cruel God with a curling lip saying to the soul of a sinner a few seconds after death, 'Depart from me you cursed, into the everlasting flames of hell.' He could protect her while on earth but he was helpless against a divine maniac, a hell packer.

'You shouldn't talk like that about her, she never harmed the hair of anyone's head.'

But the woman was not to be intimidated.

'I'll say what I like about her. It was I who brought her into the light of day, nursed her, loved her, spoiled her. She is as much mine as yours. But she belongs to neither now. She is God's. What'll she say to Him when He asks her why she never even baptised that poor child up in the bed?'

She splashed more water around defiantly. He just stopped himself in time from telling her to leave. But what was the point of a religious argument? It was the same all over Ireland. Men without hope for the good things of this world clung to the promise of the next. Superstition was part of their quotidian. And each day as Ireland grew poorer the beasts of Lough Derg slithered eastward more and more. It was his duty as a member of the minute educated classes to raise the standards of reason and to clash with the forces of evil. But Julia saw some advantage in his failure to reply and she pressed it.

'And no first communion. The day that every child in the parish is leppin' with joy you took the child to the zoo in Dublin. She'll answer to the Lord for that I'll tell you. Monkeys instead of the grace of God.'

He leaped up from the table.

'Enough is enough. That's it. I'm going to ask you to leave this house now, Julia – this minute.'

She looked suddenly crushed and she sat down at the table.

'Yes, yes,' she gulped as she fought back the tears, 'I want to leave too. But I can't.' She looked about the kitchen. 'It's this place, her cups, her saucers, it's all I've got that reminds me of her. And all her clothes in the wardrobe.' She pulled a handkerchief out of her sleeve and dabbed her eyes. 'My advice to you is to get rid of all her clothes – anything that reminds you of her that you don't need. Give them to the poor.'

'Certainly not,' he said. 'I like being reminded of her.'

'You should heed what the old people say about these things. Get rid of her clothes, shoes, perfume, otherwise they'll drive you mad. The old people have wisdom as old as the fields.'

He began to understand Julia better each time she opened her mouth. She wasn't a person any more, just a mobile parish-lore unit that consulted the *is* of the moment with the *should* of local tradition and matched them up willy-nilly.

'Everything stays as it is.'

'Have it your own way then.'

'I will.' He would just, especially the light blue frock with the Helen of Troy sleeves that revealed chinks of skin made golden in the Mediterranean sun. Suddenly she was splashing again; that meant she was about to have another go at him.

'You're going to have to think about what you're going to do. I mean you and the child.'

He detested the peasant way of referring to a young boy as a boy, but a young girl as a child, even though she was six. It offended.

'We'll manage quite well, thank you,' he said.

'Well, I'm sorry but you're not managing too well at the moment. The child is out of her mind with loneliness.'

'We'll both have to get over it.'

'It's not going to be easy for her. She needs a woman.'

He glanced across at her sharply. 'Meaning?' he said testily.

She grabbed a tea towel and wrapped it round her wet fingers. 'Would you not think of letting the child back to Ballinamarach with me for a few months? She will get the care and loving attention of six women. It would be good for her. Women need women in times like this. A man is no good.' There was pleading in her voice.

He looked at her for a long time just to make sure she was serious. Such an act would be to condemn the girl to the world of the pishogue, magic, the attitudes of the culturally deprived, hobgoblins, a world of enslavement for women, a world of slyness and rascally brutality for men. 'No!' he said firmly. 'We will adjust in good time. Róisín has the resources of her mother. She is intelligent and adaptable.'

'She is only six years old. She wouldn't even know the meaning of these words. Give her at least a month in Ballinamarach.'

Yes, and she'd come back with miraculous medals sewn into her clothes. It would be like 'taking the soup' in reverse. He arose from the table and thanked her for the meal. He said he was going up to tell Róisín her usual story. Julia reminded him that she was in his bed, refusing to go into her own. Then she turned back to the dishes.

It was a four-poster that had gone for a bargain at the auction of furniture of the last of the Bingham-Woods at Killscorna House. He peeped at her from the doorway, clutching her teddy fiercely, white faced and so alone in the big expanse of bed. Her eyes were large and puzzled. It occurred to him that he had hardly seen her in the past few days – since the Trouble – she was still in shock. He pushed open the door and beamed at her as he moved up to the bed. 'Hi, honey,' he said, 'come into my heart and pick sugar. Any kiss for Dally?' He leaned over and pecked her on the cheek.

'Hallo, Dally,' she said without a trace of warmth. She clutched her teddy all the more and he thought he noticed an imperceptible move away from him into the pillows. He searched his mind for the small talk that is the essential currency of getting through to children. He was always uneasy when alone in her presence, never having mastered the subtlety of the child's imagination.

'You look lovely in your pyjamas, you know that, just lovely. Do you remember where you got them first?' Suddenly he realised his mistake. Emer had pounced on the psychedelic floral pattern in Sacramento last summer. It had been a sunny carnival of McDonalds, Disneyland, the ice-cream parlours. Now, damn, he had done it as he watched her eyes cloud over and then precipitate into a mist of tears.

'Where is Mommy? I want Mommy, what have they done with her? They said she's sick. I'm afraid, Dally – I want her.'

He almost reeled. He looked open-mouthed at the hurt innocence of her eyes. Jesus Christ in heaven, had nobody told the child her mother was dead. Now what am I going to do? He walked to the window to think as fast as he could, but all he could think of was how swift the night approached from Cloon Wood. It was late autumn. The house shivered. He walked back to the bed and looked down at the quietly weeping child. She was the sole issue of atheists. And atheism was merely to bite the bitter truth. Out, out, hobgoblins! He cleared his throat. 'Róisín, pet, Mommy is no longer with us.'

The child tried to focus on his face, tried to wring meaning out of his words but failed. 'What do you mean? What do you mean?' she whispered aghast. 'I want Mommy to tuck me in.' She almost wailed the last words.

He gulped and looked around the room. He knew it was brutal. But children had to have teeth pulled, the quicker the better.

'You remember Shaska, the dog?'

There was the faintest flicker of recognition. 'Yes, Shaska was a nice dog.'

'That's right, he was a nice dog, but he died, and we buried him in the garden, in the ground. Shaska is no longer with us.' He waited for that to sink in. He was sure it wasn't too obtuse. The child hugged her teddy all the more fiercely and backed farther into the large pillows, away from him.

'Is Mommy under the ground?' She looked at him as if he were a ghost. She was a bright child, he thought, she got the message, thank God for that.

'Yes,' he said simply.

'Will I ever see her again?'

He paused as he mastered all his strength. 'No,' then quietly, 'never again.'

She looked up slowly at him, her tears gone, with an open uncomprehending expression on her face. It was at this precise moment that he saw for the first time the resemblance between her and her mother. Emer had sort of looked like that at times, such as when he tried to explain to her how he made bridges that wouldn't fall down.

'Why never again? What did I do?' She cried again quietly, 'What did I do wrong? Why won't you let me see her, Dally, please, Dally, just once?'

He needed his wife badly now, even more than the child. What would he say? Words were summoned to his lips, each more useless than the next. Words from a brave world. Words from the world of storm-trooping humanity. But the world of a six-year-old was equally valid.

'Róisín, little apple, Dally is going to look after you. We are alone but we are together – we're going to be happy.'

'Mommy,' the child said dumbly. 'Just Mommy, I don't want you, Dally.'

'It's going to be all right, Cherry. I'm going to look after you.' He picked her out of the pillows and put his arms around her, hugging her tightly. She began to wail for her mother all the more, her body bundled into tautness. Then the wail turned to sobs which made her body convulse in his embrace. He became frightened. He had never seen her like this before. The sobs became gasps. He thought she was having a fit. He ran for the door, opened it, and shouted, 'Julia!' But she was there outside the door, waiting. She took her from him. He noticed how the child relaxed and clung to her granny.

'I told you she needed women. Now go and take a walk and leave her to me.'

He moved downstairs and out into the garden. He was shaken by this first enounter with his daughter. It made him feel helpless. He wondered if he was about to become a wreck. Without Emer would he revert to irresponsible bachelor drinking with the boys and going to discos. He shuddered. His memory of those days was a mindless *carpe diem* of pints of stout and sexual exploits. He looked about the garden. It was almost dark, but he could make out her half-built rockery, her fountain, her vegetable patch, all hers;

he began to realise that his life had been mostly hers and that without her it would automatically collapse. He was in dread of not being able to cope. He was trapped in this garden, trapped in the half-realised plans of someone now gone. Torment took control and steered him across the road and up to Shanahan's field. He could no longer see the cattle, but he was close enough to them to hear their heavy breath shake the dew off the grass. He hoped that distance from the house would give him peace. He decided that if he could walk to the end of Shanahan's field without thinking of her once it would be the beginning of independence. After ten successful steps he felt it reminded him of the ruined church of St Fachtna, where it was commonly believed that if you could walk around it three times without once thinking of a woman you would be assured of eternal salvation. Everybody tried it but most gave up honestly after a few steps. The few who achieved it were accused of telling a lie for which they would be damned all the more. Emer had dismissed it as a typical expression of ecclesiastical chauvinism. Damn, that did it, he had thought of her. He stopped in the middle of the field and turned round. In the distance a light shone from the upstairs window. Somebody drew the curtain, nearby a cow belched. He was afraid. Now he knew he was afraid they'd get the child. He was afraid he wouldn't be man enough on his own. He decided then to march back and take control of his own house, to establish his own word as the only law. However, before he would march back, he would march forward a little more because he needed time to think. Soon he found himself at the edge of Cloon Wood. He ventured in till his eyes grew accustomed to the total dark. He leaned his back against a tree and peered at the distant window through the twigs. He moved deeper in and then he turned to look again. Nothing. It was a beginning.

Later he wandered into the kitchen and sat beside the big range. Julia was knitting beside the table. No word passed between them. After a while she coughed and said, 'Wouldn't you think of taking off your shoes, they're sodden. Leave them there near the range, they'll be dry in the morning.'

She couldn't keep it in, he thought. Years of fighting damp, of outmanoeuvering draughts, of sitting in the shade in summer – all punctuated with cups of tea – had dulled her mind to all other sensibilities.

'They're sodden and I'm glad of it,' he said, and he spread his feet in front of him in order to observe the water trickle onto the floor.

'That's all very fine now. But you might have a cold tomorrow, where would you be then? A chill is the beginning of the end of us all. That's what happened Jack, God rest him.'

He thought of her husband, a silent man who had spent his time on this earth walking about the haggard with bucketfuls of this, that and the other.

'I thought he died of cancer.' There was the smallest trace of malice in his words. She almost dropped the knitting.

'None of our family ever died of cancer. He got cancer all right, but it was pneumonia that got him in the end.' She said it with a certain note of triumph. You had to be careful how you lived in Ireland but you had to be even more careful that you didn't die of the wrong disease. She continued to knit. Click clack went the needles, never dropping a stitch. He listened to the sparring needles in a bemused fashion until it occurred to him that something was wrong. Suddenly he knew what it was. The clock, the big two-hundred year old Dublin regulator was stopped. It had been an extravagant purchase of Emer's in the early days. She had always kept it wound up.

'The clock is stopped,' he said. She didn't look up at him but continued to knit. He got up and walked to the corner where it stood, mute as a milestone.

As he reached for the key, she said, 'Would you not think it would be a great honour to the dead to let the clock hold its peace for a month?'

He thought about it. Killing the clock, gramophone and radio for a month was a commonplace practice. But it was superstition and had he and Emer not fought superstition as ruthlessly as Julia had fought damp and chills? Anyway, it had a grand generous tick and tock which had punctuated the happiest years of his life. He wound it up slowly. Then he had to move the hands and realised his mistake as the clock chimed all the way up to 10 pm. It chimed all over the house, in each chime a message he daren't interpret. Then it settled down to its tick, tock. He sat beside the range again fearing he could do nothing right. His feet were freezing but he couldn't take his shoes off now, it would be a defeat, in spite of the fact that everything she said made sense. He glanced at her out of the corner of his eye. Did he imagine she had a self-satisfied look about her? He was sure of it. She'd have to go, that was all – he'd manage quite well without her. He would master basic cooking in a few days – laundry and things like that would not be too difficult he decided. Beyond that there was little else to housework. Still, he'd have to go back to work the following day because the bridge over the new bypass was reaching a critical stage and the sub-contractors were beginning to give hassle. Maybe he'd let her stay a few days, maybe even a week. His feet were so cold he had to get up and stamp the floor. He walked to the clevy and took down a bottle of Crested Ten.

'Would you like a drink?' he said as a truce gesture.

'A solitary drop of that stuff has never dampened a tooth in my head and never will till the day I go under.'

'OK,' he said as he poured himself a very large whiskey. He tossed it all back neat in rare abandon, winced and then waited for it to expand within. It did, and he exhaled in gratitude.

'I've heard it said many a time that a man in the grip of fresh sorrow would be better off to go dry, at least until he is on his old mettle again,' she said blinking between stitches.

You're as dry as an old limeburner's boot yourself he said to himself as he topped up his glass again.

'All my life I've watched men drink their way through farms and fields.'

'For Christ's sake, Julia, give me a break. You're playing the tune the old black cow died of.'

'That's all very well to say that today,' she said, 'but where will it all end? That's what I'd like to know. Where will it all end?'

Emer, girl, he said to himself, you were a sparkling trout out of the genetic cesspool – the others were all perch and pike. All your brothers and your mother are fatheads. They all live and you die – another proof that God does not exist.

'Look what happened to Paky Connor,' she said.

'Who's Paky Connor?' he asked in desperation.

'He was a second, no, a third cousin of my own dear Jack, God rest him. He was going out with a no-good hussy of a girl who left him down. It was the luck of God that she did for if she had married him there would be no end to the calamity. She was a stupid ignorant gligeen who wouldn't know B from a bull's foot or C from a chest of drawers. Anyway, he took to the drink until he got himself and the farm into such a state that one night they had to tie him to a chair until the van called for him.'

'What van, for God's sake?'

She put her knitting down on her lap and looked at him as if he were a tramp who called to the back door. 'The van from the mental asylum of course. He's in there to this day and I'll tell you one thing for sure, he's living a very dry life.' She resumed her knitting. 'The brothers signed him in and I'll tell you thing for sure, if they ever sign him out, 'tis out in a box he'll come.'

He looked at her open-mouthed. 'And I suppose the brothers are looking after the farm.'

'Yes,' she said, 'It's as green as holly and not a *buachalán* or a weed in sight.'

He poured himself another whiskey. 'That man was just suffering from a nervous breakdown, it's disgraceful that he should spend all his life in the asylum.'

'Well, that's one name for it, but we call it going insane. Thanks be to God for mental asylums or the countryside wouldn't be safe for a body.'

'Jesus, sweet Jesus,' was all he said. What a paradox Ireland was he mused. His job called for a mastery of the most up-to-date computer technology, but at night he'd have to come home to this bronze age view of life. What a pity machines couldn't change people. He knew that in the year 2087 things would be just the same. Tools and machines might change but they would never lick the bronze age. He got up and corked the bottle and put it back in the clevy.

'Well I'm going to bed,' he said. 'I'll have a peep in at Róisín and see how she's doing. I might tell her that story if she's awake.'

Julia became as alert as a cat, dropped her knitting and said in a threatening tone, 'Wouldn't you be advised by one in the know and leave well alone.'

'How do you mean?'

'She's satisfied now, she's in her own bed. If you go in now you'll start the whole thing again.'

He resented her tone and the implication of her control. If he left her away with this she'd have him wandering around the place with buckets, same as she had her unfortunate husband.

'I'll see you, good night,' he said and trudged up the stairs.

The nightlight burned beside her bed and she lay between the sheets clutching her teddy and sucking her thumb. Her eyes darted towards him, but no flicker of joy appeared as it used before. He moved quietly up to her bed and bent down over her. Her eyes were focused somewhere in the dark part of the room.

'How about a little kiss for Dally?' he said as he nudged her teddy.

She continued to suck for a minute without looking at him. All of a sudden she raised herself up on her elbow and said accusingly to him, 'Daddy, you told me a lie.'

'Why don't you call me Dally, as you used to?'

''Cause, Gran said that was wrong, only babies say Dally, it's Daddy.'

He felt like rushing downstairs and throwing Julia out into the garden for good.

'Call me Dally. Now what lie did I tell you?'

'You said Mommy was like Shaska in the ground.'

He sat down beside her gently, hardly daring to ask her what she meant. 'I'm afraid she is, pet. That's the way it is and we must put up with it.'

She backed away from him, a hurt look crossing her face. 'She is not, she is not. She is in heaven with Holy God and all the holy angels.' She presented him with the left side of her jaw in defiance. The thumb popped in for three more sucks then out again. 'And if anybody goes near me or hits me she'll send an angel down to stop him.' The thumb was jammed back for refuel.

He never knew how to react quickly when taken by surprise – it was a failing. He began to stammer, then stopped himself and asked coldly, 'Who told you this nonsense?'

'Gran,' she said defiantly, but her mouth quivered with lack of conviction. Then she continued but there was pleading in her tone as tears began to spring at the corners of her eyes. 'She is up there now and she is looking down at the two of us and she is laughing – and one day Gran and me and you will die and we'll go up to her – and we'll have a great time. Isn't that true, Daddy, please, Daddy?' Her little face quivered shades of hope, loss, and shaky defiance. Her thumb went in and she looked up expectantly at him. He looked at her but he hadn't the courage to hold her eye. He took her hand in his, it was as limp as a sock.

'The fact is,' he said, 'the fact is,' but he didn't know what the fact was, except that he was tired and would have to put an end to this once and for all. 'The fact is, I'll have to close the window because you'll get cold.' He got up and crossed the room and looked out onto the garden. There was nothing to be seen except a moth which banged against the windowpane to escape the autumn chill.

'The window is shut already,' the child said.

'And so it is,' he said and came back slowly and sat down with a sigh beside her.

'Look, we've got to be brave about this, you and me,' he took her hand again, but she pre-empted any strategy by starting to cry out loud. He had no defence against tears. Once only Emer had to resort to them and he conceded the universe. As for a crying child he usually handed it over to a woman. But he wasn't going for Julia again. He took her in his arms and this time she did not resist. But she continued to cry and sob.

'Sure Mommy isn't out in the cold ground?' she pleaded.

He hadn't considered that aspect of it, it could be upsetting for a child. Anyway Mommy was nowhere.

'Mommy is not out in the cold ground.'

'And she is not where Shaska is.'

'No.'

He could feel her relaxing in his arms. She was soft, cuddly and yielding. She put her thumb in her mouth and sucked on this new confirmation. After a while she asked only just a little tearfully, 'She is in heaven with Holy God?'

Heaven was a mere metaphor for the dark eternity of non-existence. Children above all needed metaphors. Santa Claus was one, so were witches. He had never questioned stories about witches and magic before, why heaven now? A witch was a metaphor for the forces of hazard. We were all victims of hazard.

'Yes,' he said almost inaudibly, 'she is in heaven.' He was an atheist who felt he had just committed mortal sin.

'Why didn't you tell me that before? Gran was right.'

'Call me Dally,' he said simply.

'And is heaven full of angels?'

'Yes.'

'And will they look after me if I cut my knee?'

'Yes.'

'And is Mommy laughing?'

'Yes.' He felt like a thieving dog. What had he stolen? He had stolen away truth and put in its place a lie, hoping that it would not be discovered. It was the same as stealing his wife away from life and putting in her place some rags and bones. He felt he was stuffing the effigy of Emer Riley in the name of peace. The crying had stopped now. She sucked peacefully beside him.

'What dress is she wearing?'

'What do you mean?'

'In heaven. Now.'

'She's wearing a new dress. It's pink and long and sways as she walks.'

He had bought it for her fifty billion years ago way out in the Crab Nebula and she would wear it for all eternity and it would always blow gently about her legs in the cosmic breeze. The child was asleep.

Only five days gone and already philosophy had caved in at the knees. Heaven had arrived. Would hell would follow in its own good time?

Then all the coldness of the last few days turned hot and flowed with ease down his cheek. It was good to cry. It was warm. It was warm also to think of her in heaven and not in the cold cold ground.

She had a favourite proverb for calamity. 'If the skies were to fall we'd catch larks.' Well the skies had fallen, and he had caught a lark – a lark from the clear air.

He held her in his arms and looked out the window. There was but one star shining. It shone like a cat's eye from under a bed. It was an evening for oneness, one star, one man, one child, one lost love, one lark from the clear air. And one faith. Faith in the goodness of all things. He felt himself repeat her favourite lines:

'Twilight and evening bell
And after that the dark
And may there be no sadness of farewell
When I embark.'

Translated by the author.

Rushes

Éilís Ní Dhuibhne

We are picking rushes in the field behind the pub. It is New Year's Day. The light of evening is sliding off the land down into the sea. The water is the colour of cold iron.

'*Tá mé* freezing,' says Fiach, my son, looking sulky. 'This grass is like a sponge.'

'We won't be long,' I say, philosophically.

'My trainers are *ag sinkáil*,' he says. It's true. The field looks like an ordinary dry field but really it's just a marsh in disguise.

'Why are we *ag bailiú* the *luachra* anyway?' he asks. 'You can get them anywhere.'

'No,' I say, emphatically, as I cut a bundle of rushes carefully with my nail scissors. 'You can't get them anywhere. When I go looking for them at home I can never find any.'

'*Tá mé* bored,' he says. 'Can I *ól* a Coke?' He looks longingly at the pub.

We walk to the cottage of Mícheál and Pádraig, the 'Christian Brothers', as they call themselves. I knock at the door, then lift the latch and step right in, like Red Riding Hood. Fiach is trotting behind me, an armful of rushes under his oxter.

Within these things: light and shade. A turf fire. Mícheál and 'Peig Sayers', the cat, on one side of the hearth. Pádraig and Jim – my husband – on the other. An oil lamp on the table. Three faces gleaming in the twilight. Three glasses of whiskey also gleaming. Yellow, brown, gold, black. Dutch interior.

Pádraig jumps up and offers us drinks. I don't feel like drinking whiskey but no matter. He has Coke for the women and children. Pádraig offers me his comfortable chair by the fire, and he goes to sit at the kitchen table. Fiach sits opposite him. The men have been chatting about the old days on the Great Blasket, as they always do when Jim comes calling.

'We used to be playing cards. Twenty-one. Forty-one. Forty-one is the game they played most of the time. They were very fond of that, indeed and they were!'

Mícheál does most of the talking. He is a big strong man. A kind face, broad and without a wrinkle. Intelligent blue eyes, full of wisdom, but there is some sort of disappointment in them. Maybe because he has seen so much of life. He is over eighty years of age. But perhaps the sadness is just due to the burden of insight that falls on the eldest in any family. He is the senior one. His brother is a few years younger, still in his seventies. He doesn't say much, but he has the light carefree look of the younger child. He laughs a lot.

'Used they play for money?' Jim asks.

'Oh, indeed, it was for money they would be playing. For the pennies,' Mícheál says.

'And late at night?'

'Until two or three o'clock in the morning! They never wanted to go to bed, they did not!'

He speaks quickly. Each sentence starts in a low tone, rises in the middle, and then falls back again towards silence, so that it can be hard to catch everything he says. The rhythm of his talk is like that of the waves. Or the rise and fall of the wind.

It takes me a while to get in on it, to become accustomed to his Irish, although I have heard it very often. Fiach doesn't understand a word needless to say. His Irish is different, the *Gaeilge líofa lofa* of his Dublin school. He is sipping his Coke slowly, making it last. Fiddling with the rushes that are lying on the table.

'What will you do with those rushes?' Pádraig asks him.

'What?' Fiach looks at me for help.

But Pádraig asks the question again, in a loud slow voice, the sort of voice you'd use if you were talking to a foreigner, or somebody who was slow witted.

'St Bridget's Crosses,' answers Fiach, loudly, in English.

'Oh, very good!' Mícheál butts in.

'Used they make St Bridget's Crosses on the island?' Jim asks, with a sidelong glance at Pádraig. He makes those swallow-swoop glances when he suddenly clocks something interesting, then decides, just as suddenly, to let it pass.

'They did,' says Mícheál. 'They used to make them. They would make them and hang them over the byres and in the dwelling house as well. Yes, indeed they made St Bridget's crosses on the island.'

'And what else did they do on St Bridget's Day?' asks Jim. He switches on his tape recorder.

There's no electricity in this house. The kitchen looks exactly like it did forty years ago when the brothers came in from the Great Blasket after it was evacuated. The walls are a yellowy white, that colour you see on walls in villages in France or Italy.

There are many beautiful kitchens in this valley. Some modern, some old. The personality of the owner stamped on every one of them. But this one is the most pleasing of all. It is elegant and noble in its simplicity. Every single thing in it is functional. The skillet hanging from the crane over the fire is the sort of thing you would normally see in a museum, but Pádraig bakes bread in that pot oven every day, great golden loaves. The turkey was roasted in that pot on Christmas Day. There are no ornaments in this neat house, but every single thing in it is beautiful.

The brothers are conservationists. They have never changed a single thing in the cottage, but they haven't allowed anything to deteriorate either. You can sit in it now and understand how people lived a hundred years ago. A hundred years ago, five thousand years ago.

As I sit by the fire drinking my Coke, I go travelling. Back though the kitchens of the ages. I feel connected to the first settlers who landed in this area thousands of years ago and with the monks who lived in the beehive huts in the Middle Ages. Even with the cave dwellers. I slip back through time, and Mícheál's voice, rising and falling, encourages my dream, the way a piece of music by Mozart would.

Something is happening at the table.

Pádraig is working with the rushes, snipping and twisting them, and Fiach is keeping a close watch on what he is doing.

Pádraig has long thin hands, hands which are good for making bread. The sort of hands a violinist or a pianist might have. The hands move slowly, so that Fiach can take in their movements. Even so, it doesn't take long for Pádraig to make the little cross, a St Bridget's cross, one of the ones that look like a windmill. The cross that is not really a cross at all, but the pagan symbol of spring.

'We used to eat puffins,' Mícheál is saying, to the tape recorder. 'They were tasty enough, roasted, with a pinch of salt, although they were always a bit too greasy.'

Pádraig gives Fiach a few rushes and silently signals to him to have a go at making a cross himself. Fiach starts twisting the rushes, but he's in trouble before long. Then Pádraig takes Fiach's hands in his, and for a while the four hands work in unison, Pádraig's long thin hands and Fiach's little white ones. There is not a word from either of them. They don't understand each other's language. And anyway, they both know you're not allowed to talk while the tape recorder is on.

On the way home I tell Jim my thoughts about the house of the brothers.

I remember what happened when we ourselves came down here to the valley, to our own house, a week ago. The electricity wasn't working. The pipes had frozen and there was no water in the taps. The telephone was out of order. It's often like that when we come to the summer house, especially when we come in winter.

I sat down on the floor and started to cry. I declared that I was going to turn around and go back to town straight away. I said – screamed, actually – that I would not spend one more minute in this ghastly place.

'I'll go with you,' Fiach had said. 'I can't *imirt* my Sega Mega without electricity.'

'But even so,' I say to Jim, as we drive back up the hill. Even so I can take a precious jewel when someone puts it in my hand. I know that nobody and nothing can reproduce the thing that Pádraig and Mícheál have created, even though many people attempt it. Their house is like a painting by a

Dutch master. It is like this and it is like that, but it is not the same as anything else on earth. It is, simply, itself. A wonder. It is like the pyramids in Egypt, it is like Brú na Bóinne, it is like the mountains and it is like the stars. I would love to celebrate that beauty, to sing its glory, to recreate it. But how can I? How could anyone?

Next day we go back home. Dublin. Rotten rainy weather. Everyone has the flu. We visit the doctor, we devour antibiotics. Fiach goes back to school, and I go to work. Jim heads off to a library in Sweden to read documents they have in the archive there relating to the Blasket Island. Letters from Peig Sayers to Carl Vilhelm von Sydow, I think – they're in the library in Lund.

The rushes are thrown on the floor of the garage. From time to time Fiach goes out and brings in a few of them. He takes them up to his room where he sits on his bed watching *The Simpsons* or *Friends*. His hands keep busy, though, working with the rushes.

Out of the blue, a spring day arrives, as they do sometimes towards the end of January. Mild weather. Suddenly all the gardens are filled with the green spikes of the daffodils, pushing up from the winter earth.

The phone call comes soon after that. A Sunday night. A friend of mine in the valley. I know someone has died as soon as I hear her voice. They only phone from the valley when there's a death.

Pádraig. He got the cold and it turned to pneumonia. 'The old man's friend,' she says. He was in hospital for two weeks.

I don't go down for the funeral. I'm too busy and I have no leave left. Jim is still in Sweden, reading Peig's letters. So I send a mass card in the post and think about Pádraig as I go to work on the DART.

The day of the funeral is bright. On the streets of the city the sun shines and the optimism of spring is in the air. On the weather map on television I see that the sun is shining everyway in Ireland, even down in Corca Dhuibhne. The sun is shining in Dingle and shining on the Great Blasket. I know it is pouring in through the kitchen windows in Dún Chaoin like honey from a jar.

On that day Fiach gives me six St Bridget's Crosses, as a present, to comfort me.

'You can give them to your friends for a *bronntanas*,' he says, 'on *Lá 'le Bhríde*. I made a big pile of them for you.'

They are small and tight and perfect, every single cross. They make my heart lift with pride and happiness. Suddenly I decide to have a little party on St Bridget's Day. A glass of wine with some of my women friends who like St Bridget because she was a strong woman. I'll make up take-home bags for them. When they leave they'll each get a St Bridget's Cross. The cross that is not a cross, but a windmill.

I wonder if I should tell Fiach about Pádraig's death. I dither, but in the end I do tell him. In the end, there is not much I keep from Fiach.

He hasn't a lot to say.

'Who'll give the catfood to Peig Sayers?' he says, although I know he knows the cat will be grand. Then he starts working with a few straggling rushes that are left on the floor, rushes that are all different lengths and brown and withered looking, the dregs. He weaves the strands, green and brown and yellow, together, to make the last cross. It's a funny, bockety, multi-coloured cross, this little one.

That's the one we'll be keeping for ourselves.

Translated by the author.

THE DARK ISLAND

Angela Bourke

'Dark Island,' I heard one of the servants call my father's kingdom. I didn't like the name much, but I saw what he meant. The sun hardly ever shone there, summer or winter. Inside the high walls, where the old stories say there used to be a garden, nothing grew but nettles and briars. Sweet-smelling herbs grew there long ago, they told me, and roses, and my mother used to pick them. She was good at healing, they said. Not that it was any good to her when she caught the sickness herself.

The old people in the kitchen used to say that the place wouldn't have gone to wilderness if my mother hadn't died. When she and my father took over, they said, you'd see them walking around all the time, hand in hand in the sunshine. The flowers weren't only in the garden then; they were all over the meadows too, and sea-pinks and all kinds of other plants grew in clumps among the rocks above the stony beach, where the cormorants make their smelly nests now and everything around them is burnt bare. The other name for sea-pinks was thrift.

I can hardly remember my mother. I have two pictures of her in my mind, but that's all. She used to be asleep beside my father in the big bed if I went into their room early in the morning when I was small. I remember the way her arm used to stretch out from under the quilt to pick her nightdress off the floor, and the way she would slither it over her head while I was pulling my father's beard to wake him. He used to make hills and valleys for me in the bed then, with his knees bent up under the quilt, and I used to climb up, and slide down, and fall over, up and down, screeching and laughing, delighted with myself.

'When I'm big,' I said to them once, one of those days, lying flat on their bed on my little fat tummy trying to catch my breath, 'I'm going to marry Daddy.'

I remember my mother laughing then. 'Well, love,' she said, 'that's one thing you won't do. You can marry any man you like when you're big, if you want to, except Daddy. You can't marry Daddy.'

The other memory I have of her is going for eggs. She used to take me to the hen-wife's house, with a little basket of my own. She carried the big basket, full of eggs, but she used to put one egg into my basket, with a wisp of straw wrapped around it, and that would be my boiled egg for supper.

I was afraid of the hen-wife. Her fingernails were black and hard, and there were whiskers on her chin. One day when we went to visit her, she was eating her dinner. A boiled pollock: the whole fish lying dead on a white plate in front of her. When I saw her put its eyes into her gummy old mouth, I felt so sick that I had to run out of the house. But my mother came after me, and this is my second memory: the way she gripped my shoulder, and the angry look in her eyes.

'If you can't have manners with the hen-woman, you'll never come with me again,' she said. 'She's old and she's poor, and the likes of you has no business criticising her. Grateful to her you should be.'

When she'd said that much, she brought me back into the house so that I could say goodbye properly, and I saw her giving the hen-wife a kiss.

I often thought of that after Fionnuala came to live with us. She was my mother's stepsister, but a good deal older, and my mother had been dead a year when she came. Looking after us she was, according to herself, but all she did was torment us.

'The poor orphan,' she called me, in the sort of voice that let me know an orphan was something nasty and worthless. She never stopped giving out to me and to the people who ran the house. I was spending altogether too much time in the kitchen, she said, and the household staff ought to know the difference between themselves and us.

Fionnuala wouldn't let me go near the hen-wife. She hated her. Not that I wanted to go near her. I was still young and easily frightened, but I thought of my lovely mother when I heard Fionnuala talking to my father.

'You wouldn't know what diseases she might pick up down there,' she said. 'You ought to run that disgusting old hag out of the place and knock down her dirty little hut.'

I listened carefully to hear what answer my father might give, but he didn't answer her at all.

The cook's theory was that Fionnuala was out to marry my father. He said it one day when he didn't know I was listening, so I just stayed behind the big kitchen press, listening.

'Don't you know,' he was saying to the butler, 'that a king has to have a wife?' He was making bread, thumping the dough over and back on the table. 'A king that's not married has no luck in his kingdom. Did you not notice there are no swallows this year? And it's June! And it's two years since I heard the cuckoo!' He sifted a handful of flour over the dough and divided it into two loaves, shaping them between his hands. 'Do you not see the way that Fionnuala one dresses up at dinner time?' he said then. 'The way she's always looking in mirrors? You can be sure the king never sees the cranky side of that lady!' And he put the two loaves beside the fire with a clean cloth over them.

I ran up the stairs and out.

I watched Fionnuala at dinner time that evening. She had her hair twisted up onto the top of her head, with a gold ornament of my mother's pinned into it. There was mascara on her eyelashes and three different colours of shadow on her eyelids. Every time my father looked the other way she cleaned the blade of her knife on a piece of bread and looked at her reflection in the shiny metal, checking her eye make-up.

If my father married her, I'd be finished. I couldn't stand it. She'd be with us forever and I'd never get away from her. I took a deep breath.

'That's my mother's gold hairslide,' I said out loud, pointing my finger at her hair. She started to laugh, but her face went red, and my father looked at us both.

'What's she talking about?'

'It's only this little thing,' she said, 'a little trinket my sister had,' and she took it out of her hair. She laid it on the table and my father picked it up. That was the first time I noticed how thin his fingers had got, and how pale he was.

'I didn't give anyone permission to touch the queen's jewels,' he said at last.

Fionnuala was trying to laugh, trying to speak lightly, but her face was very red. 'But sooner or later you'll have to,' she said. 'You'll have to think about marrying again, for the sake of the kingdom, won't you?'

'I won't marry again,' said my father, and I saw some of his old kingly authority coming back to him, 'until I find a woman like the one who died. A woman with fair hair to her waist, and blue eyes. A woman who can wear the queen's clothes.'

I looked at Fionnuala and Fionnuala looked at the floor. Her hair was black, with some grey in it, and her eyes were green. I thought of how tall my mother had been and I felt delighted. Fionnuala was small and skinny, she wouldn't have come within six inches of her.

She didn't stay long with us after that. My father gave up coming to the table in the evenings. He used to eat meat and bread in his own room and throw the bones to his dogs. The room smelled awful, but he wouldn't leave it. He wouldn't even open a window. There were big heaps of bones in the corners that he didn't even notice. I used to go in to see him, but he didn't talk much to me. He didn't talk at all to Fionnuala, and when the winter came, with fog and rain and storms of wind, she left. She said there was a leak in her room, and broken glass in one of the windows. My father didn't give any instructions about getting them fixed, but he didn't mean anything by that. Her room wasn't the only part of the palace that was leaking by that time.

Little as I liked Fionnuala, I missed her when she went. The only woman left around the place now was the hen-wife, and there hadn't been another child on the island apart from myself for a long time. The cranky old cleric who was supposed to teach me Latin and reading never spoke to anyone. The only pastime I had was to go up to a little room in the tower and rummage in boxes of my mother's things. There was nothing valuable in them (all the jewels were in a glass case downstairs), but there were dresses, and a few books, and I was able to get through rainy days by reading.

I spent a lot of time walking around the island, talking to the workers. That was when they told me about the flowers, and about when my parents were young. But they were superstitious. They annoyed me sometimes. They used to say that the welfare of the land depended on the woman, on the right woman being queen and being married to the king, and that there were no more flowers because my mother was dead. They used to look at me then, and say it wouldn't be long now till I wasn't a child any more. They'd show me the odd little flower, eyebright, and scarlet pimpernel, and another little one that was called milkwort in my book but that they said was the little sisters. They said these things grew in the places where my foot had stepped.

When I started to bleed I thought I was dying, like my mother. I spent two days in bed, I felt so weak and so ashamed, but it stopped, and for another month I was fine and healthy. When it started again I didn't know what to do. I remembered all the things the servants had said about women. I thought about the island being a wilderness and the house falling into ruin, and I started to clean.

I cleaned a bathroom. I washed sheets and curtains. I cleaned the windows in my own room, and in my mother's little tower room, and I started to organise the stuff that was in her chests and boxes. I bathed myself from head to toe, as the old stories say – washing my hair three times a week and brushing it till it was smooth and shiny.

I started going for walks again, and taking an interest in what was going on in the island. My own clothes were too small for me, I'd grown so tall, but I found lovely things in one of my mother's boxes. I felt fine and proud wearing a blue dress of hers, and when I met the hen-wife cutting nettles one day I greeted her cheerfully.

'What are the nettles for?' I asked, curious.

'To make soup,' she said. 'Come on into the house if you like, and see how to make it.'

I hadn't stood in that house for ten years, though I'd walked past it every day, but I liked it straight away. I recognised the delicious smell of fresh bread and my eyes got used to the darkness. The hen-wife put me sitting by the fire, and showed me how to make soup out of the young nettles that grow in spring.

I went back often after that, learning to make pancakes, and home-made bread with soda and buttermilk. Making that bread felt like magic to me. We'd had nothing but potatoes in the palace for ages. The cook had left and he was the only one who knew how to make the yeast do its work.

The hen-wife told me stories, and we spent long evenings talking about the ways of the world. She had known my family a long time, so she knew a good deal about the doings in the palace. I liked her stories better than the ones I heard from the servants. They weren't that different basically – stories about the island in times past and the life people lived then – but to me they had a different flavour. The hen-wife listened carefully to what I had to say about them, but when I told her about the servants who'd said flowers grew where I placed my foot, she shook her head sceptically.

'Sunlight is what makes flowers grow, darling,' she said, 'enough water and the right soil. But some of those lads get a kick out of frightening a young woman.'

Bit by bit I came to trust her.

If it wasn't for her I wouldn't be here now.

I told her about the bleeding every month, and she said it was a good and healthy thing. She told me about the work she used to do long ago, when children were still being born in the island. She was a midwife, helping the mothers. She even helped my mother, she said, when I was being born.

She told me about the people who used to live on the island long ago, women and children and young fathers, and about how one after another they lost heart, sailed away and left their native land. She spoke about the difficulties people had in dealing with life and with each other, and how much it hurt them to have bailiffs over them who didn't treat them justly.

The hen-woman was sympathetic and understanding, but she had a sense of humour too. She would take the pipe out of her toothless mouth sometimes and throw back her head, laughing at some of the things we talked about. It's not surprising that she was the one I ran to when suddenly in the middle of the night I had to leave the palace for fear of my father.

I look around at this new country and I don't know whether it's good or bad. But certainly I couldn't have stayed on the island. I feel a little breeze on my head and around the back of my neck. It reminds me of the scissors and I'm suddenly very lonely. I'm still not used to having short hair.

'But what does he mean? Is he joking?' I asked the hen-woman that night. It was like having stones in my throat and needles in my brain, I felt so disgusted and so heartbroken. 'He can't marry his daughter, can he?'

'No, darling. No, he can't. But still we'll have to do something. You're not safe in that house. Your father isn't well these days.'

The red veins in his eyes were the first thing I'd seen when he woke me, trying to get into my bed. I felt the heat of his body and the sour smell of his breath, and I slid out from under him, still half asleep. I managed to get away from him, into the corner of the room. He was always slow on his feet and the drink had made him dizzy.

'You're the woman,' he kept saying. 'You're the woman. You're the woman. I won't marry any woman but you.'

The hen-woman took the big scissors out of the dresser drawer. I jumped, but she laid them on the table. She took a comb out of her pocket and began to do my hair.

'You're too like your mother, darling. This long hair is too heavy a load for you just yet. You'll be better off without it.' She made it into a long plait, tied it with a red ribbon, and cut it with one swipe of the scissors before I realised what she was doing. She put it into my lap, with another bit of the red ribbon.

'Tie it up now, good girl,' she said, and I tied the other end of the dead plait of hair. 'You can keep it now, in memory of your childhood days, if you like, or else I'll keep it for you. It'll grow again anyway.'

'You keep it,' I said. Tears were blinding my eyes, but they were like what a little girl would cry who'd had her hair cut against her will; nothing like the heart-scalding tears of terror I'd been crying just before.

'It's no wonder you'd cry for your hair, darling, but you'll get over it. Wait till you see how nice and light your head will feel in the summer. But listen, we have to make a plan.'

My father had said he was going to marry me, and the hen-woman advised me not to argue with him if he started on that notion again. I would tell him my hair had got burnt by accident, and that I'd had to cut it. I'd pretend I was prepared to marry him, if only everything was done correctly.

'Tell him you need proper clothes,' the hen-woman said, 'and a trunk of your own. And tell him you can't stay in the same house with him between now and your wedding day.'

I sat then and took my soup, a crop-haired barefoot waif beside the fire, listening. The hen-woman was planning in detail what I'd say to my father, and what clothes I'd have to ask for, but I listened as though her talk was just a story, words that would give me consolation until the light of day would come.

When I sneaked back into the palace at dawn, my father was in the hall. He got a shock when he saw my short hair, but he wanted to apologise.

'I'm sorry, sweetheart, if I frightened you last night,' he said. 'It won't happen again. When we're married you'll see that it's all for your own good.'

'You can't marry your daughter, Daddy.' I still had no shoes on and I was shaking.

'I can,' he said sharply. 'The king can marry any woman he wants. Anyway it's necessary, for the sake of the kingdom.' He walked to the door. 'Tomorrow,' he said. 'Tomorrow will be the wedding. Get dressed now.'

I remembered what I had to do and I ran after him.

'Daddy, I can't get married till I have proper clothes.'

He stopped.

'Do you know what I'd really like?'

'What?' He was looking at me kindly again.

'A dress made of bog-cotton.'

'Bog cotton, is it? You really are a little girl still, aren't you? But why not! There's plenty of bog-cotton on the turf-cuttings. I'll have your dress made for you.'

'Daddy?'

'What is it now?'

'The bride shouldn't stay in the same house as her husband before they're married. Do you think I should find some other lodgings for myself?'

He laughed again. 'Whatever you think yourself, sweetheart. Do whatever you like.'

He had a light and a liveliness in his eyes that I hadn't seen for years, and the love I felt for him was breaking my heart, but I remembered all the hen-woman had told me. I ran up the stairs and filled a bag with books and clothes. Down again then, and out the door before he could stop me.

I stayed in the hen-woman's house. She told me to call her Betty, she said that was her name, and as time went on I got used to it. Every time my hair grew down to my neck, she cut it again, but I didn't mind any more when I saw those little brown feathers on the floor under my chair. The blond plait was still in the dresser drawer, tied up with its two red ribbons. It seemed to me now that it belonged to someone else entirely, to some lonely, childish little stranger.

I used to go out for walks, getting to know places in the island where I'd never been before, but I avoided my father whenever I saw him. He had taken to going walking himself. I pretended I was just shy, but I heard that servants were out cutting bog-cotton, spinning it and weaving it, and I realised I wouldn't have my freedom much longer.

Betty understood very well how worried I was, but she didn't let on until one day when we were bringing in some sheets that had been drying in the air.

'A queen has to have her own trunk,' she said. 'Listen. When your father brings you the dress, tell him that he'll have to get you a trunk, and that it must be well made, strong and waterproof. And when you see the dress, tell him it's lovely, but that you need something even whiter and softer than bog-cotton – that you must have a dress made of swansdown for your wedding.'

When I heard the plan she laid out, as we sat at the table with the folded sheets between us, I thought she must have lost her reason, or that she was making fun of me. When the trunk came, she said, I'd have to leave the island in it. She would shut me into it and the tide would take me to Ireland.

'But I'll be drowned. The trunk will break up.'

'It won't break up. Wait till you see. I haven't given you bad advice yet, have I?'

'No, you haven't. Oh, but Betty, you're not serious?'

'I'm completely serious,' she said, and I realised that she was. 'You can't stay here. Even if your father hadn't taken bad the way he has, there's nothing here for you. All that servants' talk about wild flowers growing under your feet! Honestly! If you're not scrubbing and cleaning for them they make a saint of you, and I don't know which is worse!'

That made me laugh, as she knew well it would.

'When I was young,' she said, 'people used to come and go from Ireland all the time, and we used to send messages on the tide, sealed up in bottles. If you throw a bottle into the sea at Rinn Mhór during the spring tide, it washes up safely on the Birds' Strand in Ireland.'

She walked to the door and looked out at the sea. That sea looked dangerous and unfriendly to me, but Betty took hold of my hand and promised me that it would carry me to Ireland.

I had to send a coaxing message to my father to make him accept the second delay, but he had changed a lot in those weeks, his hair and clothes were clean and his beard was trimmed. He knew I was frightened of him, so he was trying to be nice to me.

He ordered the trunk made, and the second dress, and Betty began to tell me about the journey I would have to make. Now I had two things to be frightened of, one competing with the other, and gradually I came to the decision that I would be better off taking my chances on the sea than submitting to my father's will. This had been Betty's plan for me from the very first night, if I had only known, but she waited to tell me about it until I had recovered a bit – until my arms and legs had got strong and my skin had turned brown from being out in the wind.

One afternoon I walked as far as Rinn Mhór and threw some scraps of wood into the tide. They floated clear of the rocks, as Betty had promised me they would. I watched them moving out of sight towards Ireland and I knew that I'd be following them soon.

The trunk came, and the second dress, and then we had to think up another plan, because I couldn't leave before the spring tide. But I was getting braver. I spoke to my father myself, standing at the gate of Betty's house.

'The two dresses are lovely,' I said. 'The bog-cotton one will do me for walking, after we're married, and I'll wear the swansdown one around the house. But do you know?' I said, and I didn't call him 'Daddy', 'ordinary people get married in white. The proper and fitting thing for a queen would really be a dress in the colours of the sun and moon.'

I looked him straight in the eye, and he gave in. He ordered the third dress made, and Betty and I rushed to get the trunk ready.

We took it down to Rinn Mhór on an old donkey-cart and I laid my mother's blue dress and my own two new dresses into it. We tied a rope to it to see if it would float, and it did. We hauled it back in and tried again, this time with heavy stones in it. It floated nicely, and when we pulled it in to shore again it was as dry inside as it had ever been. We made holes in the lid, so I'd be able to breathe, and then I got into it.

It was a trunk made for a queen, from sweet-smelling planks of cedar, and inside it was wide and roomy. Even after Betty shut the lid down, some daylight came through the holes. Underneath me was swansdown, with bog-cotton beneath that. I lay back and closed my eyes, and drew my breath gently and evenly.

That was five days ago. I had to wait for the spring tide, and for the full moon that would come with it. Betty and I were anxious, but we managed to convince the people in the big house that it was only wedding nerves.

Yesterday morning my father came to the door with my wedding dress. All the colours of the sun and the moon, just as I had asked, and my own father looking at me as proudly as a child.

'Tomorrow,' he said, and left.

I started to cry then, and I would have lost all my courage, but Betty sent me out in the open air. I spent all the rest of that afternoon walking around the dark island for the last time, and came home quietly in time for supper.

When the moon rose we were ready. Betty gave me a special drink to make me sleepy, and put me into the trunk, with a little packet of food and a bottle of spring water. My book on herbs and my book of stories were wrapped in a silk handkerchief beside my head. Before she closed the lid, she laid the new dress with the colours of the sun and the moon in beside me. 'You never know when you might need it,' she said, and she kissed me three times.

I remember crying quietly in my downy bed before I fell asleep, but most of the time after that I was dreaming. All that night I was thrown from wave to wave on the sea, but I only woke up properly when one wave threw the trunk right up on this beach.

I'm assuming I'm in Ireland. It's quite like the place I've come from, except that there's one patch in the sky that's as blue as my mother's dress.

Fionnuala lives around here somewhere, but she's not the one I want. I'm going to make my own way as best I can. I know how to make a loaf of bread, and how to cook nettles. I know Irish, and some Latin, and I have new clothes in my trunk that are fine enough to take me anywhere.

Translated by the author.

CANNIBALS

Mícheál Ó Ruairc

It was six o'clock in the evening when the yellow van pulled into one of Dublin's posher housing estates. It cruised into the middle of a small square on the south side of the city and parked. The van had come to a stop in a place that had all the trappings of vacuous modernity. The empty square boasted a mock-fountain complete with artificial cascades, its tackiness courtesy of some filthy-rich chancer who had once passed himself of as a property developer.

Nothing happened for a while. Then people began to make their way towards the van in their dribs and drabs. Before long a fairly large crowd had formed a semi-circle around the parked van. The crowd was silent. It waited patiently but there was no movement from the van. The windows of the vehicle were blacked out. Nothing happened for a long time. The evening sun disappeared over the horizon and the dark shroud of the night came in but still no-one stirred. Then, just as it looked as if nothing was ever going to happen, a small hatch in the side of the van suddenly flew open and a bald middle-aged man poked out his head. He let a roar out you could hear half a mile away.

'Have your money ready now, you lot!' He produced a piece of paper and proceeded to read out a list of names. 'McAndrew, ten girl-cutlets – one hundred euro; Hyde, three son-steaks – eight hundred and sixty euro; MacMahon, seven kilos of minced refugee-meat – thirty-five euro; McFadden, daughter-flavoured female-child calf-meat cutlets – ninety euro; Naughton, baby-liver-cutlets – one hundred and twenty euro; O'Neill, boy-child-ribs son-flavoured – two hundred and fifty euro; Treacy, ten T-bone boy-hand boy-child steaks son-flavoured – one thousand five hundred euro; Humphries, twenty refugee burgers – twenty euro ...'

With each name that he called out, the bald man threw a brown parcel into the waiting crowd. As each person collected their parcel, they slunk quietly away – back to their upper-class houses.

Exactly twelve minutes after that small hatch first opened, the crowd had completely disappeared again. There was no sign of the yellow van. It was as if it had never even been there.

Vivian Buckley, human-meat glutton and consumer, and his wife, Treasa, a non-human-meat eater (she herself much preferred the term 'vegetarian'), stood at an upstairs window of their eight-bedroomed mansion complete with swimming pool (to buy this house would have set you back a cool twenty million euro). From their elevated vantage point, they surveyed the small square that lay opposite their home. Vivian shook his head, a disgruntled look on his face. Times had changed since all of the new prohibitions had come in. Life was much tougher now since the ban on the eating of meat, poultry and fish had been instigated; the same with the daily ban on sex between 6 am and midnight; the ban on alcohol consumption between 6 pm in the evening and midday of the following day; the annual ban on foreign travel between May and November; the law that insisted all couples have no fewer than six children living together in any one house. Yes, there was no doubt about it; life had become more difficult for everyone.

Vivian and Treasa were lucky that they only had the one child, a daughter named Rachel. Vivian shook his head ruefully again. The smoking ban was the root-cause of all this craziness, he said to himself; if they hadn't initially accepted that ridiculous proscription, they would never have found themselves in this mess in the first place!

Bans! Bans! Bans!

The ban on eating meat had put the kibosh on it altogether. It made no sense at all. Worse still, in Vivian's opinion, was the fact that this particular ban had been brought in deliberately in order to destroy the farming and fishing industries. The Coalition Government consisting of the Grey-Greens had got sick of forking out the various grants to support the development of stock – whether sheep, cattle, poultry or salmon – especially when all the farmers had retired to sun themselves on the Costa del Sol. A new European regulation was issued putting an end to all grants relating to these industries. This was all the excuse the Coalition needed. They decided to institute a complete ban on all farming and seafood produce. This new legislation was resented greatly, but the Grey-Green Coalition stood firm on it, just as they had done on a regular basis in relation to the other bans and prohibitions previous to this. A year or two went by. A few people here and there tried to break the law; a couple of people made official complaints about the new legislation, but most people just accepted it quietly. Then a butcher from Cork – a man who was also a senior member of the Cork County GAA Committee as it happens – identified a loophole in the legislation. Most types of meat were covered under the provisions of the ban – animal-meat, bird-meat, fish – but what about human flesh? Nobody had thought of this option. The man from Cork took his case to the High Court which found in his favour. The High Court ruled that it was permissible to consume human meat between Thursdays and Mondays, provided that people abstained on the other days of the week. This ruling proved a radical legal move, without a shadow of a doubt. Sure, similar legislation had already been implemented in Turkey, France and Holland, but they were the only countries that had permitted such a ruling. A divisive and somewhat tedious debate dragged on for weeks in the Irish media where the ethics of this pro-cannibal judgement and the morality of cannibalism were debated at length. As usual, however, the left-wingers won the day and people on the right-wing of Irish politics had to just grin and bear it. One or two groups organised protests against the new legislation, but they were only wasting their time. A majority of the Irish population were dying to sink their teeth into some meat again and they couldn't wait for the new provisions to be implemented. One difficulty still remained, however. While it was now legal to buy and to eat human-meat, it was still illegal to kill people for this purpose.

In order to negotiate a solution to this legal quandary, members of the Grey-Green coalition government were forced to cut short their holidays. Disgruntled, they left their chateaus and villas behind and hurried back to Ireland on their private jets. The government minister in question had ordered them all home in order to resolve this damned question once and for all. The fact that they were the only members of the Irish population permitted to take foreign holidays during the summer only made them more aggrieved than they were already. Following urgent discussions the solution that the government arrived at was as follows: Families with more than four children between the ages of five and fifteen could be culled under new legislation. In the case of non-national families (i.e. those families with children who were born outside Ireland) the age group for the cull was broadened to include children between the ages of one-and-a-half and nineteen.

Children with disabilities or children from well-known wealthy areas (the same districts where members of the Grey-Green coalition government and their families lived, as it happens) were exempt from the new regulations and it was against the law to cannibalise them. The new Cannibalism Bill was submitted to the Oireachtas for approval and it passed all stages. The opposition made no objections to the new legislation, partly because they themselves were in a bad way given the chronic meat shortage. The various Coalition ministers returned to their chateaus and villas again, secure in the knowledge that this cannibalism issue had finally been put to bed. One problem that immediately raised its head, however, was the fact that most butcher shops had already closed down because of the meat shortage. Most butchers were very reluctant therefore to re-open their human-meat supply chains or to go back into the cannibalism sector again. That said, it wasn't long before a few new butchers supplying human-meat did spring up again here and there. It wasn't long, however, before these same businesses found themselves under pressure again. These butchers were inundated with new orders for human-meat, and demand for their produce far out-stripped supply. They just couldn't cope.

You had the occasional protest against the new legislation by vegetarians in those early years, of course. The Society Against Cruelty to Children (the SACC) organised a couple of street protests as well but without any success. At the same time as this was going on, very strict legislation had been put into place prohibiting the killing or eating of all animals, including birds and fish. Anyone caught breaking the law in this area would be immediately exiled to Africa as punishment for their crime.

Within a year or so, everybody in Ireland who wasn't vegetarian was consuming human-meat at a great rate. They tucked into cannibalised meat products in restaurants and takeaways everywhere. They gorged themselves on the stuff in hotels and pubs up and down the country. They wolfed it down in the privacy of their homes too, of course. Human-meat was very expensive, but that didn't seem to curb people's appetite for it. The more expensive the meat was, the more the demand for it seemed to soar. As you'd expect, there was a wide range of prices relating to quality and product-type. Some types of human-meat were far more expensive than others. For example, delicacies such as girl-meat or daughter-meat were a good deal less expensive than boy-meat or son-meat, for which punters could pay astronomical prices. Boy-child meat was particularly costly given its unique texture and could only be found in the most high-class restaurants. Even then, this variety of meat was extremely expensive indeed and was far outside the price range of most foodies. Refugee-meat, black-meat or asian-meat were all fairly cheap and it was mainly the poorer or more run-down restaurants or takeaways that served this type of food.

Vivian Buckley gazed out at the square where the crowds queued for the takeaway van on a regular basis. Secure in the lush comfort of his post-modern, mock-Tudor house, he marvelled at how other people could eat refugee burgers and chips, never mind black-sausages or asian-rinds. The whole thing was just beyond him. Even his own daughter liked the stuff. She regularly sneaked out of the house at night and headed for the local chipper to get a takeaway for herself. As for himself, he'd initially kept his distance from this new food trend. He'd begun eating human-meat only occasionally at first, but before he knew it he'd developed a taste for it. It wasn't long before he actually developed a craving for it. These days he had absolutely no qualms about admitting to his friends that he was a 'confirmed human-meat-eater' and proud of it.

Everything was going fine for a year or two. Then things changed. People noticed that the quality of the human-meat for sale had declined greatly. It didn't taste nice any more. It was bland and stale. It had become completely flavourless. One night Vivian was at home watching television when everything became clear to him in a very profound way. Most of the human-meat that was on the market was the coarse meat that some people referred to as 'the leavings'. It was just gristle, fat and bone, all formed into one inedible mass. This meat was the rough stuff and the kids butchered for it were the hard-chaws who came from the flats and the disadvantaged housing estates of Ireland's cities. In the final analysis, their meat was not fresh because these kids weren't raised in a natural and healthy environment. Their flesh tasted artificial and manufactured because that is what they were – they were a mass-produced product. They weren't 'free-range', so to speak.

As a consequence of this decline in quality, the demand for free-range meat went through the roof. This was the catalyst for the boom in the yellow-van phenomenon. A few chancers saw a gap in the market and decided to go for it. They pooled their resources and bought a fleet of refrigerated yellow vans. They hit the thoroughfares of Ireland, big and small. This new company really went for broke. They travelled every road, motorway and lane in the country. There wasn't a major housing estate or backwater village that they didn't drive into and flog their wares. Rural children! Free-range children! This was the major new market; this was the new boom! Free-range kids that were born and raised in the countryside and fed on the finest and most natural of produce! The cream of the crop – lovely, healthy country-bred kids that would provide the best of feeding and sustenance to the masses.

The finest of son-meat and girl-meat. This was it! This was the real deal! Every illegal market and auction in the country now had their agents who scoured the countryside; every single small-holding and family farm was combed in the search for prime country-kid-flesh. They paid top dollar for these kids, but you get what you pay for – isn't that what they say?

All of these kids were butchered in the most humane and efficient manner possible – with a quick bullet to the head. They were all beheaded almost immediately in a butchering process that was as meticulous and systematic as their sourcing had been the first day ever. Nothing was wasted. One pile was made of the skulls, another of the other bones. Another pile then consisted of the flesh and the torsos. The skulls and other bones were fed to the dogs, while the carcasses were hung on racks in the back of the refrigerated yellow vans, all arranged carefully in terms of their quality. The owners of this fleet of vans were well aware that their activities were against the law, specifically the stipulation that each human-meat vendor have an official licence as issued by the Human-Meat Association of Ireland (HMAI). They didn't care, however. Business was booming and that was all that mattered.

Weren't the cream of Irish society amongst their most regular customers? Politicians from the Grey-Green Coalition, judges, business people – even the Garda Commissioner himself, Mr Michael Adams. At the end of the day weren't they fulfilling the mantra of the Human-Meat Association itself? – 'Be humane in all human affairs'. Didn't they also butcher all of their produce in strict accordance with all of the regulations and in the most humane manner possible? After all, they didn't ever degrade themselves by resorting to cruelty, kidnapping or other illegal measures. They adhered carefully to all of the regulations with respect to the boning of human-meat and the age limits as relating to child-meat products. Taken together, each of these facts were enough for the authorities to turn a blind eye to the fleet of yellow vans that criss-crossed the country on a daily basis.

'Vivian! Vivian! Are you deaf or what? Come down here immediately! Your dinner is ready.'

Vivian snapped out of his reverie. He'd been daydreaming for the guts of half of an hour. On his way down their pure-mahogany staircase, the smell of roast meat came to him and his mouth began to water. Initially, Treasa was very quiet in herself as they sat at the table. Their daughter Rachel was silent also, but that was nothing new of late. Rachel was at that awkward age. She was sixteen and madly in love with some lazy chancer her parents couldn't stand the sight of, a dark gap-toothed Moroccan individual with body odour. This evening Rachel was in an even more foul humour than normal. Apparently the chancer hadn't phoned her in three days.

Just the previous Monday, Vivian and Treasa had rowed badly about the effect that Rachel's new boyfriend was having on her – and on everyone else. At one stage Vivian had lost the run of himself and blurted out.

'If he was just a year younger, then he'd just be sausage-meat or a burger down below in Schelazi's fridge in the takeaway at Art's Corner – instead, he's trying to get the leg over our Rachel!'

Vivian's outburst caught Treasa by surprise; she nearly fell over, she was that taken aback by what her husband had said and the venom of his outburst. The biggest insult that one could give to a vegetarian or a human-meat-abstainer (a term which Treasa had never liked) was to mention them in the same crude context as human-meat-flesh. If, for example, you were to say a phrase such as 'she would make a lovely slice of girl-meat' or 'I'd love to have that young lad on my plate seasoned in a nice pepper sauce', you could really offend certain people. Treasa had just recovered from Vivian's outburst when, next thing, she caught her husband completely by surprise.

'The same thing crossed my mind, Vivian. Can you do anything about him? You couldn't have a word in the ear of one of the Grey-Green councillors or something, could you?'

'You know full well that the likes of that is against the law Treasa,' Vivian said.

'Against the law is it! Yourself and the law. Never mind the bloody law. Sure nobody obeys the law here any more. The law is an ass in this country, everybody knows that.'

'But what can I honestly do, Treasa? Let's face it. This guy's parents are over in Morocco. We'd have to get permission off them for a start – '

'Get their permission! Are you out of your mind? Where do you think most of the refugee-meat that they're eating up and down the country comes from, for God's sake? Are you telling me that all of the meat producers of this country are going around asking refugees' parents for permission to do their butchering? Some chance! And what about the yellow van that comes here once a week? Do you think that the people in that have got permission before they start doling out that human-meat of theirs?'

'I'm sure they have, Treasa, because – '

'Will you wake up, Vivian, for God's sake! Those vans operate a "shoot-on-sight" policy when it comes to refugees, that's what I've been told! Anyway, aren't half of the refugees who come here either orphans or homeless people?'

'But I'd have to get in touch with some back-street butcher or other and give him Kwaki's address ...'

'You will not do that! That'd be far too risky!'

'Sure, what else can I do then?'

'Weren't you an apprentice butcher for a while when you were a teenager? Don't tell me that you've forgotten everything you learned back then?'

'Well ... well ... but that was more than twenty years ago now.'

'It is very difficult to completely forget the basics of any trade. I've often said that myself. If things continue as they are, you'll regret it, that's for sure. You saw the way that he was looking at her the other night. That lust-filled look in his eyes. He couldn't take his eyes off her haunches all evening. Before you know it, he'll have her up in the bedroom with him and it'll be too late then. God knows that they've plenty of opportunities as it is, we're away often enough.'

'Don't say things like that, Treasa. Can't we just tell him to get lost?'

'But Rachel is mad about the idiot or haven't you noticed! We'd be wasting our time. There's only one way left to us now, Vivian, and it's up to you to get it sorted out as quickly as possible.'

'How do you mean ... how do you ...?'

'I'll tell you what. I'll phone him tomorrow when Rachel is gone to town for ballet practice. I'll invite him over to dinner and I'll tell him to bring his overnight bag with him because he'll be staying the night. Once he's here, I'll tell him that you're down in the basement fixing Rachel's moped and that you could do with a hand. He'll be down to you straight away.'

'I don't know Treasa ... I don't know ... and what about the tools I'll need?'

'Don't you have a shotgun and plenty of ammunition for it? And there are two metal saws in the garage and there are plenty of carving knives in the kitchen. Haven't we two freezers down in the basement, one of which is empty at the moment. What else do you need?'

'What else indeed?' said Vivian to himself, 'just the guts necessary to do the deed.'

The moment of truth was at hand and Vivian knew that he would just have to steel himself and get the job done.

'This son-meat is absolutely beautiful,' said Vivian at the table, attempting to prompt some conversation from the other two. Treasa shook her head quietly. As a vegetarian, she disliked any references to human meat while at the table.

'You sure eat enough of it anyway,' she said, a wry smile on her face.

'I suspect that you now like human-meat way more than you ever liked regular meat.'

'You're probably right about that, Treasa.'

The pair of them were caught completely by surprise then when Rachel spoke up. It was such a long time since she had spoken to either of them that, for a moment, the sound of her voice appeared almost alien to them.

'You needn't worry about me any more,' she said in a chirpy tone.'

'How come … how come?' said Treasa, a distinctive tremble in her voice.

'Myself and Kwaki have split up.'

'How do you mean?' Vivian asked, a look of terror in his eyes.

'He hasn't contacted me for three days. He must have a new girlfriend, I'd say. I couldn't care less. I don't love him any more. Anyway, Richard Hyde – yep, you known him, the son of the senior counsel – he's been texting me non-stop for the last week or so. I think he really likes me. And I like him too. I invited him over to watch a DVD here later tonight. Is that OK, Dad? OK? OK?'

'That's … that's … great news, Rachel. That's … deadly altogether! He'll always be very welcome in this house, Treasa, won't he?

'Absolutely! Absolutely! He's a lovely lad. He's going to college in St Patrick's at the moment, isn't he? And unless I'm badly mistaken, he's a fine rugby player, too. I've spoken to his mother, Tina, once or twice on the golf course.'

'By the way, Dad,' said Rachel then, a more talkative jib about her. 'Where did you get these refugee burgers? They're bloody delicious! I've never had burgers as nice as these before in all my life. They're even nicer than the ones you get below in Schelazi's takeaway.'

Her parents glanced across at one another, a secretive smile on their faces.

'I'm glad to hear that, Rachel. I got them from the yellow van there last week. I'm thrilled that you like them so much. As it happens, we have plenty more of them in the freezer. There's plenty more where they came from, girl!'

Translated by Micheál Ó hAodha.

SORELY PRESSED

Dara Ó Conaola

It was the great Daniel O'Connell himself who caused me my misfortune, well beloved and all as he was by the Irish race. Sure they thought he was the Almighty. I had great praise for him myself. I'd work for him for nothing. I would – until that night.

'Where was I again?'

'You were in the big city, of course.'

'That much I know – but where?'

'You were in that pub you're always in. Didn't you spend the day there?'

'Where did I go after that?'

'You said, eventually, that you were heading off. Nothing would keep you. You vamoosed. That's all I remember …'

I suppose since we can't recall, I'll never find out for sure where I went. I must have been in a few places and whiled away the time somewhere. I've never heard of a couple of hours that went missing in this life without someone using them up. I suppose I came by Trinity College. Down then towards the bridge they call O'Connell Bridge. The bridge of Danieleen of the Gaelic. Wasn't it the Gaelic saved him!

'Daniel O'Connell, have you Irish in your head?' said the maid from Ireland to him, in the old tongue.

'What's on your mind, let it be said,' said Daniel, not thinking of anything in particular, no more than I was that night.

'Ah,' says she, 'there's poison in your cup to kill you stone-dead.'

It's a long time now since I heard that tale from Darky John.

'It was, you know,' said Darky, 'it was the Gaelic what saved him …'

And may God rest Darky John, Daniel, the maid from Ireland, and myself …

I remember the Bridge. Not a sinner or a ghost, not a car or a bus, nothing at all to be seen but the empty bridge. Daniel himself was there, of course, and his monumental angels …

I spoke to him. It must have been Irish or English I spoke, because I haven't Latin, French, Greek or the language of the seagulls.

Whatever tongue I spoke, he took no notice of me. There's nothing I find more annoying than being given the deaf ear. I knew well that a bronzed man wasn't capable of much talk … But couldn't he pretend? There's more ways of killing a dog than by hanging … He could have spoken to my heart – and my heart is always open to receive pleasant tidings in a discreet fashion …

He could have said that he had got my message, that he was grateful, that I should be going home now to my wife and family, if such I had … or the likes. He'd have said all that if he were anyway decent …

Since God granted me patience, something I've never ever got any credit for, I said to myself I'd give him another chance …

'May God and Mary bless you, Daniel O'Connell,' said I in the sweetest Gaelic of the Gaels of Ireland, word for word as my grandfather would have said it, and God rest him too; and they say the Irish spoken in his days was far superior to what it is now … But if I spoke to him in the language of Brian Boru himself, the great Liberator was impervious to me.

'Well may God never put luck in your way,' says I, angrily. I was going to give him a piece of my mind that would knock him off his pedestal. I was totally pissed off with him. I suppose anyone looking at me would say I was a proper madcap or, in civil service terms, out of order.

It wasn't long before I was surrounded by an unruly mob – they were coming at me from all sides. O'Connell's elite guard. I drew my silver-hilted sword before you could say 'Emancipation'.

'Lay down your sword in the name of the law,' said one of them.

'Let ye stay the blade's length away from me,' says I with a boldness to match.

'You've broken the law,' says the other, 'and we'll have to be taking you in.'

'Ye won't be taking me in if ye're not taking yer man in,' pointing to O'Connell, 'or it's certain ye won't be having me without a fierce battle.'

'We'll take him in, too, only throw away your sword.'

'All right so, if you swear before all present.'

He swore. I threw away my sword. They leapt on me. They caught hold of me here and there. One fella grabbed my ear. I was thrown into the big, black car that people call the Black Maria. I was captured. Off she goes, Maria …

O'Connell was left behind in his victorious, stately posture. I wasn't too pleased with this injustice, for all their promises.

'Yeres is a crooked law,' says I. They said nothing. 'But it's not as crooked as yerselves ...'

The answer to that was punches in the ribs and a barbecue sauce of rich expletives. I'd a sauce of my own to add to it. They made it clear that all the cursing and swearing was another case against me.

'If that's the way,' says I, 'I might as well earn it.'

Every foul word, so to speak, that I ever heard since I left home became part of a litany – and I got a lovely 'Pray for us' in the ribs with each response. They didn't leave off until we arrived at the station – that's what they call it, the station. I call it the barracks. The drink had cooled down in me at this stage. I remember the barracks well. They dragged me into a back room. Three of them in front of me and one behind. The interrogation began. Name? Who are you? What have you in your pocket? ... Are you a member of an illegal organisation?

I was the master now, and would be until they got information from me – something I had no intention of giving them.

'Even if I had committed a crime, ye'd never find out by such a feeble line of questioning,' I declared. One of them went bananas and gave it to me straight in the kisser. A half an hour they spent beating me and questioning me. But I said nothing at all.

Eventually they lugged me down to a cell. I was given a blanket and ordered to go to sleep. With this I complied. I was just about to nod off on the hard wooden bed, when I heard someone coming again. It was a middle-aged man this time. Far more civilised than the other lot. He was half-way towards being pleasant with me. But I wasn't going to be deceived – I remembered the way they tricked me before, not taking the Liberator in, as they had promised. But I knew, all the same, that they'd give me no rest.

'I'll say nothing tonight,' I told him, 'but if ye'll arrest O'Connell, as promised, maybe tomorrow after I've consulted my solicitor, maybe I'll talk then.'

He was happy to get that much out of me. Off he went and that's all I can recall until the following morning. The court. That's what was facing me next day. I'd spent the morning being transferred from cell to cell. From car to car. The waiting was worse than the court itself ...

I was first put into a cell in the courthouse. Two members of the Travelling community there before me, asleep. Three wooden beds. I lay down on one. The great door opened. Tea, would you believe. The Travellers were quickly on their feet when they heard the tea coming. A small pot of tea and a slice of bread were placed near me. Up I stand like a crowing cock. I give the teapot a good old kick. The Guard says nothing at all. But I can see from the way he's looking at me that he won't forget – it will go on my account, as they might say in the bank ...

I was called at last. I was brought to the bowels of the courthouse.

'Up you go now,' says one of the Guards. Up I go. Into the court. The Judge is there before me. A clerk by his side. Another clerk on the other side. Other state functionaries sitting by the wall, standing by the door. The audience seated behind me ...

'So this is the nameless one,' said the Judge.

'He is, your Honour,' said the Guard, 'he won't talk until he sees a solicitor and hmm ... hmm ...'

'Yes?'

'There's another condition as well, your Honour, but I'd rather not mention it at this time for fear it might raise laughter. I'll be asking for permission to have the case adjourned until ...'

'And this other condition refers to ...'

'The Special Crimes Act, your Honour.'

'Case adjourned to the Special Court at high noon. Next!'

'Down. Down. Down,' says the Guard.

Down again. Down the stairs. Up another stairs. Into another big cell already occupied by one detainee. They closed the door. Another wait. Exchange a few words with the other fella. I didn't bother with the lunch. The other man worried about the Special Court. Worst court in the world he said. The one with the least mercy. The Judge with his name in Irish – if we appear before him it's a life sentence ... A long wait. Listening to the other fella is punishment enough.

At long last the door opens. The other fella is taken out, my turn to go down. I'm standing by the iron door of the court. In I go – the Guard with me every step of the way, like my shadow. What a shock. Sitting beside the Judge in all his composure, who should I see, but the bould Daniel.

A little scarecrow of a man came up to me.

'I'll be speaking on your behalf,' he said. 'You say nothing except you're guilty. I'll do the talking. I know how these guys work. This is the Special Court. The Judge uses the Irish form of his name! You've only a squeak of a chance.'

'How did they manage to bring yer man along?' I asked him, referring to the bould Dan.

'Special Branch. They can do that kind of thing ...'

'Silence in the court!'

'What's the charge?' asked the Judge with his name in Irish.

'Five in all, your Honour,' said the Guard.

'Which are ...?'

'One: Insulting a leading statesman in O'Connell Street Metropolitan. Two: Attacking a leading statesman in said street. Three: Attacking officers of the state in said street. Four: In possession of deadly weapon. Five: Resisting arrest.'

'Guilty or not guilty?'

'Not guilty,' said I.

'What did he say?'

'Guilty, your Honour,' said the solicitor

'Has he ever been charged before?'

'Never, your Honour. My client comes from a very respectable background, incapable of imagining such offences. I request he be freed under the Probation Act ...'

The Judge laughed.

'Let him go free so as to insult our statesmen, the Noble Gods of our ancestors, such as the heroic gentleman among us today, courtesy of the Special Branch? The Probation Act isn't worth sixpence in this Court. It is the act of Special Crimes we deal with here. Do you follow?'

'I follow, your Honour, but ...'

'Life imprisonment,' said the Judge and pounded the bench with such vehemence that O'Connell himself got a fright ...

I was rehearsing a litany of abuse, seeing there was no more satisfaction to be got ... but, I suppose, they were expecting as much. Suddenly I felt something like a towel gagging me ... I was dragged down stairs. Then down another stairs. They knocked my skull in. That helped me to sleep.

Translated by Gabriel Rosenstock.

WHATEVER I LIKED

Micheál Ó Conghaile

He asked me if I had ever used a shotgun before. I told him I hadn't and if I was clumsy with it, then so much the worse for the person I'd be using it on. There's no law that says murder has to be tidy ...

Now that I've been convicted by the court and received a life sentence, I have plenty of time to think about things like this. The horror of it. I have all the time in the world, except for whatever portion of it I can manage to fritter away in this narrow little cube of a cell where they have cooped me up. It's all my time now – and that's the damning and the saving of me all at once – even though they tried to take it away from me. I might as well tell the truth now, at this stage of my life, or some bit of the truth anyway. Just as it comes to mind.

'Are you guilty?' the Judge asked. I remember that part very well.

'How do you mean "guilty"?' I asked him. 'What sort of question is that?'

'Are you guilty of the crime that you're accused of here today ...' He looked down at the sheet of paper in front of him, as if hoping for some silent support from it. 'That you murdered your parents on the fourteenth of March ...' I don't remember what he said the rest of the date was.

'You couldn't call that pair parents,' I said.

'That's no way to talk in a court,' the Judge said, a hard edge coming into his voice.

'It's the only way to talk about those people.'

'I'm asking you one more time: are you guilty?'

'Guilty of being alive?' I say. 'I am. If that's a crime I'm guilty of it. I am, your Honour. And those two you mentioned earlier are even guiltier of that crime, too, if we accept that it is a crime.'

I remember I gave a big long statement then with a passion that surprised even myself. Maybe 'statement' isn't the right word. It's too official a word, too legal-sounding. I made a speech, I suppose. A speech that wasn't all that coherent, or maybe that was coherent enough at the time, but I can't seem to put the sentences together right now, so many days later.

Let the Son of God be the first to judge me, I say. Sentence me to death, and he can pass a true verdict on my whole life from the unlucky night I was conceived, a judgement free from prejudice and bias. And I remember someone shouting out then that there was no death penalty in this country, more's the pity.

'More's the pity,' a second voice echoed in support ...

'More's the pity,' a third time, I answered, or retorted, to be precise.

'Even a blind man can see he's a nutter, a complete madman,' a voice hissed from somewhere else in the room ...

Where was I? Oh, my birth. Yes. It all began with my birth, I say out loud. It was all wrong. I was born to those two after their bit of grappling ... or to that woman, I said then, correcting myself, since he had taken himself off to the ends of the earth by then, as per usual. That birth should never have happened. That birth was a bad start, ruined everything else, it was nearly the finish of me. An ill-fated birth.

'Here's some breakfast for you, if you want it,' says the middle-aged warder in his light-grey uniform, hunkering down to shove the tray under the iron grating of the door. That's about all I get from him, apart from hearing the rustling tread of his footsteps as he walks away. I stare at the brown tray with its white bowl of porridge, its plate of scrambled egg, two reddish-brown sausages, a couple of crisp slices of bacon. On a smaller plate beside it lie two slices of half-burnt toast, a pat of butter wrapped in mocking gold-coloured paper. In the corner of the tray sits a cup of black coffee, with a little tub of milk lined up behind it, as if in its power. It's there if I want to use it. Two white cubes of sugar lie under the handle of the cup. I get a whiff of breakfast smells as I lift the tray and put it down on the little square table that's only just wide enough to hold it. A mix of different aromas at first, but the hot coffee smell is the strongest of all. My gaze falls on the plastic armoury of knife, fork and spoon ...

I lose interest in the food all of a sudden, just as soon as I pick up the fork. As if something's stopping me. Something inside me telling me not to eat it. Not to touch it.

One day when my father came to see me he brought me an apple that tasted of fish. An apple from out of his pocket. A soft yellow apple that tasted of fish. I like fish, but when I take a bite out of an apple, it's the taste of apple I want. It startled me. That's why I threw it at him, after taking just the one bite out of it. A bite I hadn't chewed. A bite that I spat out rudely, in a temper, my face roaring red.

'Now, now,' my grandmother said, coaxingly. 'This is your father. You have to be nice to your father.'

'Sure he's no different to anyone passing by out in the street', I said ...

My grandmother had a flat three floors up and so I had a good view of all passers by. Those flats were knocked down a long time ago – there's a swish hotel there now.

And nobody could believe I had done it. At first anyway. Until they started bringing out the evidence. He wasn't someone who would commit a crime like that, a lot of people declared. A quiet fellow. That lad was well brought-up by his grandmother. Lad, I thought ... Eighteen years ...

'Could any family member commit a more horrible crime?' the Judge asked.

'They could, your Honour,' I say. 'What about forcing a book on someone who can't read. Except a picture-book, of course.'

He called for order in court then because some people had started to laugh.

'Amn't I right?' I say. 'There aren't too many pictures in that big Bible of yours now, are there, despite all its thin transparent pages.'

My father gave me a hundred euro that day. He said it was from the two of them. A little present from the two of them, he said. They had got together to celebrate the day with me in the hotel. Their long-lost son.

'Neither of us had any idea what you might like,' he said.

And how could they have? As if there was any need to say it.

'If we give you money you can buy whatever you like. You're all grown up now, God bless you. You're a man. You can do whatever you like. Make your own way.'

You'd swear it was he who had raised me, and that I was just taking my leave of him, that he had reared me and was going to miss me.

'So you see, your Honour, he told me I could do whatever I liked. He gave me that freedom. Didn't he say I was grown up? Wasn't it he himself who gave me the money. Who said he didn't know what I liked or what I wanted but that I would know that myself. I would know what I wanted.'

'What you're saying makes no sense at all.'

'What I'm saying makes a lot more sense than my life does. My life doesn't make much sense, maybe, but there's some sense in what I'm saying in this senseless life.'

Now I notice the reddish-coloured sausages on the plate across from me. I'd forgotten about them for a while. I pick up one with my spindly fingers and start to eat it. It's cold, gone hard and greasy. I eat the second one and one slice of the cold toast. I drink the bitter coffee in two gulps, shaking my head involuntarily at the black taste of it. It gurgles its way down through me. I put the tray under the grating of the door. The warder will collect it later on. Maybe he'll chat to me, stay and make some remark about how much or how little I've eaten … or maybe not.

It was when I realised that they were going to sleep together again that night, that I went out to buy the gun. That was what made me lose it altogether. I knew I could get one from a guy that used to hang around the alleyways. If he didn't have one on hand he could get one for me within the hour. But as it happened he had one. He took me to a derelict house and pulled a board up out of the floor of an upstairs room. Ninety euro. I had ten euro change out of my father's hundred. He loaded it for me for that price. He asked if I needed more cartridges. I told him there was plenty in it, that I'd only be using it the once. He asked me if I had ever used a shotgun before. I told him I hadn't and if I was clumsy with it then so much the worse for the person I'd be using it on. Serve them right.

'You killed two people,' the Judge said. 'Even if there were any sense to your ravings, even if you thought you were entitled to revenge, why did you have to kill both of them?

Why tear two families apart! They both had young children! You left two more people widowed.'

'What has to be has to be,' I say.

'Even if you insist you didn't want the life they gave you, that doesn't give you the right to take two lives in its place.'

Would a judge say something like that in court? You wouldn't imagine he would. He'd hardly say something like that out loud, even if it's what he was thinking. Maybe now that's not exactly what he said at all ... Or maybe it was the lawyer who was talking at the time ... I see now that I could be getting a bit confused again – maybe the description I'm giving isn't all that accurate. If I was to write these thoughts down some other day of the week ... But the bones of the story are sound, not like my own tired, sore bones. I'm certain of that. Isn't that enough, after all? The overall picture is right, pretty much. Sure what do the niggling little details matter? ... just like it hardly matters whether I say the cup on the tray here beside me has tea in it and not coffee ... as long as there's a cup there. But to come back to what the Judge said when he said something about two people. Two.

'Since I didn't ask them to give me a life I didn't want, then didn't that give me the right to take their lives?'

'Two people. Two.' The Judge said 'two'. I'm positive of that much.

'To be fair,' I said, 'if I had half-killed both of them, that wouldn't have been the same as killing one of them completely. Even after half-killing they'd both be alive. Wouldn't they? That was the problem.'

'The problem!' The Judge said the word. He repeated it a few times from his high desk, his eyes popping. I still see those big eyes, popping like two white, hard-boiled eggs.

'They had a hand – if that's the right word – if not a say in creating me,' I say. 'They share the responsibility, half and half. Someone like me wouldn't happen to be here without the two of them working hand in glove. I'd be doing an injustice to both of them if I discriminated between them. Half and half, that's the way it was. Side by side they stood. It would be unfair to the one who was put to death, if the other one was left alive. It would be unfair to the one still alive if I'd killed the other one. Wouldn't it, your Honour?'

The Judge didn't answer me. He had his arms folded, like someone listening because he had to, but who wasn't really hearing me. In one ear and out the other.

'It's the same whichever way you look at it,' I say. 'My conscience wouldn't let me act any other way except the right way, the kind way. Be kind to the people you meet in life, even people you don't know very well, that's what my grandmother used to say to me when she was alive. She's dead a long time now. You never know who they might be or what sort of dealings you might have with them in the future, she used to say ... How do I know whether or not they had planned to spend the night together in the hotel? I don't think they had – I think it was just at the last minute that they decided to stay with each other. It had been two years since they'd last met before that ... and before that again who knows how many years. And both of them with young families at home.

'What I wanted, your Honour ... what I wanted was to avoid them replicating me. I happened so easily, so simply, like something that sprang up overnight. I did. And it was part of my revenge to make sure that the likes of me wouldn't be cast onto life's stormy waters so casually again ... just for the likes of them. For their temporary relief. Them and their shenanigans. Their gratuitous pleasure. Having sex without a second thought, without paying the price. That's all they wanted. Sex without strings, without consequences. But everything has its price.'

He asked me if I had ever used a shotgun before. I told him I hadn't and if I was clumsy with it then so much the worse for the person I'd be using it on. Serve them right. There's no law that says a murder has to be tidy ...

They're fast asleep now, and I've just tiptoed into the room. This is the moment. They look so peaceful, lying there by the light of one of the bedside lamps that they've left lit. Her head on his breast, her dark hair tossed loosely all around her. Her face completely visible. His right arm is around her, under her breasts as if supporting them. His left hand cradling her head. I think to myself it's a strange way to fall asleep, the way his left hand cups her head. The smell of drink. I didn't realise it would be so strong.

'And after all that you stole the money that was in their pockets,' the Judge said.

'I didn't steal it, your Honour.'

'Wasn't it found in your possession?'

'It was.'

'Well if it was found on you, didn't you steal it?'

'The money found on me was my own money, your Honour. They were dead, your Honour, weren't they? As the legal heir to those two that was my money. I only took what was mine, your Honour. Isn't that the law? Your law?'

The state pathologist said they died almost instantly – from bleeding from the brain. Bleeding that started from the shot at point-blank range that they each got. He couldn't tell who was hit first, or who died first, but there was very little time between them. Seconds, he reckoned.

For quite a while I couldn't make up my mind who to shoot first. It didn't occur to me, when I took the gun out of the deep pocket of my coat, that this was a decision I'd have to make. Lack of experience, I suppose. If I shoot him first, I'll be strong enough to deal with her, if I have to. But I'd be afraid she'd start screaming and yelling the place down, and causing a big rumpus. Everyone would hear. That's how it happens in films. He wouldn't be like that, I don't think, if I shoot her first. More likely he would try to do something to save his skin. As I raise the gun I realise now I have to make a decision and aim at one person before the other ... before I aim at myself maybe.

I didn't see much blood. And nobody said a word. I heard little choking snorts. Gurglings in the throat. Do you know what I did then? I put the point of the gun on the light-switch – that had caught my eye – and put the light out ... leaving them completely in darkness. Goodnight, my parents.

I hear the warder making his way back to me, pushing his creaky trolley ahead of him as he loads up all the trays. Stopping, pushing on. Following his routine. Since I'm in the very first cell inside the main door, I'm the last person whose tray he'll collect. He'll be off out the big iron door then ... Out ... Out.

He still doesn't know how much of my breakfast I ate and how much I left for him to take away. Just as that pair didn't know what kind of end was in store for them that night. Just as the State Pathologist doesn't know which of them I killed first. Just as the Judge doesn't know whether I was sane or mad at the moment I pulled the trigger. Just as I don't know where'll I'll be tomorrow. Yet.

Translated by Katherine Duffy.

THE STOLEN ANSWER-BAG

Micheál Ó Conghaile

Why is the world overpopulated?

How many bridges have yet to be built?

Who painted the sky and the sea blue?

Why do some people have all the luck, while others find themselves on the slippery slope?

Why should a cat have nine lives and man but the one?

How many packets of steroids, or bags of angel dust, were given to that holy cow that jumped over the moon?

Why are you reading this now and not later?

Where *do* people get the neck – yourself included – to ask questions that haven't got answers ... unless they're at the bottom of the stolen Answer-Bag!

These are just some of the questions that are bothering the good people of Virtue Valley. They are experiencing something of an answer famine since these questions were first asked. They are of the opinion that the answers do, indeed, exist – scattered somewhere, in some shape or form, or in someone's possession. Yes! Someone has them, yourself maybe? They're keeping an eye on you as well. So, if the stolen answers are in your possession, you'd want to watch out!

You'd think they were easy enough as questions go. So they are – in a way. They're no mystery, even to the plebs. Most of them aren't worth putting on an exam paper, in a crossword, or on a TV quiz-show. But that's not how the people of the Valley view the matter. The world may well be overpopulated, but there are still too many questions around – more than people can bear. Every sinner in the Valley is pregnant with questions. Little questions. Big questions. Complicated questions. Questioning questions ... questionable questions. And with no answers, the people of the Valley are up the creek.

Each citizen of the Valley – with the exception of the Question Officer, of course – must put their back or their shoulder to these boulder-questions and bear the burden as one. Questions are spreading, locust-like. The people are in a tizzy, to say the least, and maybe even in danger. The weight of the questions, you see. Each one is apportioned his own lot and very often a good deal more than that. There's some people going around not with one hump, but five. Others are strained beyond belief, dragging these questions behind them. Some fall by the wayside, and if the fall doesn't kill them the Question Officer is quick to kick them to their feet again. For some, the questions go to the brain. The result is dizziness or delusion. You see them from time to time, meandering like lunatics or zombies. Spaced out. Often in their search for answers to these questions their stomachs are affected by painful spasms. What can they do to ease their load? They suspect that nothing can be done. They begin to accept the questions with great reluctance and continue to bear them, just as one puts up with an ingrown toenail or a disease. What choice do they have? You can't throw these questions aside – as you might throw a sod of turf on a rick – for anyone to pick up and examine, or use in some clever game like Scrabble! What they didn't understand from the beginning is precisely that. Questions are not sods of turf to be neatly piled one upon the other and left to dry. And even if that were possible, they wouldn't stay put. These questions pursue people and follow them around. Dog-like: kick them as much as you like and tell them to go home and they're still at your heels, or twenty metres behind you, never letting you out of sight.

Down the nights and down the days they follow, some of them weaving a spider's web in your ear. Others make their way into open wounds; others still turn up in pockets or take the shape of a hood, or mufflers, that are worn. One man was nearly completely muffled altogether on a frosty morning and on another occasion a ticklish question lodged in a fellow's throat so that he had to be hurried to hospital in an ambulance for an emergency operation. Twenty-two stitches it took to restore him to comparative normality. Some questions are as heavy as a wet overcoat and the odd one – very odd – is no bigger than a cap on the crown of a cleric, but as powerful as a priest's curse nonetheless. You'd hardly notice it at all on your head but, small as it is, it's there and it becomes a burden.

Why it is I don't know but the questions most plaguing the good people of the Valley are those for which they seem to have an innate antipathy. They seem to bring them on themselves, knowing that the result will be nausea and severe headache. People simply go off their rocker!

The other night in Hotel Virtue this fellow takes his jacket off, throws it on the floor and challenges the question there and then to a bout of fisticuffs – or out on the street if it were more convenient. Some people started laughing their heads off at him – tourists, wouldn't you know! It was no laughing matter I can tell you when another man's house went up in flames and all because of an awkard, nagging question that was hovering about and that he decided should be burned alive. On top of his trouble, the insurance company wouldn't cough up a cent, claiming in court that the man was nothing more than an amateur arsonist. He explained his case as honestly and as accurately as he could: that he did indeed manage to set fire to the question, but it dived into a tub of water and got away with only a scorching.

'And why didn't the question drown?' he was asked, 'or is it the way it was waterproof as well as being fireproof?'

'I don't know,' your man said in his melodious Kerry Irish. 'N'fheadar,' he said, 'unless maybe the question has nine lives like the cat and if so I'll have to confront it another eight times and by then we'll all have run out of plans how to deal with it. N'fheadar,' he says again, 'I can't say why it didn't drown because I didn't ask it and I don't think it would be fair to be questioning a question in that way. It's reasonable enough to answer a question with another question, whenever possible, and some are expert at the game, certain nameless politicians, but no one should ever question a question for fear of not getting a straight answer. That would only create another question – and we're looking for answers here, right? We don't want any more questions! All I wanted was a simple answer on that cursed day when the question burned down my pleasant little abode situated in a shady nook in the Valley.'

'I'm afraid your insurance policy does not cover such a wilful act,' said the justice, not without some pity. 'I regret to say that I cannot judge in your favour and that the insurance company is not obliged, under law, to give you a red cent. You are without a roof over your head now.'

'Thats OK, your Honour,' said your man, 'of far more value to me than the house would be to get an answer to my question, and since this court is bursting with brains – judges, lawyers, senior counsels, junior counsels – who knows if you all put your clever heads together you might be able to come up with an answer, thereby bringing much mental relief to yours truly. I'll be perfectly happy to live out my days with the sky as my roof and die happy, if die I must, as long as I have an answer to my question.'

And he raised the question. They apportioned it out in clauses and assembled in a circle and spent a long time dissecting it and exchanging insights with red-eyed determination. They were still at it the following day and returned on the third day, but to no avail, though they argued that they had come close a few times. They went their way morosely. 'For such a question a hotel should be burned, not to mention a humble cabin,' said one of the senior counsels as he left the court-room through the back door.

'Now,' says your man, his thumb out wanting to get a lift home to his pile of ashes, 'I'm not the great *amadán* that people think I am at all. Maybe I'm cleverer than those that answer easy questions every day of the week and get well paid for their trouble – and double pay, sometimes, for coming up with a bogus answer. Am I not as sane as the man who goes out to the ditch every night with his rifle, firing pot-shots at questions, never reaching the target, hitting nothing if the truth be told except that one time when he shot the blind cat next door that popped out of nowhere, frightened by the shopkeeper's alsatian.' He smiled, self-satisfied. 'I'm no worse than him to be sure, nor am I worse than the lad who was so tormented by a question that he took his boot off and flung it with such force at the question that it ended up in the porridge over the fire; or the old woman walking the roads every day and – God forgive her! – the language out of her, and the curses that would wither the leaves on the trees as, with each dragging step, she tried to rid herself of the questions that were hounding her, tooth and claw.

'Yes, indeed,' he reminded himself again, 'maybe I'm not the worst after all. Who wouldn't set fire to his house if it meant burning or choking a question? Let the experts say what they will – experts sexperts! I'll continue with my search and I may get an answer yet before my death, whatever life, death or rebirth is yet my lot. If it's true what they say, that the Answer-Bag was taken from these parts a long time ago, maybe it's hidden away somewhere. If a person could only find it, lodged in some crevice or other, or buried in a cut-away bog or underground tunnel, or it might be in some security vault in a bank somewhere. Bankers can't be trusted and maybe they intend to hang on to it and sell it for a fortune on the black market. Some would be bold enough to put it on auction or raffle it, a thousand euro a ticket. And there's those that would buy it, wrong and all as that would be. I'm telling you now, it would be an evil thing if the bankers had it – it would be far better if the fairies had spirited it away. It's possible to bribe a fairy but who could bribe a banker except another banker or a politician, perhaps. Answers should not be valued in monetary terms. If there are answers they should be freely available to all, anyone who bothers searching for them …'

And off he went, but when he reminded himself that he had no home to go to, he decided instead that he'd go to the Community Centre, where once a week the people of the Valley had their Question Confession in the hope of finding out had anyone come up with an answer that might ease their load.

No sooner did he reach the Community Centre when he heard the hubbub and the uproar, the sweet rumours flowing from mouths like honey. The Answer-Bag had been found – well according to rumour at any rate. They had caught Wily Willy Withershins, as he was known in the Valley, the night before, trying to weasel his way through the town at dusk. He reacted violently to his arrest, but for all the tea in China he wouldn't part with the bag on his back. But the bag was to be opened tonight in the presence of honourable witnesses, Valley people all of them, and Wily Willy Withershins would be interrogated and given the opportunity to apologise for whisking away the bag in the first place.

The citizens of the Valley all assembled – even the raving old dotes who'd never stir a limb except on voting day, Pattern Day or bingo night, each with their own encumbrance of questions, and some of them very angry indeed, fit to be tied, having wasted their lives carrying questions devised, worded and framed by other no-gooders. Many wanted swift revenge.

They couldn't wait until Wily Willy Withershins was hauled before them, all except the Question Officer, who was beginning to get worried about his job. It looked like he might have to live on the dole, with regular visits from the gauger. They began to quake and roll as though on some electric, automatic device, whispering and nattering to each other, looking at their digital watches every so often, calculating the time with deadly accuracy.

They all gathered in a ring when they observed the shenanigans going on in the corner. Suddenly Wily Willy Withershins was seen being dragged roughly towards the middle of the park. Everyone gawked at him in wonder. They pasted him with cow dung and donkey shit as he was forced through the crowd. Some tried to trip him up and give him a dig in the ribs. Small and hunched, his two eyes were popping out of his head at the massive throng that had gathered to ogle him. And the bag! He clutched the magic Answer-Bag close to him with one hand, the other surrounding it protectively as if it were a baby, nor would he part with it or let anyone near it, though those closest to him were kicking him, vilifying him and tormenting him with questions, without giving him the slightest chance to answer. They reminded him that the answers belonged to them and their ancestors in the first place, and that he deserved death for snatching them, and woe betide him if he had lost any or sold any, that they'd pursue him out of this world and into the next after his death, straight down to hell – where he would surely be – and kill him again as an extra punishment. Wily Willy was shaking with fear. He was all curled up like a hedgehog, trying to fend off the blows and crawling about, holding the Answer-Bag like a woman heavy with child would hold her belly. He knew it would be pointless to cry out, for those who could hear would only be frenzied all the more.

'Isn't it a blessed day for me,' he whispered to himself, 'that I took a good dose of morphine this morning or I'd never stick this scourge. Thanks be to God, his Holy Mother, Saint Patrick and all the saints.'

And he held fast to the bag and wouldn't open it.

'If he doesn't part with the bag,' said someone, 'we'll have to kill him and take it from him.'

'He'll have to be killed anyway,' said another from the crowd.

'But it's my own bag,' whined Wily Willy when he found his voice during a brief lull. 'Finders keepers. I didn't steal it. I found it. There's a difference!'

'You found it?' the crowd roared back. 'And where would you find such a precious bag simply for the taking?'

'I found it on the road,' said Wily Willy Withershins, 'as I was passing through this Valley of Darkness. If it were the bag of answers, ye yerselves would have found it or is it blind ye all are?'

'Don't be cheeky,' said another, 'you've some neck! The eyes are worn out in our heads looking for answers, but we can still see – something you won't be able to do much longer. It's easy for the likes of you to be talking, someone who never knew a question or a headache or what it's like. Oh, you're the wily one to be sure!'

'But maybe what he's sayin' has a grain of truth in it,' said the man who burned his own house down. 'Maybe it's not our answers he has in the bag at all but other answers. Let's be careful, just in case.'

But the mob wouldn't have any of it.

'Rubbish!' they said. 'If he weren't trying to escape with the answers he'd open the bag. You'd think he'd give us a peep at least.'

'But it's my own private bag,' said Wily Willy, pitifully. 'It was I that found it and no one else, being in the right place at the right time. That's how it is in life. The bag is part of me now and I'll not give it up until my last holy breath. Release me at once!' And he pressed the bag more lovingly than ever to his person as though comforting it.

The mob became venomous.

'You might have been in the right place at the right time last night, but you're in the wrong place at the wrong time now!' cried another voice.

'Let him be skinned alive,' shouted someone, 'what the devil is holding us up?'

And so it was done. A volunteer gladly flayed him. Two others tortured him, goaded on by the rabble. A fourth poured a kettle of boiling water over him. A fifth – a woman, in men's clothing – grabbed him by the throat and wrung the last gasp from him.

The Answer-Bag fell to the ground with a thump like a sack of coarse salt. The crowd cheered victoriously.

'Open the bag quick,' said the man with the rifle, 'before I collapse under today's weight of questions. Give me my answers! Give me my answers quick, I say. I'm long enough waiting.'

'And mine!' said the woman famed for her curses.

'And mine!'

'Mine!'

'Mine!'

'Mine first!'

They tore the bag apart, greedily shredding it with their sharp claws until the inside was out and the outside in. Alas, their noses quickly told them what their eyes could see already, that this wasn't the Answer-Bag or anything like it.

What was it but a rotten bag of rubbish that had fallen from the County Council lorry, bursting with orange skins, used teabags, the bones and guts of fish, empty bean cans, bottles of coke, stale crusts of bread, bits of mildewed cheese, shards of glass jugs, burnt-out light bulbs, sour potato skins, rotten apples, heaps of old newspapers, bandages streaked with blood, used condoms, snotty paper hankies, torn personal letters, unpaid telephone bills, supermarket plastic bags – and, yes, pinch your nose now if you must, nappies well and truly soiled.

'Doesn't seem to be the right bag,' said someone in a hesitant voice, tears brimming in his eyes.

'Doesn't seem?' said the rifleman. 'It most certainly is not, and the battering I've given to my body, crawling on bloody knees, ten whole miles since morning under a weight of questions, believing my answers would be waiting for me here.'

'Fuck this fucking bag anyway,' said the woman famed for her curses. 'Come on, let's go on the fucking piss.'

'Let ye all have patience! Hang on there!' said the Question Officer authoritatively, pressing his way towards the centre of the crowd. 'No one's going anywhere. Aren't ye the right loodramawns! Yerselves and yer questions and yer lack of answers! What kind are ye at all? What business do ye have with answers? Would ye recognise one if it was presented to ye on a silver tray? How would ye? And ye can't see a bag of rubbish for what it is, a bag that fell off a County Council lorry when its axle hit a pothole! Eh?'

The crowd around him was silent. The Question Officer took a long deep breath and continued, his white teeth flashing:

'And on top of all our misfortunes, you have murdered Wily Willy Withershins, a wretch that never harmed a fly, the craythur. But ye'll pay for it. Ye'll all pay for it now with yer lack of answers and this new burden ye've created for yourselves. Now, which one of you is responsible for this atrocious, merciless deed, so I can sentence him to life imprisonment?'

All the people of the Valley looked at one another, their eyes dimmed by this terrible question which was beginning to form a crust on their minds, grinding numbly in their ears.

Nobody opened their mouth. They shook their heads and stared sheepishly at the ground, for all the world as though they knew nothing about anything, for sure.

Translated by Gabriel Rosenstock.

THE CLOSETED PENSIONER

Micheál Ó Conghaile

I'm living this long while now in the toilet. Well-settled in. I've locked myself in. And I've never been happier in my life. My adventurous days pass quickly. I'm not exactly sure – and couldn't care less – how long I'm here. Years maybe. What difference does it make? Time doesn't count here. No clock on the wall in front of me. Or alarm. Or Angelus. No deadlines. No calendar, moon or tide. The only date I remember is the day I finished with the civil service – that fateful day on which I took early retirement; and strode straight into the jacks with a purposeful stride. Just like that. The same evening! Now that was something. And I'm thriving ever since.

Sure, they tried to stop me. Head me off at the creek. Over and over again they pleaded with me to reconsider. They put me under a lot of pressure, lots of warnings. The little woman had the biggest problem with it, and soon the whole family were behind her.

'You're a thundering disgrace!'

'What will the neighbours say?'

'Have you no sense at all!'

'You can't stay there, you know!'

What a chorus.

'And why can't I?' said I. 'Who's to stop me?' I was getting bull-headed. 'It's my life and I can do what I want with it. Get a life,' I told them, 'every blasted boring one of you. Anyway, don't ye go into the upstairs loo yerselves!'

That got them. They went ape-shit altogether. They started kicking at the door like a child locked in his room after being beaten for no reason.

'Going to the toilet is not the same as taking up residence there,' suggested the missus, 'everybody goes to the toilet once in a while and it's an acceptable fact of nature.'

'I don't, do I? You're wrong again, woman, as usual. Isn't that one of the reasons I'm here. I'm here because I'm here, because I decided to go on early pension and settle in here. I won't have to go out to the loo again for the rest of my life. Let ye be off now and mark my words, ye pack of divils!'

I believe this sermon sobered them up a bit. They knew well I was right. They left me for a while. I suppose they thought surely I'd get fed up in time and come crawling out. But I'm not in the least put out here, and there's no danger of that either. That's where they were wrong from the beginning. They thought I'd emerge in the middle of the night or early morning at the latest, with my tail between my legs. I much prefer this place to the outside world. I'm as oblivious as my arse ... except when they start annoying me out there.

Of course, I'm not actually sitting on the toilet all of the time, only some of the time really. I keep myself busy. I'd go crazy otherwise. I've the walls covered in grafitti. Tiredness of the wrist is all that stops me from writing. I listen to the flush every time I pull the chain. I know how many drops it takes to fill the cistern. Much puffing and snorting dispels odours.

And thinking – I do a lot of thinking, thinking about women I fell in love with, conversations and arguments I had, going out visiting at night, days in the office ... there's no limit to me at all and the thoughts crowding my head. And dreaming as well – my imagination taking flight, from birth to death, the whole shebang. My head is always bursting at the seams with the strangest dreams of every variety. I've them all well listed by now – stored away and graded under each subject category. There's more of them than would fit in the most powerful computer. New dreams are filed away each morning when I awake, and I make a comparative study of them. But there's more than dreams to keep me occupied. I sing songs and recite reams of poetry, dredging them from the recesses of my mind, blowing the dust off them. I say my prayers, of course, a few times a day like a good Christian and say the rosary every night, counting the *Aves* on my fingers and thumbs. I myself respond to the prayers, naturally enough, and sometimes you'd think there's more than one of me in the toilet. I pray most fervently and most piously, and the orisons rebound from the companionable walls.

Other times, as a brain-limbering exercise, I'd ask myself a riddle and try to figure out the answer ... which is the longest, the goose's beak or the gander's? Which cow yields the most milk? What goes up, but doesn't come down? Which is closest to you – yesterday or tomorrow? Working out riddles is great sport entirely. I make up a number of new riddles for myself as well, in order to create answers which turn out to be right. And who can contradict me? I don't suppose anyone else makes up the same riddles, not to mention the answers. I drive the wife round the bend when I shout one of my riddles. They nearly always get it wrong outside, and even if they get it right the odd time, I tell them they're greatly mistaken and make up a new answer on the spot. Sure, they wouldn't know the difference, the poor misfortunates. And that's how it goes.

When I need a rest from the riddles, I try out some other trick – I've no want of pastimes. The family tree – I've worked out who my great-grandfather was on my mother's side long ago ... I count all the cousins. Classify distant relations. Working out exactly who is related to whom around here. Those who were engaged once and never married. Those who don't talk to each other, and why they might have it in for each other. Those who don't talk to each other, though their families do. Those who usedn't talk to each other but do now, or those who were the best of buddies and wouldn't look at each other today, crossing to the other side of the road if necessary. And necessary it is ...

Now, how could I be fed up with life and all that going on? And that's nothing. Whatever the way it is when I start on the physical work, time flies in the toilet. It's essential I keep myself fit and supple at all times. And I do. A couple of hundred press-ups daily – sit-ups, heel-ups and whatever's up with yourself. I'd do an hour of stationary jogging a day. The equivalent of a good few road miles and it's better at it I'm getting. Getting faster all the time. If I'd a stopwatch I could judge the progress I'm making, but I haven't. A pity I haven't one of those bikes that are stuck to the floor. I could stick it to the ceiling and be pedalling away for myself. Not to worry, I'm as fit as a fiddle the way I am, and as healthy as a trout. I'm much better off here. Now! And they thought I could do nothing inside here, apart from the obvious. But I can have a full, creative life here in the toilet. Anyone thinking of going out on pension should think of the toilet, I tell them. I'd be dead and buried long ago if I were anywhere else. I haven't aged a bit in here – *au contraire*. That can't be said about the others ... They're sprawled on the couch, enthralled by satellite television. If I were one of them, sure I'd only be another slave. A zombie.'

'Wouldn't you think of going to Spain,' says she, under the door.

'I could think of it,' says I. I gave her some rope, knowing she'd soon hang herself.

'It would do you good. A lot of pensioners go to Spain. They like the heat. I wouldn't mind it one bit myself.'

'I know they go,' says I, 'especially if they have the arthritis. I never stopped a pensioner going to Spain, did I?'

'You didn't, dear,' she said gently, knowing well she had to agree with me.

'Well, let no one stop this pensioner retiring in here then,' says I.

That was the end of Spain. A bloodless victory, I'd say. It wasn't quite as easy to rout the parish priest when she brought him to hear my confession and to prepare my soul, as she said, seeing I hadn't been to confession in ages.

'Divil a confession,' says I. 'Pull the other one. What sort of sinning could I do here? Did I steal something or covet the neighbour's wife? Did I kill someone in here? Did I tell an injurious lie? Did I drag God's name through the mire for no reason? Did I give bad example? Was I gambling in here or driving at a hundred miles per hour? Or any of the other thousand extra sins in the revised catechism? Huh! Half of them weren't even invented when I came in here. How could I commit sins that weren't there? Do ye know anything? Sure the toilet isn't an occasion of sin. This place is free of the devil's wiles and temptations.'

'Fine! Fine!' It was the priest who spoke, trying his best to placate me. 'We're here for your own good. We know the regard you have for the place you find yourself in.' He began to brown-nose me then and called me a gentleman. 'We're all sinners, each and every one of us. But if you like, sir, you can make your confession from where you are. You don't even have to come out. You can bend a knee there inside the door and I'll be able to absolve you through the keyhole. In that way you can cleanse your soul and stay where you are. It's your soul I'm trying to save.'

'Cleanse my soul,' I shouted, 'through this measly keyhole. My soul is it? Piss off now or it's my hole you'll be hearing from, a forceful fart from my hole, through the keyhole and into your earhole. Feck off with you!'

'Now, now, patience, my son. No need to be rude. Your lady wife and myself are only thinking of your welfare. You're there now years. It is not good for man to be alone.'

'Don't be stupid,' says I. 'Aren't Elvis and Rushdie in here keeping me company lots of the time. We play cards too. You bet. Big time.'

'Now, now,' said the priest, 'it's not any younger you're getting but – alas – older like the rest of us ... You know what I'm saying. You could ... you could ... God between us and all harm ... you could kick the bucket any day now.'

I laughed out loud. I laughed and laughed. 'Bucket-schmucket! It chokes you to say it, doesn't it. I could DIE, DIE, D-I–E,' I screamed, luxuriating in the word and in its echo all round me, before collapsing in another paroxysm of laughter.

'Holy Father,' says I, standing on my head at this stage with stitches of laughter and speaking through the crack in the door.

'Father,' says I, 'I'll tell you something seeing as you don't know ... Do you hear me?' I took two sharp breaths. 'People don't die in the toilet. Do you understand? Oh, they die in the bedroom, the sitting room, the dining room, the kitchen, out on the street or in the garden, sometimes on the stairs if they fall down and even in the bathroom. Yes, the bathroom, if they slip coming out of the bath or drown in the tub or – God look down on us – if they cut their wrists, but not in the jacks ... Not in the jacks! People don't snuff it in the jacks, end of story. Right?'

I was breathless after my monologue. I drew my breath again as quickly as I could, so that I could launch into the rest of my eloquent speech.

'People do not die in the toilet,' I reiterated. 'May God give you sense, Father, and may His Blessed Son take pity on your empty head, but did you ever hear it tell, "Mr X died today ... at home, in the jacks." Did you ever hear that? You never did. Never, and do you want to know why? Because it doesn't happen, see? Not even in America or in the English tabloids. And anyway, even if it could happen – or was about to happen – it wouldn't be allowed to happen, because they wouldn't let a person snuff it in the loo. People would think it was a disgrace or a scandal or ... impolite. And people don't want to be impolite, do they! He'd be taken out of the toilet before he breathed his last, so that they wouldn't have to admit that it was in the loo he died ... Anyway, they wouldn't announce his death before they got him into the bed. Father, dear, who'd admit a relation of his died in the toilet? Who ...? The smart alecs of the town, some TV smarty pants, asking was he standing up or sitting down when death struck, was it Number One or Number Two, Father – we'll say nothing about Number Three. Oh, no!'

The poor priest never came back and my soul is still unshriven. I don't think he was much taken by my brand of wisdom. He didn't say so as such, but that's my conclusion. I suppose he's busy now sucking a confession out of some old wretch before he croaks it, and before a spirit within him soars free. My spirit – if such a thing I harbour – is perfectly OK thank you; and if it's not, it won't be the confessor that will make it whole or wheedle me out of here.

They all have a plan to get me out. People have so many plans, all of them. Even my solicitor, he's full of plans, nice ones though, but my poor old solicitor won't get me out either. He was outside the other day ... the other something anyway. He knocked on the door – something the others hadn't the manners to do – a sprightly little knock as he whistled gaily.

'Excuse me,' says he, interrupting me in the middle of the rosary, 'I wonder could I bother you a moment!'

'You're bothering me as it is,' I replied, 'so it's a bit late for excuses or wondering could you bother me further. Who the hell are you anyway?' – pretending I didn't recognise his voice.

'Your solicitor, of course, who else? Don't say you don't recognise me? Wouldn't you be inside a little cell for life long ago in the security wing if it weren't for all the court cases I won on your behalf? I wouldn't mind but you were guilty of each crime and other crimes that never came to light.'

'True for you,' says I in a hushed whisper, 'but don't forget you did well out of it yourself, a few backhands which we needn't mention now ... and what about that scam ...? Never mind. I thought I'd seen the last of you, but you're a good man. What do you want?'

'A signature, what else?'

'What else. How foolish of me. What else would a lawyer want but a signature. What do I have to sign this time?'

'Your will, what else?'

'Not a good sign. But at least I've a will and where's there's a will, there's a way. You're a much squarer bloke than that rogue priest who was here a while ago wanting me to sign my soul and, sure, whatever soul I had I left it outside when I came in here.'

'I'm glad you're willing to sign it,' says he. 'What'll you leave the wife? I'll take a note of it here.'

'A single bed, heaven closed to her and hell as her reward,' says I. That much I knew for sure.

'I'd leave her more if I had it, but I haven't. Let her be grateful for that much itself. Everything else is gone.'

'She'll profit rightly by you it seems,' says the lawyer, 'only maybe you're giving her too much.'

'No way. I was never one to give her too much.'

'Now if you would sign these documents.'

'Shove 'em under the door.'

He did.

'But you'll need a witness.'

'Aren't you a witness?'

'But I can't see you.'

'Close one eye and look through the keyhole.'

'OK, it will have to do, I suppose.'

'It will.'

'Well then, everything is settled except for the matter of ... where do you wish to be buried?'

'Buried! In the name of God, I'm not going to be buried, unless they bury me alive. I'm as buried as I'll ever be here.'

'Everyone gets buried.'

'They do if they die, but people don't die in the toilet. What do you think I'm doing here only keeping myself alive? To die in here would be too traumatic for a living person and too dramatic for his family!'

'It would to be sure. You're perfectly right there. But, what would you like us to do with you?'

'Well, nothing really ... just leave me be ... but, of course, should you, or I, wish – later on – or should it become necessary, ye can cremate me. Alive, of course.'

'Cremate you alive! But that's totally –'

'No it's not. C. U. Burn Crematorium. I've come to a special arrangement …'

'All right! All right! Very nice, it can be arranged for a reasonable sum, I suppose, but then what do we do with your ashes? Oh, of course, they could be scattered to the winds or exhibited somewhere. It wouldn't be necessary to bury them, but some arrangement would have to be in place.'

'Sure, there wouldn't be a whole lot of me. Keep a pinch for yourself and store it in the egg-timer. You can use it every morning and watch me trickling down.'

'Lovely! Thanks very much and may you have a long life. You'll be very useful to me in the egg-timer – but the rest of the ashes … not too nice to leave them lying around. Your wife, you know, the family, or the greedy rogue priest. You wouldn't want them sinking their claws into you – or your ashes!'

'Not to worry. There's an easy way out of this,' I said. 'I'll be able to plan it all myself. All you have to do is stuff what's left into a condom, when it's cooled of course, and bring it back here to me. Slide it carefully under the door. Be sure it doesn't burst. OK?'

'OK. OK.'

'I can flush it down the toilet whenever I feel like it … *if* I feel like it.'

Translated by Gabriel Rosenstock.

THE WORD CEMETERY

Micheál Ó Conghaile

Focaleen was just like everyone else when he was young. No sooner had he been thrown from a human mouth, than he sprouted legs and wings and flitted lightly all over the place. Indeed, he could be in lots of different places at the same time. Nothing could stop or deter him – no wall, moat, drain, fence, ocean or frontier, however mighty. Instead he enjoyed lots of exercise, leaping out of everyone's mouth – everyone, that is, apart from dumb people.

He travelled on a single shout sent up in the heat of conversation, on a timid whisper, mingling happily with words of all kinds. Sometimes he acted as a bridge between them, other times he worked side by side with them. At odd times, he stood up on his two hind-legs, as onewordallalone.

It wasn't that Focaleen didn't have a happy childhood. He had. He had free rein and *carte blanche* to make his mark on the wordy world of Irish, from the very first moment of the very first day. When he had some free time he would be quiet – happy to hover among other words, ready and waiting to be called up or given the nod. When a message or a hint came through from the watchword, there'd be no time to waste, no chance to think things through or count the beats. He would rise to the occasion with perfect control, recreating himself again and again like a clone. Then he would rest, although he never really needed to. And in his own time he would dream silently. He would wander off in his mind. Sometimes he'd be on a hillside, running about, hopping and skipping, never too far from somebody's thoughts somewhere. Sometimes he had nothing at all to do, though he was there on offer to everyone, on the verge of being summoned ... Until one day there was trouble in paradise – unpleasantness, violence, uprising. And then the Great War of Words. Focaleen was the worst affected. People started laughing at him. It wasn't long until other words were laughing at him, especially the ones who were older, more firmly established, better known than he was. The offspring of these words followed their elders' example and carried on as if he was a bad word. As time went on he almost began to believe himself that there could be such a thing as bad words and good words. It was cold comfort to him when the High King of Words made a proclamation clearly stating all words were equal – big or small, high or low, young or old, with or without pedigree, dependent or independent, whether acting as a crutch for other words or born of the coupling of two words in a compound word. None of this was any use to him. Focaleen was left lame, little-used, heartbroken, ostracised.

Gradually he became odd. He didn't hang out very much with his fellow words. He started to avoid them, and ended up being thought even stranger as a result. He became shut in on himself, reserved – withdrawing like a scallop that's been teased too much into his shell. He was beginning to be forgotten ...

Then one day while he was loitering about on the hillside, fed up with himself, fed up of being idle, didn't he slip.

Before he knew it, he was tumbling head over heels down the side of the hill and, because he'd been so seldom called on in those days, he wasn't able to let out a screech. He was dizzy before he was even a quarter of the way down and he couldn't tell the rough, craggy ground from the foreboding, thundery sky over his head. The big protruding boulders knocked lumps out of his ribs and spine and he fell into a coma. Finally he was pitched, arse in the air, into the lake at the foot of the hill. And there he sank, down and down, to the bed of the lake.

That's where he stayed, unconscious, lost without hope for years and years. There wasn't a stir nor a budge out of him. Above, life and the world were transformed with the passing of the years. A hole opened up in the ozone layer, the earth's climate and weather changed. The lake dried up, and suddenly its muddy marshy bed was revealed for the first time in thousands of years. And stretched out there, embedded in the middle of it, was Focaleen's wasted body.

A group of words passing by recognised him immediately as one of their own and a big crowd of them gathered around, weeping and wailing, trying to resuscitate him by blowing and giving him airy kisses. They came from every art and part and nook and cranny of the human face. They huddled close together in a circle – words from every hollow and bump of humanity's many unpredictable expressions.

They nearly snapped the limbs from Focaleen's desiccated body, hauling him up out of the muck banked around him. They scraped it off slowly, studiously, carefully, bit by bit, nail by nail. They worked on unceasingly until he was stripped, and he stood before them, naked as the day he took flight. The crowd gathered around, marvelling at him, stroking him, talking to him, but they couldn't identify him or tell what age he was, or figure out his birthday or the day he died, since he couldn't move or speak for himself. It was thought that maybe he wasn't real – just a scarecrow of a word.

They decided to convene a big International Word Conference and sent out signals, signs and summonses all across the world inviting every kind of word – of all ages, of all colours, of all languages, from every dictionary – to see if he could be brought back to life. The monster meeting lasted three days and three nights and there was plenty of drinking and singing and pontificating and shenanigans, but nobody was able to make head or tail of him. In the end there was nothing for all the foreign delegates to do but to make their long return journey to their own lands, after insisting that it was imperative that expert reports be compiled and studied and that another conference be held again soon.

'And what are we going to do now?' asked And. 'Now that we're all on our own?'

'We'll keep on trying to make some sense of him, trying to get him to function,' said Utterance. 'Sure, isn't that the least we can do for our poor little fellow-word?'

'It looks like he must be one of us,' said The. 'Since the foreigners didn't recognise him it's unlikely that he belongs to another race.'

'Well if that's the case where's his Irish etymology?' Howdy asked.

'God knows,' said Why. 'One thing's for sure – he's not from this century or the last. Sure we'd recognise him if he was. For all we know he could have been stuck in the muck of that lake since the time of ogham or Old Irish.'

'Well what else have the Old Irish crowd got to say on the subject then?' asked Seek. 'Eh?' He wanted to get rid of the problem by dumping it on a crowd who were always making themselves out to be so much more knowledgeable.

There was a silence, at first. Then loud, sharp words that were not quite intelligible could be heard far away, clashing, as if they were killing or stabbing each other. A few words hanging around in corners were seen to give each other an elbow or two in the ribs, glaring at each other sideways, full of intolerance and doubt.

'Put the question to them ones in English,' an echo of a faraway voice was heard saying. No name was given, but the general opinion was that it was Prattle.

'Sure isn't English an official language too?' asked End.

'I wouldn't hold my breath waiting for an answer from them,' said Pillage. 'That Old Irish lot can never agree on anything, and behind their false words they always have the knives out for each other.'

'Now, now, one word, one voice. Are we on the same side or aren't we? Couldn't it happen that Focaleen here will get us all bonding and forging new friendships?'

'I don't know him from Adam,' said Old And. 'I can't recall ever seeing or hearing him and I'm on the go a long long time. Maybe he's not a word at all, just a fragment?'

'Maybe there's too many of us here, all talking at once, not stopping even when we've nothing to say, and never giving silence the respect it deserves?'

'Can you even make out what sort of a tool he has?'

'Is he feminine, masculine or neutral?'

'He could even be a castrato, or a word that got a sex-change, the awful way the world is now.'

'Do you think he had a guardian angel?'

'If he had, where was it when he needed it most?'

'Maybe he committed suicide,' suggested Bastard, his voice full of pity. 'People are very hard on some of us, accusing us of being bad words. It's only people that attribute badness to us.'

'True for you,' said Gratitude. 'True, by dad.'

'At least we're not people, at least we don't have their sins on our conscience, isn't that right?'

'That's right,' said Rest.

'But words don't kill themselves,' said Alive. 'We couldn't even if we wanted to, that's the problem.'

'Well if we can't, people can kill us. They snuff us out wrongly all the time, without giving a second thought,' said Illegitimate sourly. 'Look at me, the way they treat me lately you'd think I was a hangman. A word-robber gets more respect than I do.'

'Was some word among you talking about me, you backbiting backbiters?'

'Illegitimate is right,' said Queer. 'Look at the way I'm ridiculed nine days a week. Nobody says me out loud and clear; most of the time I'm sent sprawling from people's mouths in a malicious mutter.'

'That makes two of us,' says Gay. 'I was stripped down and remodelled altogether.'

'Now, now,' says Union, 'we're not here to fight or argue among ourselves. Let's leave all that to idle, silly people. At the end of the day they're the ones who create us, not the donkeys or the sheep or the pigs or the cows, however friendly they might seem. They have the power, whether we like it or not.'

'But they don't own us.'

'But what if we rise up! What if we rise up against them?' It was Fighting who spoke.

'Declare war on them,' War said proudly, bursting to begin.

'Teach them a lesson.'

'Get a fair deal for all words from now on.'

'Stop them from letting any one of us ever be forgotten or misused again.'

'Exactly,' said Morsel. 'We can make ourselves stick in their throats, in their gullets,' and he was thrilled at the idea.

'I'm with you completely,' said Tarmacadam. 'And I'd be great at that myself. And I know plenty of other long-winded complicated words. We have a whole clan living in Muiceanach Idir Dhá Sháile na gCloch beside the roundabout at the bridge where they put the traffic lights recently. Words that are all up and down and upside down. Words that turn around a few times on their way out of mouths. We'd be well able to make them tongue-tied.'

'Me too,' said Fuck, 'although I'm short and sweet, I'm sharp too.' He was itching to be in the thick of the aggro. 'I'm a thin, slippy word and I'd be great at slipping out and saying my piece right where nobody wants to hear me. I'm good at embarrassing people, famous people too, especially when I hop out of their mouths when they think nobody's listening to them or no cameras are watching. I can be deadly altogether, my friend, at causing trouble.'

'You'll be the boy to catch out certain politicians, such as the Junior Minister of State for Words,' said We. 'You'll put the wind up him.'

'We could metamorphose, change our sense and meaning overnight, without their knowing,' said Gay, 'just like they do. If enough of us did it, the mis-meanings would put them all astray and at odds with each other. They would. Before long they wouldn't be able to trust any word. No word would be politically correct.'

'Then they'd have to keep us pent-up inside them – that would shut them up.'

'They'd be in a right mess then, their stomachs all full of pains, they might even explode.'

'And there'd be such hassle and trouble among them.'

'Such argu– '

The word, the talk stopped abruptly. There was silence among them. An occasional syllable falling to earth startled them, making them take a step backwards ...

Argument sat down in the middle of everyone and addressed the crowd. 'Don't you know well that we're the only ones who'll suffer in the end,' he said, 'if there's any argument? They'll take their wrath out on us. They'll use and abuse us to insult and hurt and damage each other. They'll misuse us like footsoldiers in a nuclear war. They'll wound some of us. They'll castrate more of us. We'll be subjected to translation and standardisation and misquotation. We'll be slaughtered. Weapons are all we'll be to them at the end of the day. Weapons to be put to fight against each other until some of us beat the rest of us. Until half of us murder the other half. Until some of us are swallowed by others of us. Until some of us are reduced to a pulp. Until the heavy words sink to the bottom and the light ones rise to the top. Until certain words get ahead of other words and others fall behind. We're just pawns in their game of chess. A game to the death.'

Argument sat down. He heaved a sigh of relief.

Authority got to his feet. He cleared his throat.

'But do we really belong to people?' he asked, assuming the mantle of philosopher. 'That's the primary question. Wasn't Utterance here in the very beginning along with God, if what we're told is true?' He paused. 'Where do we come from? Who are we? Where are we going? What is our mission? Do we own ourselves any more, or did we ever? Were we here long before people or were people here before us? Do people depend on us or do we depend on them? Are humans our masters now, our God, or is the God of humans our God also? Or is the devil lording it over us now, and over the whole shootin' gallery? Is there another life for us after this life, if we die? Who is older now, word or man? A year in the life of a person isn't the same as a year in the life of a word. I believe it's the word. The word is older. In the beginning was the word. If that wasn't the case, man couldn't have got hold of it. We've always been here, silent, in our own shapes, in the air, and all we needed was a person's mouth to pronounce us, to bring us down to earth. Millions of us hovering lightly in the air, ready to slip into mouths and come out again whenever they wish.'

'But wait,' said a voice from the crowd, 'where would we be without people, without the shelter and warmth of their mouths? What other being would pick us up, use us again and again? The animals never took any notice of us and we spent millions of years just waiting in the cold and the heat, the frost and ice. And anyway, wasn't it the mouths of humans that shaped us, planed us down, polished us up, gave us definition, created our beauty, made us sound sweet? We are theirs and they have the power to do as they please with us. They can spit us out like phlegm if they want to. We really do belong to them. Isn't it we who are dependent on them?'

'But are we?' asked Authority. 'Isn't it we who give humans their freedom? We ennoble them, raise them above the animals. We make the difference between "yes" and "no"? Aren't we their very soul and spirit? A person without words, without the power of speech ... Don't you remember the first lot of them that came down from the trees? The state they were in! The grunting and groaning and moaning they went on with. They were no better than wild animals, having to rely on signs and grimaces and gesticulations even to get the simplest message across. And they were a million years or so at that carry-on before they figured out how to use us, before they embraced us in our droves as we brought them freedom and confidence. Only for us they'd all be mute, their lines of thought and imagination going nowhere. Every last one of them! We're the most powerful tool a person has, the basis of all their dealings. We give the world civilization. There's no end to the possibilities now, and it's all thanks to us.'

Some words agreed with this, others differed.

'Don't you understand?' Authority said, straining to explain. 'There are all sorts of us here. High words and low words. Technical words, mechanical words, political words. Loving words and fearful words. Every one of us has our own shade of meaning. Our own type. We are full of syllables, symbols, and ornament. Stress and sound, accent, idiom, diacritics, intonation. We are the poetry of the human soul. The true sweet essence. Where would they be without us, without words of love, holy words, gentle words, or exuberant curses? Where would they be if we went on strike?'

'Strike! Strike!'

'Stop it, stop it!' screamed Rambling. 'All this talk is misleading. Our thoughts are all over the place. It's too high-falutin'. It's all hot air. This discussion has wandered way off the point. There's no point asking ourselves where we came from and which of us is the oldest. Or indeed where we'll end up, since maybe there'll be no end to things at all. If we keep going the way we're going, soon we'll be as bad as those eejits of people that are always trying to figure out which came first – the chicken or the egg. What the hell does it matter which came first? The hen doesn't care anyway, as long as she can go on saying chuck-chuck. The egg doesn't care if it never hears the same chuck-chuck, doesn't give a hoot that it's without ear or beak or neck. Chickens and eggs exist and they are the way they are because that's the way they are, and that's that. Maybe the day will come when there'll be hens that won't lay eggs for love or money, or maybe the day'll come when every egg will be addled.

Maybe the day will come when there'll be no such thing as chickens or eggs at all and that'll be the end of it. But nothing matters except the fact that they do exist at the moment. Right now. It's all the same to us. We're here, however many of us are here, and those of us who aren't here, we're not here any more, and I don't suppose we will be again, even though we were here once. Remember, the fact that we existed that time doesn't mean we don't exist now or even that we must exist again. If we exist again the chances are we'll be having a different conversation altogether. And what about poor Focaleen here, who's been forgotten while you've all been losing the run of yourselves? This meeting was called to try to help him, not to be trying to put the world to rights with mad theories when the world can never be put to rights and when words have no business giving themselves headaches trying. Now is there anything at all we can do for poor Focaleen here?

They all looked around.

'Where's he gone?' Question asked.

Focaleen was nowhere to be seen. Not a hide nor hair of him could they find. They looked east, west, north and south. Not a taste of him, not a smell or shadow of him. But wasn't he here, they said, just a little while ago? It was for him they had gathered together to find out his meaning, but they had gone off on a tangent with all their digressing and discussing.

Humans, they said! It'll be the greedy bloody humans who are behind this. They'll have taken him away, body and bones, to make use of him. If that's the case, we won't be able to do anything for him. Because if they get some sense out of him, they won't get any sound out of him, or they won't pronounce him properly. They'll pin him down on a bit of paper, that's what they'll do. And then they'll shut him up in a dark dictionary where he won't get fresh air or see the light of day. What sort of life is that for any poor word, living or dead? All words are entitled to a natural death, at the very least, instead of finishing up silent and stagnant, in a coma forever.

They were right. People had got hold of Focaleen by now, or of what was left of his frail frame. A hunchbacked old man who had been pottering about looking for treasure with an illegal metal detector had found him. He scooped him up immediately, thinking to himself he'd never need to do another day's work. He tried to sell him to a word collector on the black market, but the Office of Public Works took him to the Supreme Court, claiming that Focaleen belonged to the nation. That he was a national treasure.

But then the National Museum said they didn't want him – they were stuck for space anyway. And if he was a word, wasn't the National Library the place for him, they said? But the National Library said that books were their preserve, not strange, stray words and he was packed off swiftly in a black taxi to the University where there was war between the Department of Modern Irish, the Department of Old Irish and the Department of Folklore before he found a resting place. He was given into the care of a hungry bunch of scholars. They had a meeting to see if they could revive him, make him perform, get some mileage out of him. They grabbed him from each other and passed him back to each other again. They put vowels in front of him and consonants behind him and loaded him down with diacritics. They tried prising open the spaces between his ribs, and then they tried filling them up again. They stretched him and they twisted him. They turned him inside out, back to front, upside down and arse in the air. They shook him till his teeth rattled, hoping some extra letter or key to his meaning would fall out. They spelled him back to front, diagonally and bottom to top the way words and scrolls are spelt in other parts of the world. And they pronounced him in every way possible, but he didn't sound like anything they'd ever heard before, and he wasn't shaped like any word they'd ever seen collected.

'To hell with it,' said the Professor, exhausted and pouring with sweat.

'It's not worth bothering about any more,' said the newly-appointed unannounced Associate Professor, who had the shakes from drinking and wanted only to throw in the towel so he could go off to the pub.

'A waste of time,' said the Doctor of Rare Words, once he'd grasped that there was nothing in it for him, since Focaleen wouldn't fit in his unpublished new collection.

'Hah ... hah,' said the Senior Lecturer, agreeing with all of them.

'Huh … huh,' said the postgraduate. 'Who cares whether it lives or dies? I have enough words for my thesis without it.'

'I'm not qualified to voice an opinion,' thought the undergraduate, silently, lazily, without opening his mouth, and he didn't even look at him, but chewed away noisily on his chewing gum. 'Anyway, for all we know it could be a word without any letters at all.'

'Throw it out on the skip then and nobody'll ever know that there was a word like that and nobody will be any the worse off without it,' said the Word Caretaker. 'It won't do anything for our reputation to be minding a word nobody understands.' Once he got the nod, he'd be able to lock up and go home in time to watch the soaps with his wife and kids.

But before he could take him by the scruff of the neck, didn't the impatient Professor pitch him out the window, sending Focaleen skimming out over hill and dale and over the swamps and plains of the midlands. He didn't stop until he had landed head over heels in the middle of a Mayo bog.

Sitting on the wall, mooching about and smoking a joint was a well-off secondary school student. When the blur of Focaleen whizzed by with a swishing sound, taking a strip of skin off his ear, he picked him up, thinking he'd come from outer space. He didn't manage to figure him out but, more importantly, he realised quickly there was nothing for him to sip on, nothing to sniff or inhale. Still, he carried him home to throw to the baby in the cot to keep him quiet. It was the youngest, the newest, the least-prejudiced child in the country at that moment and everyone gathered around him to see if he could spot any life or squeeze any sense out of Focaleen. 'Certainly,' he nodded, gesturing to say as soon as I learn to talk, I'll say him right out. He took hold of Focaleen and crammed him into his mouth like a new toy. They waited in a circle around him, afraid he would choke himself, for a year or so until he learned to speak, trying to read the different expressions on his face. Then they pricked up their ears until they were as high as a horse's when they sensed that his sweet little mouth was assembling Focaleen's syllables ready to speak.

'Focaleen fucked,' the infant cried out, propelling the word out of his mouth with the force of a whip, up into the dark sky. He kept going until he belly-flopped into the soft muck at the bottom of Muicíneach Idir Dhá Sháile na gCloch where he had been found in the first place. In the take-off and descent he had shed some of his syllables.

'That's that now, thanks be to God,' Focaleen said to himself contentedly. 'Isn't it great to be alive again and free of all of them, words and people, and able to go my own way just as I please. Although it did no harm to spend some time as a pretend word with no real duties. Being there and at the same time never having been there. Instead of having them examining and bothering and dissecting me. But I'm free now from their greedy paws, from their sharp teeth and their rough tongues and they can't tie me down or shut me up or put me in a hole. And to make sure no living being can ever misuse me again I'm going to turn myself to powder right now.' And he puffed himself up until he was a huge big balloon and – laughing all the way – burst into smithereens.

Translated by Katherine Duffy.

The Banana Banshee

Deirdre Brennan

Anyone watching would have sworn I was giving Val my undivided attention. My friend Fidelma, an inveterate matchmaker, had just introduced us. Her choice of men for me usually left me cold and this was no exception. I was actually drifting in and out of listening as if I were coming out of an anaesthetic. The evening was a bit of a yawn and it took all my willpower not to retreat into myself, to ponder the futility of life and to count stars shooting against the velvety darkness of my brain. Val's voice jolted me back like a dig in the ribs.

'Did you know that it was the Pilgrim Fathers themselves who invented it?'

What on earth was he on about?

'I'm telling you now. They used to make a concoction of pine needles and the chippings of walnut trees. Oh, yes. The cocktail's sure come a long way!'

I laughed with relief. Encouraged, he leaned closer towards me.

'Here, have a slurp of my Alabama Fogcutter. It's the drop of vermouth that makes the difference.'

The idea of a cocktail hour had been dreamed up by Fidelma as a fundraiser for the local musical society, trying to recoup losses on its most recent production, *Hello Dolly*. She had modelled the evening on the Plaza Hotel, New York in the 1930s, which was why I was standing there, all six feet of me, *gottied* up in short black silk, ballooning out in layers of fringed chiffon and thinking only of escape.

'So, what are you drinking?'

Wow! There was actually a gap in his knowledge!

'Banana Banshee,' I said sourly, licking what tasted like a lemony orange froth from my lips.

'Can I have a taste?'

I handed him my swizzle stick knowing he couldn't possibly taste much.

'Mmmmm ...' he sucked, 'nice tension there between the ingredients.' He scanned me up and down. He had an aquiline nose that gave him a greedy look as if he wanted to possess me. In what sense I wasn't sure, but I had these vibes that lodged somewhere in my guts. I clung to my glass as if it were a strong stake anchoring me.

'What do you do?' Val questioned.

'I'm an artist,' I said evasively

'Me too.'

'What kind?'

'Oh, groovy. Contemporary. I express bodies and feelings and how they relate to each other.'

'Christ!' I said under my breath. What kind of a nerd had I been saddled with! I stood up as if summoned by an unheard bell, said I had to go and Cinderella-like made a bolt for it.

I didn't see or think of Val for another six weeks. Not till Fidelma came round one evening after work.

'Hey, Lynn,' she said, 'we're having a sixties night for the musical society on Saturday. Say you'll come.'

I groaned audibly. I was suffering.

'Val'll be there. Isn't he drop-dead gorgeous and he really fancies you!'

'I can't,' I blustered. 'I'm off to the country to visit the folks.'

I could already see spring outside the train window, fields of winter corn flashing past, a dusting of catkins on the trees, my folks making a fuss of me. I didn't need man-hassle. How could I, after Martin ditched me almost at the altar and took off for Australia with a girl he had known a mere few months.

Fidelma refused to listen to me.

'You're cloistering yourself. All work and no play. You might as well be a bloody nun. You'd have more sport in a convent. Cop yourself on girl! Your folks will still be there next week.'

I yielded, painted butterflies on my big toes, put on a purple mini, a long string of green glass beads swinging down to my stomach and headed for the fundraiser.

When I spotted Val, I wondered was it him at all. He had a more highly evolved look about him than I remembered and seemed less overpowering, merging with the crowd, listening, rather than holding forth. To my surprise, I found myself hoping he would come in my direction, but when he did as if on cue, I didn't let on I saw him.

'Well, if it isn't the Banana Banshee herself!' he whispered.

The ice in my glass shivered slightly as my eyes swam into those greedy ones trying to possess me. That's when I knew he was still quintessentially him. He certainly looked different without the thirties gear.

'How's the art going?' he asked knowingly. I realised Fidelma had split on me, so I stretched out my sandalled feet. The glorious butterflies looked as if they were about to take off. I had studied their every movement in the Butterfly Centre in Carraroe. Watched them as pupae hanging from a twig in the overheated glasshouse; sketched the first flutterings of wings, their flight, and now the captured stillness on my toenails. Stillness and patience was what it was about. If you work in miniature as I do, you must do your homework with precision as well as imagination.

'You're a manicurist?' Val was enquiring.

'A nail artist.' I corrected. 'Flowers, butterflies, cartoon characters – whatever turns you on.' I had no notion of elaborating.

'I think we've a lot in common,' he said smiling.

From that night in the Plaza onwards, Fidelma was forever begging me to give him a chance. It was on account of her and our friendship that I decided not to run him. There was no way I was bowled over.

Within two months Val and I had become an item. I never fell in love with anyone quicker. And that brought me back to the old chestnut, of speculating about love and puzzling whether it was possible for a man to love a woman without trying to possess her. Love is a discovery, one of the other. My experience had always been that the less you give away the better since familiarity invariably breeds contempt. That is why as a rule of thumb I keep an escape route at the ready, an emotional trapdoor that I can drop through at will. No man on earth was going to hurt me again. What I didn't realise was that by being evasive and trying to conceal myself, I was in fact revealing far too much to Val and that by moving quickly he had battened down my trapdoor before my very eyes. I might have been one of my painted butterflies. There was no escape. I tried not to panic.

Little and all as I gave away, I was conscious that Val gave less. He was ostensibly open, loving, frank, talkative. It was clear that he was very taken with my height. When he invited me for the first time to his workshop in Kilkenny, I was flattered but not prepared for what lay ahead. Bear in mind that I thought I was visiting some class of art gallery, but this place smelled as antiseptic as a hospital. It was obvious from the inks, the needles, the general equipment, that my loved one was a tattooist. Sketches of the Sacred Heart and all kinds of religious images mingled with anchors and roses and snakes on the four walls. I could have murdered Fidelma. The bitch! Of course she knew. I felt such a fool.

'So, you express bodies and feelings and how they relate to each other,' I said with as much sarcasm as I could muster when I found my voice.

'Do you have a problem with that?' he said.

Of course I didn't, but yet I did. I'd thought that Val might have wanted me as an artist's model; that I might have become famous like the wife of the French artist Pierre Bonnard who painted his wife languishing in the bath or draped against the garden vegetation.

I had met the real Val at last. Gone was the poseur and know-all. He explained how he listened to music as he worked; how he used the rhythm of the music, transferring it to his subjects. He demonstrated the amount of preparation work that went into his pieces; how he realised his responsibility to his customers whose chosen designs were as much an expression of themselves as they were of him, the artist.

I think I was two months pregnant when I next visited the workshop. I looked squarely into the liquid eyes of the Sacred Heart, Padre Pio, St Christopher and a pantheon of unrecognisable saints. Did priests and nuns really wear the holy ones under their garments? There was Cú Chulainn too and Mona Lisa, and St George and the Dragon. Val himself was wearing a yellow cutaway singlet which showed off to perfection a bunch of bright bananas on his left forearm and my name under them. His assistant had designed it under Val's direction. I began to laugh hysterically. He loved me. I thought how angry and defensive I had grown after the Martin experience. Now I had renewed confidence in the world. Val and I had a kind of ceremony.

'Does it hurt?' I whispered, looking at the needles and inks.

He tenderly swabbed my upper arm close to the shoulder with disinfectant and deftly traced on it a single banana, his own name in the folds of a leaf. He worked gently, competently. I didn't feel a thing and the tattoo was very pretty, really much nicer than a ring.

Fidelma was gobsmacked when I showed her.

'Jesus, Lynn, you've tied yourself up good and proper! Why didn't you use one of those transfer tattoos? I never thought you had it in you. There was no need to go over the top.'

But, there was. She didn't understand at all.

She continued, 'I can tell you I wouldn't do it ... not for Val, nor any other man.'

'I'm not tied in any way,' I said proudly. I wasn't going to say anything further.

'Would you give over,' she laughed. 'Where else have you got a tattoo?'

Once we had a home together, Val developed a passion for gardening. Not on a big scale, you know, but in window boxes. The following spring, he had parrot tulips that would take the sight from your eyes. He was fascinated by their abandon and flamboyance. He looked at me longingly. Oh, I wasn't mistaken. It was my skin he coveted. Six feet of prime canvas. But it was mine. In the beginning, I was reluctant, but in the end I gave in. I let him tattoo a yellow-red parrot tulip down my backbone. I lay on my belly, thinking of the child inside me and taking comfort and happiness from Val's hands drawing fine lines on my skin, the swirl of feathered petals swimming between my shoulders.

As for my own art, I shared it with him. Lovingly, meticulously I adorned his finger and toenails with wild flowers and insects of every kind. On the first anniversary of our meeting, I pierced the third nail of his left hand and hooked in a thin gold ring. Fidelma said that was different since it wasn't permanent.

By the time the baby was due for delivery, my body was a riot of colour. All of Val's personal feelings for me and our child were transferred to my skin. My gynaecologist's eyes widened somewhat when she examined my abdomen for the first time. Beneath her fingers, a serpent writhed under an apple tree and Adam was half hidden in Eve's tangled hair.

It was a wonderful picture. Eve's face resembled mine. Adam's face was Val's.

'Why did you do such a thing?' the doctor questioned.

'My husband,' I said, 'he's an artist.'

'Good God! And you allowed this? You do realise, Lynn, that tattoos like this are irreversible?' she murmured.

I understood. When I saw her worried face it got me thinking once again of love and commitment and possession. Val was so obsessed with the living canvas of my body, would he ditch me when the canvas was full, or would he need me as his life's masterpiece? I got a chilly little feeling in the pit of my stomach when I faced the fact that our sharing was not quite equal. He could erase my nail-paintings with a ball of cotton wool soaked in polish remover. In his mind, love and the realisation of his artistic ambitions were one. I prefer to think that he loves me in his own way. However, I decided not to hand over any more canvas for the time being.

The baby was born. She is now three years old. Sometimes I see her father look at her longingly, greedily as if he can't get enough of her. I see her eyes swimming into his. I keep a sharp eye on them. These days he is teaching her to draw little yellow bananas.

Translated by the author.

GREAT AND SMALL

Daithí Ó Muirí

I am a film actor but do not know if filming is still taking place or if it is to continue. The film director is missing. I would gladly discard the script and seek out another film, but I fear I may be called on – I may be asked to recite my lines, or be given new lines, be asked to portray arrogance or humility, self-importance or self-effacement, some one of my stock of characteristics – but I would not be available. And what use would I be to the film if I was not present to accept the directions?

In seven minutes' time a scene is to be filmed, but perhaps today's schedule has been postponed. Or perhaps they were unhappy with my efforts in the scenes already filmed in the village, the scene in the shop, the scene in the public house, the scene in the street. Perhaps a new actor is coming to take my place, a fresh new talent come to light among the Flahertys, one of the Conneelys, the Feeneys, the local people who were recruited to fill the minor parts, to provide another vague face in a scene dotted with faces, or to roar unheard above the great roar of the crowd, or even to say a few lines, a few inches of filmstrip to be discarded among the waste on the floor of the editing room, the people who have not the least understanding of the art of acting, who want merely to add a few extra pounds to their dole.

The director is a perfect gentleman, but he is hot-tempered. He can become very annoyed if he is thwarted, or if the art he is responsible for is thwarted; an art which he respects more than anything, as he explained to us, an art with a special significance, a significance beyond the person who lights the set, a significance beyond the person who handles the camera, beyond the person who writes the lines in the mouth of the actor, the person who ties together word and deed, who suits expression to gesture, yes, significance beyond the director himself, beyond the actors who play their parts, even though it is they who often seem the most prominent aspect of the film. He made us aware that this is a film of the very highest artistic merit, a film of a kind never seen before and never to be seen again, that we must be prepared to lower our self-respect, that we must comply fully with the mastery of the director – however easy or hard we might find that – in order to give precedence always to the film. And we had faith. His words inspired our full confidence in him as a director, we placed our trust completely in him, we vowed to do everything possible to achieve his aims, to yield to his will, almost to sacrifice ourselves for him, but now, now he is not here and the only guide we have is the schedule.

... I asked my colleagues, the other actors, five of us wandering aimlessly about by the side of the road in the hollow of the valley, scripts in our hands, looking at the hills surrounding us, at the great high-peaked mountain to the west, at the clear blue sky, the dazzling sun rising higher and higher as time passes, that is all that is to be seen – I asked them, all of us anxious, what we should do. But each of us is in the same predicament. An hour ago filming was to have commenced, but the director has not arrived, nor the crew nor the technicians. Perhaps distant cameras were filming us, hidden microphones recording us. Perhaps it was a stratagem of the director's in order to confirm our loyalty. We did not fail him, if that was the case. We donned our costumes, recited the lines we had dedicated ourselves to learning by heart, we made the gestures, yes, even though no camera was evident, no recording equipment, even though we were not asked to adapt or improve word or deed.

In two hours' time the next scene is to be filmed in the forest on the side of the mountain to the west. All our ears are listening intently, expecting to hear the drone of the minibus coming northeast over the hill, the labouring of the equipment truck's engine in the narrowness of the valley road following behind. But only the light breeze can be heard. Soon we must proceed up towards the forest if we are to reach it on time. Perhaps the cameras will be there waiting for us, the director eyeing sharply his wristwatch.

The last time I saw the director was here this morning. An enormous golden sun was rising over the brow of the great hill to the east. It was precisely nine o'clock – the clock on the village courthouse was ringing it out a few miles to the east in the silence and stillness of the early morning. The director's nine soft footsteps, like echoes of the distant clock's nine muted peals, were extinguished suddenly by the crash of the minibus door being closed. He spoke a few words to the driver and was driven northeast towards the main road which leads to the village.

... In the forest a foot cracked a fallen twig which raised a screeching of birds hidden by density of foliage, which snatched, in the blinking of an eye, some dun-coloured creature from sight. We were spellbound at the magic of the trees, at the play of light filtering through gaps in the millions of leaves. That was not in the script. And what of the nest of the ants? We overturned a stone and observed their pointless toil. That was not in the script. We forgot the schedule and ran disoriented through the forest until we found ourselves at its perimeter. Before us, to the west, high above, lay the mountain peak. It was not in the script but we decided to ascend.

The thunder, the tremors in the earth, the first issue of smoke from the mountain top, evoked fear. Fear: the head half-thrown backward by the contortion of the neck, a shoulder hunched up, a claw-like hand tearing at the hair, an eye suddenly blocked by the closing together of fingers, the breathing laboured and interrupted, plaintive whimpering, the eyes casting about on all sides, the upper lip raised above the upper teeth, the eyelids drawn back to reveal an expanse of white, every part of the body in a shudder, over there the black semicircle of a mouth, here the uncontrollable swallowing of saliva. Nor was that in the script.

But, as we race downward through the heather with the mountain hare far ahead of us and the waves close at our heels, it is the scalding of the foot soles that will generate the real screams.

I am the tiny twig lying under the shadows of the mountain forest – my spine was snapped when one of the actors trod on me. But no heed was paid to this appalling act. The birds – it was not the snapping of my spine that sent them screeching upwards, but rather the interruption of the silence – before long they alighted on the high branches once more. They did not mourn me, they did not loudly broadcast my demise throughout the world, they did not attack the trespasser in a cloud of beating wings, they did not leave him pitted with hundreds of beak-stabs. The animals of the forest – they fled the scene in order not to hear my death rattle, so that it would not be related in times to come that they witnessed the injustice, but did not tear the guilty one apart with sharpness of tooth and claw. The trees themselves –

they remained unconcerned, standing with their old steadfastness, they did not bow their heads, they did not bend their knees in respect to me, they cast down not one single branch to crush the bones that trod me mercilessly under foot.

But before giving up my spirit I made my complaint to the mountain. This was my final prayer:

Although I am but the lowliest thing on your sloping back – the weak desiccated twig in the midst of the mighty oaks, the leaf-stripped branchlet hidden by the green luxuriance of the horse chestnuts, the lowly little stick half-enveloped by the earth beneath the height of the towering pines – hear me, O long-slumbering mountain, I beg you to listen to my request; although I am hardly more than the tiny inconspicuous wisp of straw entangled in the fur of the cape as it is draped over the shoulders of the great noble by the keen-eyed servant, despite that, O rock-hard giant, despite that and all else, O most great high cairn, give ear to my demand; although I have left no mark in your noble ancient war but the prick of a tick behind the knee of the great warrior from which was drawn the least vital drop of blood, unlike the living stream from bone-deep wounds, the unrelenting flow from a slashed belly dousing red the innards as they hang below the trembling knees, but be that as it may, O stone stack heaped with the hardening of the ages, although I am esteemed by neither flora nor fauna in this mountain forest, but hear you, O giant of the sky-piercing summit, hear you the tiny whisper in your great ear.

Stretch your shoulders rigid with age and startle the hearts of those who have invaded these secret grounds that have been defended and preserved since ancient times; part lips closed for eons with a slow-awakening yawn that will send tremors and shudders up and down your old bulk and will fold under with terror those legs that have violated injunctions created long long ago, so long that only you know the why and the whereof; ignite yourself, O long-slumbering volcano, stoke up the murky abyss of your belly, set a torch to the musty old gruel that has lain there since the creation of stone and clay, before plant or person was engendered, heat it until it glows red, yellow-red, yellow, white-yellow, white, so bright white that it seems blue – belch up the boiled pulp with the churning of your belly, send it up through the gullet to your throat; open wide your maw and puke out your rotten poison vomit amid clouds of ash, amid incinerating heavy rain, overflow yourself with liquid steaming burned mud flooding down from your mouth in thick bilious waves; char that absconding foot which was so bold as to overthrow the least conspicuous, but the most loyal of your subjects with a proud careless footfall; submerge every creature and every thing in the fluid crematorium of your vomit, with complete willingness will we sacrifice ourselves under your fiery crimson cascade in order to wreak your revenge; fill the valley with the lava of your fit of anger so that it will congeal and become a flat memorial stone that will remain as a mark of your humble might for all time, after plant and person have been swept from the earth, for ever and ever, until neither stone nor clay exist any longer.

I am the film director. I have nothing to add to what I have already said in the press statement, which is to be released tomorrow. It was not I who told the people to go west to the valley, to stand there in the sun and that they would be paid well for it. Certainly, I assured the community association that a few local people would be employed in the crowd scenes, some customers in the shop, some young men in the public house, but I made no mention of children, dogs or cats. It was not I who told them to drive the cattle, the pigs, the sheep, the hens west with them. Certainly, I took advantage of the opportunity when the mountain exploded to shoot some fine footage. It is true, and what a disastrous loss it is, that the camera went missing afterwards and it is also true that a reward will be given to anyone who can help the police in locating this priceless footage. I beg your pardon, sir, but I just happened to be on the hilltop above the valley at the opportune moment, that is all, it was a complete accident that I myself did not die tragically in the valley along with the other people. I beg your pardon? I went west to see what was delaying the actors, that was the reason. The road? The road ... of course, it was blocked by the people with all their animals going west to the fair in the valley, that was the reason, and, as I have said, it was not I – a man I met showed me a short cut, but, as it happened, it was not a short cut – I got lost, I say, that is the reason I did not reach the valley before the people. I was very angry because almost the entire day had been wasted searching for the actors – I have not the faintest idea what they were doing in the valley – yes, that is true, it is true that I went out with them early in the morning, but we were just looking at a location. Why did they not return with me in the minibus? I do not know. I do not, and that is the truth. Actors are a strange breed. Possibly they were just accustoming themselves to the place. They were very zealous. They were wandering all around and I became impatient waiting for them. Damn them, I said, damn them, and I ordered the driver to drive. Let them walk, if they so choose. At least the driver fulfilled his duty. And the minibus did not break down, unlike the equipment truck yesterday. I beg your pardon, sir, but there was ample time ... I was waiting for them in the courthouse at midday, as we had arranged, but when they failed to appear I went west. I did not bother to question the people who were walking west. No. I do not know. I assumed it was a fair or something of that kind and that I might as well bring along the camera –

that is what I thought, yes. By Christ, how should I know why they might have a fair in some deserted valley, I am a city person, I am ignorant of these matters. Yes, ignorant. I was there by accident – by accident, I say. Yes, I carried the camera two miles west, yes ... Foreknowledge? Foreknowledge, you say! Hah! How could I have foreknowledge? Do you think I am a prophet, that I managed to predict a volcanic eruption when not even the cleverest geologists did ... Do not listen to that nonsense, there are so many rumours going around that no credence should be given to any of them, none whatsoever, no more than to the superstitions of old country people ... Please excuse me, excuse me, Mother of God, I no longer care, everything has collapsed, everything has been topsy-turvy since my arrival here, all sense of order ruined by headstrong actors, even the parish priest interfering – yes, I am aware that he is not here to furnish you with his own account – and now, the crowning misfortune, the most significant piece of footage I have ever made – more significant than the people who perished in the valley; more significant than birth, life and death itself – while all of you try to demean me and the work I am undertaking; you who understand only the commonplace struggle with the commonplace responsibilities of life, but I, I have a responsibility beyond that, I struggle with the Film, the Film that will be remembered by hundreds of generations to come, generations who will be grateful to me, my name will be spoken everywhere when all of you will be remembered only because you tried to thwart me, to place obstacles before me, obstacles that I will overcome, by the devil I will, I will overcome them, I will overcome the whole world with my own blood if needs be. I will ...

I am the volcano. I tried to clear the mucus in the back of my throat with a bark of a cough, kneading it into a single lump that I might expel in a high-rising, far-travelling, heavy-falling spit. But with the feebleness of old age I produced only a rasping croak and a dribble of spit which rolled down my chin and came to rest in the hollow of my neck.

Without delay the news spread throughout the country. North to Errigal. East through Derry and Tyrone. On the wind across Lough Neagh so that Slieve Donard might hear. From there down past Dundalk Bay and south to the Wicklow Mountains. When Lugnaquillia had done with scoffing he passed it along through Wexford and Waterford. Slievenamon paid no heed and the knowledge departed westward to Macgillycuddy's Reeks, where Carrauntoohil's tittering triggered some underground tremors.

All that was bad, but, to my shame, worse was to come.

On the waves of the Atlantic Ocean a statement went west, finally making land on the coast of America, journeying far west over the Appalachian Mountains, from the Great Central Lowlands through the Great Plains until, finally, it reached the Rocky Mountains. Most probably Mount St Helens heard it before it continued down the Sierra Nevada, the Sierra Madre and then, turning through the Panama Isthmus, down into South America. Down it went along the west coast, its echoes rebounding off the Andean peaks until it was forgotten somewhere in the vicinity of Tierra del Fuego.

I heard Ben Nevis recounting on all sides before the commentary went down through the Pennines. I heard the lapping of the waters in the English Channel and the underground whispering in France. It was transferred across the borders of Switzerland where it scaled the Alps. Descending southwards in a run it traversed the Apennines, slipped by Vesuvius who called it out to Mount Etna. The news travelled east then, leaping across over the Balkan Peninsula, swimming across the Black Sea. I heard the muttering on the Caucasus Mountains, the shouting on the Zagros, and, before long, the announcement throughout the Himalayas. Everest guffawed, sending snow in thousands of tons avalanching down over his shoulder blades. The knowledge was then steered through the Indochinese Peninsula and into Indonesia. Krakatoa declaimed its tale throughout the Philippines, but, finally, it yielded up its spirit on its way north to Japan, where Mount Fuji heard nothing of it.

But this same spirit, what became of it? As a ghost it passed up through the atmosphere, still telling its tale to motes of dust and pebbles before they fell as meteors. It spent an entire day spinning and weaving through the vacuum of outer space before alighting on the mountainous wall of the widest crater on the Moon. It intoned its knowledge but there was no reaction to its disclosure other than the usual silent tranquillity. Out to Mars it went, where it spent a month rambling on Olympus Mons. For a year it was buffeted by a hurricane in the Great Red Spot in the clouds of Jupiter. Three times it orbited the rings of Saturn. It spent years travelling out to the stars. Sirius drew it into the immense heat of its heart and projected it out after half a century. It paid a visit to Betelgeuse and spent a few centuries orbiting it. It slumbered for a millennium on the north pole of Deneb. It left the Milky Way itself and made explorations in galaxies so far away that neither thousands of years nor millions of miles can measure the distance. Yes, it made its grand tour until finally it lay down in the bosom of the Creature who measures neither time nor distance, and who could extinguish the stars of the Milky Way with its infantile dribbling unknown to itself.

I am Flaherty Mac Flaherty. I am an excavator of holes, a deceiver, I am an erector of walls, an upright gentleman, I am a scoundrel and a parasite. On the day in question I was living a few miles to the west of the valley that has long been such a subject of conversation. In any case, once during the week, I used to proceed eastwards to the village, in order to take care of business. Never have I paid heed to car or horse, to roadways great or small. On foot I journeyed in a straight line eastwards, across the edge of the mountain, down through the hollow of the valley, over the brow of the great hill, through the fields, one by one. I leapt the ford in the river, made my way between the bushes, ploughed through the mud of the swamp until, finally, I reached the village.

However, on that day it was deserted. In place of the cat that I used to stroke from its forehead to the end of its tail as it lay purring on the window ledge, there was a magpie attacking its own reflection in the glass. A flock of large unkempt crows were parading boastfully around in place of the dog I used to coax with tickles under its chin, while I exchanged some words with the old people in front of the post office. Down at the corner I did not get the opportunity to wink at the alert eyes of the bravest dogs as they looked up at the behaviour of the young men, because all that could be seen were the long pink tails of rats protruding from holes in old fertiliser bags overflowing with rubbish. I proceeded to the public house, but it was securely closed. I slipped in through a crack in the rear wall and consumed a pint and a whiskey for the sake of my health. Then I made my way to the priest's house. But he was not at home, nor was the servant girl, nor anybody else. For fear of hunger, I ate a fine hearty meal of sausages, eggs, pudding and bacon.

Then I proceeded westwards towards the valley – the Devil had informed me that the most advantageous bargains were to be had there, where all the villagers were gathering. I returned through the fields, one by one. On my way I encountered a stoutish fellow, filthy with mud, his grand clothes torn and tattered by briars and bushes. And such a temper he was in, swearing at a stone that tripped him, cursing at a steep incline that he slithered down – but he made sure not to relinquish his grip on a large weighty camera despite the tripping and slithering. By the providence of God! This is the kind of work that I like, I said to myself. Over I went to speak to him.

From the welcoming look he gave me he must have thought I was an angel of God come to carry him heavenward. The unfortunate creature, he was perspiring like a potato digger in hell, whimpering like a child kept home from the bonfire. Alas, alas. As it happened, I had been composing a special salutation all week, and he being the first person I had seen since that number of days, I presented it to him. But he did not show much appreciation. In fact, he did not wait for its conclusion, but interrupted my sweet melodious words, beseeching me to direct him towards the valley, saying that he had gone astray, that he did not know where he was and that he was in very great haste. And, believe me, he certainly was. For if it was the Devil who had informed me that the mountain was going to transform itself into an active volcano, the Seven Devils had informed him. I adopted a studious look while he tried to calm his laboured breathing. What would you say to a pint, I asked him? As prepayment for the information, I added, turning eastwards again. By God, I almost went deaf listening to his lies about why he was in such haste until, finally, he plunged a hand deep into his pocket and drew out a large sum of money. Money, I say! What use could money possibly be to a man like me, a man who had never paid for anything in his life? I refused it outright and enquired about the equipment he was carrying. But for all the gold in the world, for the love of God or to advance the work of the Devil, he would not relinquish the camera. If that is how you feel, I said, I will have to be satisfied with praise. The poor tormented soul, he had no experience whatsoever of good manners, and while he whimpered and sighed with impatience I explained to him what I meant. Finally he remained silent, adopted a look of exasperation, and he began to praise me. But, God help us, his praise was so weak and disheartening that it would not even raise the spirits of an ant. I made valiant attempts at inspiring him, adding a few words to his miserable attempts in the hope that he might understand my little hints. But it was work in vain. I am a man, I said, a large man, a large broad heavy man, but exceedingly swift, and if I struck you, you would not feel it, for you would soon be laid out in your coffin and there would be no trace of me. A look of terror came over him. Now, what do you have to say? He said that I was a nice person, a nice strong person. But generally, I said, I am a gentle person, a little slender person with so light a tread that I would not even bend a crooked twig lying under the forest trees. This tied his tongue completely, for whatever reason, the colour faded from his cheeks, and he knelt down before me. He joined his two plump hands together and began thrusting them back and forth, up and down, fingers woven together, and he asked me not to put him to death, he was merely recording the workings of fate, a thing that nobody could avoid, and other talk of this kind that I did not hear properly as it was smothered with paroxysms of tears. There now, I had no intention whatsoever of killing him. I am not a murderer. Then, well, I actually began to pity him. I offered to carry him west on my back free of charge. He grabbed his camera and climbed up. Off we went through the swamp, between the bushes, over the ford in the river, and up the hill until we reached its top.

In any case, I do not wish to be long-winded. Suffice to say – but you know this already – that the mountain exploded and that everyone in the hollow of the valley was drowned in the burning deluge. I greatly pitied them. They were not completely bad people. And if such was the work of fate it was bad work. That fellow recorded it all, the camera propped on a tripod, and he danced in pure heartfelt delight, tears of joy this time squeezing from his eyes. Did I say that I was a thief? While he was so consumed with his frolicking, his capering back and forth, bounding from side to side, kicking heels in the air to the right and to the left, singing *diddlee eye dee doo* and *diddlee oodle dye*, I stole the camera. I snatched it and off home I went. But alas, it slipped from my grip as I swam across the valley. Yes, it certainly did, although I dived again and again down into that lake of flames, I found not a trace of it.

That now is the simple truth, but if it is a lie, it is a straight lie, and if it is the truth, it is the crooked truth.

Translated by the author.

THE KHRUSHCHEV SHOE

Gabriel Rosenstock

Randal is one of the leading collectors of antiques and curios in both Ireland and Britain. His name is legendary among his peers.

Four or five major American museums are eager to get their hands on some of his more unusual artefacts. He won't part with anything, however, not even the most seemingly insignificant object. He would rather give away his soul than see his collection pass into a stranger's hands.

Neither the dictates of fashion nor his own feelings ever intrude on Randal's judgement, relying as he does on written reports from trusted agents around the world. Most collectors of his acquaintance and their agents tend to be specialists in their own relatively narrow subject area. Randal's collection is marked by its individuality and diversity.

After all, doesn't he own the magic wand once used by Crowley himself ('the Great Beast'), a treasure he picked up in Iceland no less! He'd been offered $95,000 for it. He didn't bother to respond to the fax that offered him such a princely sum of money, however, as the fax had been sent to him directly. He had his own agents and functionaries in various parts of the world to filter such messages.

They say that Randal was a born collector. No sooner was he snatched from the breast than he began to acquire historical artefacts and various other miscellaneous items. He collected lollipop sticks, match boxes and toilet rolls in addition to stamps, coins, dead insects and empty lipstick holders thrown out by his mother.

Later in his career, not only did he collect a variety of items, but he also noted their price (when such information was available), where he had acquired the item, its provenance and its date of purchase. Everything was carefully noted in his thick accounts ledger.

Those in the know claim that this ledger is worth a great deal in itself, never mind the information contained in the actual entries. All of the annotations were done with a scholarly neatness ... each nugget of information carefully recorded and its previous history given over the course of several generations.

Randal was never a vain individual. His morning and afternoon *toilette* consisted mainly of keeping his pencil-thin moustache neat and free from nicotine stains. His annual routine was nearly as regular as his daily ablutions. He kept his own council in controversial matters and dusted down his antique collection once a week. Once a year, on his birthday, he gave himself an illicit treat when he hired an Asian prostitute and paid her to feign an orgasmic frenzy. This year, in perfect symmetry with Randal's age, it was in room 47 of the Burlington Hotel; no sooner had he finished listening to her cries of pleasure, then he immediately booked room 48 for the following year. Randal was a man of simple needs.

Fort Knox is what his fellow antique collectors had nicknamed his spacious apartment in Ballsbridge. As implied by this nickname, Randal was also a collector of locks in addition to everything else. He collected door locks, gate locks, handcuffs, not to mention the chastity belt he had hanging on the wall. In truth, you'd have to be a Houdini of sorts to gain entry to Randal's pad unknown to him. He had a particular hatred of journalists, rumour mongers and photographers (except those photography masters whose work he collected). No fear that any of those crooks would ever find out about Khruschev's shoe, the shoe that the Soviet leader had removed to use as a hammer on his delegate desk at the UN. This shoe was the sole item in his entire collection the existence of which wasn't noted in his ledger and which wasn't always kept under lock and key. Instead, he carried it with him everywhere he went, hidden deep within the folds of his overcoat. Nobody, not even the nosiest journalist, would have suspected that he carried this shoe everywhere. Who knows? Given an extra tip, the Asian prostitute might permit him to give her ass a good leathering with it at his next birthday? What bliss!

This shoe was the jewel in his crown. It was more tempting than the devil himself. As prizes go, it even surpassed the ornate tigerskin rug from Tibet – a rug the centre of which had already been worn thin by the asses of five generations of lamas. It was even better than that enchanting letter written by the author of *The Islandman*, Tomás Ó Criomhthain …

It was two months after the fall of the Soviet Bloc that he had got his hands on this prize. He received a fax from Prague and was on the next plane. Soon after landing, he recognised a number of his fellow antique collectors who had already arrived in this ancient city. A few of them were mooching around in the guise of tourists. He spotted that agent of McGregor's, whatever his name was, and that idiot from Glasgow. Even Kleinstein himself was there, all the way from Pittsburgh. By a strange coincidence, all three of his competitors found themselves in the same pub one day, an Irish bar by the name of the James Joyce.

Randal was drinking an Irish Coffee, McGregor's agent was on the whiskey and Kleinstein was drinking wine – this in an establishment where most of the customers drank beer and Guinness. Each of the collectors let on that they hadn't noticed any of the others, while Randal had his nose stuck in a literary journal called *Trafika*, a journal published by some learned American ex-pats based in Prague. Despite his best efforts, Randal found himself unable to concentrate on the piece he was reading – an extract from a novel by a Vietnamese writer, translated into English. In fact, it wasn't long before he left the journal down and went back to his hotel.

Huh! Kleinstein! You can be damned sure that he'd swipe the journal the minute Randal was gone. Kleinstein, the specialist! A so-called expert in Church furnishings and the man wasn't even a Christian. Kleinstein was Jewish, for God's sake! Maybe that's the reason why his conscience never seemed to bother him as Orthodox treasures from Eastern Europe made their way back to his lair. Kleinstein with his chalices and icons and sanctuary lamps! And the same fellow had probably never even heard of Khruschev!

$14,000! Sure, what is $14,000 really when all is said and done? It's nothing when you had a treasure as unique as Nikita Khruschev's shoe in your possession. Come the end of the century, this shoe would have doubled in price! Questions of value and price didn't make a whit of difference to Randal, one way or another. No matter what happened he was certain of one thing. He would never part with that shoe. The Russians had sworn on 'the Czar's bones' that they wouldn't tell a soul, living or dead, who had bought it from them. And Randal had done business with them before, of course.

Sure, there were crooks and chancers amongst them … but they wouldn't let you down. The Russian Mafia knew their stuff by then. They were wise enough to know that it made no sense to fall out with Randal's agents in the antiques game, and that it was the absolute kiss of death to get into a dispute with any of the *bone fide* antique collectors. Play a trick on him? Unlikely.

Ever since the so-called Hitler Diaries made the news, buyers and sellers were extra cautious. Having checked and re-checked the available documentary evidence, it seemed absolutely certain that this shoe was indeed worn by Khrushchev himself in New York, 12 October 1960.

In a way that he could not articulate, his purchase of the shoe in Prague was the apex of his collecting career. Stations of the Cross, ornate baptismal fonts, an ancient church organ, still intact, these were the collectibles which McGregor and Kleinstein chased down, always in the knowledge that theirs was a race against time. Let them off – the fools! What business did he have with stained-glass windows and mosaic side-altars? Randal wanted artefacts to surround himself with, not to be viewed in museums and galleries. He preferred objects that he could touch and feel, antiques that he could appreciate in the privacy of his own domain.

Even today, nobody knows how Kleinstein managed to transport that fifteenth-century church pulpit all the way back to Pittsburgh. Ah, himself and his treasured oak pulpit. Some day – God willing – it will fall down on top of him!

Occasionally, Randal released Khruschev's shoe from its dark haven in the depths of his coat, exposing it to the light, polishing it gently. He would set the shoe down in front of him and worship it in all its hidden glory. This was a shoe that millions had seen when it was originally worn. It had also been seen by millions since in a multitude of photographs. In these private moments, Randal would smell that shoe, inhaling its leathery secret.

Two years later, he answers a caller at the front door of his apartment. He has already checked the security monitor. The postman is there with a registered parcel for him. The parcel is postmarked Pittsburgh. On opening the parcel he discovers a video and a note signed in Kleinstein's handwriting: 'I hope the shoe isn't pinching ...'

The bastard. How the hell did Kleinstein ... Who told him ... What the hell?

Randal puts the video in the recorder and presses play. A slight trickle of perspiration falls from the tips of his thin moustache. The film is in black and white. It shows Khruschev beating the desk with his shoe. The piece of film has a voice-over by Kleinstein, no less, the original sound-track deleted.

'That's Khruschev's shoe that you have all right, Randal ... Sure it is ...'

In the background he hears Kleinstein in fits of laughter. He is practically choking with mirth.

'But that's not the shoe he struck the table with, hah, hah! Hah! Not at all. Your shoe is the other one, you fool! The one that remained firmly fixed on his other foot!'

Kleinstein explodes with laughter again. Randal turns up the sound.

Translated by Micheál Ó hAodha.

THE THREE CLICHÉS

Séamas Mac Annaidh

Greetings! You're very welcome.

You're going to enjoy this one, for believe it or believe it not, this is a true full-blooded controversial metafictional short story, or to put it another way, this is a work of art that is totally contrived, artificial, deliberately assembled; it's pompous, self-conscious and minimalist and is about absolutely nothing, but itself.

OK, now, you can sit down and relax, for, from now on, when I say 'you' I won't actually be referring to you, and, of course, then when I say 'I' I won't mean me either. Which is just as well, as you'll soon see ...

Now, come with me, quietly, calmly, right into the heart of the first cliché. This room is the heart of so much of our hope and our fear, a hot spotless room with artificial light. There are no windows here, and while we sit here our attention will be focused on the door. We are right next to the maternity unit in an overcrowded hospital. We await the birth of a child. No smoking. Smoking is never permitted in hospitals, or indeed in my stories any more. In the other room, a girl, still in her teens, lies drugged, but still in pain. Everyone, and in this case I mean everyone, waits, always.

Very good. That didn't hurt at all, now did it? Are you ready for the next one?

Well, this time it concerns me and him. I'm the moneybags in an unspecified school and he drives a great big digger. I make sure that the teachers don't make excessive use of the photocopier and he shifts hundreds of tons of earth every day. He's great.

Anyway, we're bowled over, head over heels in love, wow! You've probably seen us in the pub in the early evenings, drinking minerals and playing energetic word games. Everyone notices us – that is to say that quite a lot of people notice him and me, for everyone doesn't actually mean everyone in this case, and we love the attention. Nobody bothers us, though I'm sure they know exactly how things are between us. Him and me, that is, not you and me.

Are you still with me? Good. Nice and softly does it now. This next one is very subtle.

A policeman.

An ordinary police officer.

And to tell the truth, that's you. You're the cop, though you're off-duty right now. That's why I'm so fascinated by you. Now, I'm sure you have responsibilities of your own, isn't that why you're here? But since I'm beside myself with anxiety, I thought it might help to concentrate on you for a while, Mr Policeman.

I hope I'm not boring you, but I thought you might find it interesting if I explained it. You see, this great world of ours is furnished chock full of stereotypes and clichés, but nobody pays a blind bit of attention to them until they run straight into each other and knock shards from their marble fingers and splinters from their wooden knobs, and you can complete the sentence yourself if you're so inclined. I'm talking to you because you are in the same situation as ourselves, because you have probably noticed us by now and you've come to the same conclusion about us. Yes, but isn't that exactly what we are, three clichés in the one room, the big strong policeman, the two silly young queers, and the child that is about to enter this world at the other side of that door.

I would love, honestly, to have the opportunity to talk to you. We don't often get the chance to meet like this, all in the same situation as we find ourselves now. You sent a little shiver through us when you walked into our local in your dark green uniform with your partner last Tuesday, even though we weren't doing anything illegal.

Now the three of us are trembling.

I don't think, in all honesty, that you really know us. I'm in my early twenties, you're in your thirties – this is probably not your first time in a place like this, in this very room, even. Have you got a little girl at home who climbs up on your knee during the News and asks, 'Daddy, what's wrong?'

Maybe it would be easier if we talked about your wife. Is she big and strong like you are, or is she very thin and fragile? Easier than talking about this gorgeous tousled-headed youth here beside me, or the girl who's lying in the other room, in pain?

You look pretty calm and collected, Mr Policeman, or is that something they taught you at the depot in Enniskillen, not to show your feelings or to let them get the better of you?

By the way, do I disgust you?

Do you deliberately choose not to notice how his hand slides into mine from time to time – behaviour liable/likely to cause a breach of the peace – dammit, man, why don't you say something?

I'm sorry. I get a bit emotional at times.

To tell the truth I'd love to buy you a drink and have a long friendly conversation with you, oh, about anything and everything. I don't really mind what, because at the end of the day, we're all just people, clichés or not.

Of course, I'm only talking to myself, pretending that I'm talking to you. Words aren't really necessary between the two of us here, him and me, that is. We've known about this for some time and at first it really frightened us. The responsibility, you understand, but then I don't suppose you've ever met 'The Mother' as we sometimes call her (a nod to Pádraig Pearse) long before any of this happened, because we were her little man-childs and she took us and looked after us. To tell the truth, and notice how often I say that and the occasional lack of punctuation from thyme to time, but, of course, this is a true metafictional story and be sure now not to forget that you're not really a policeman and that I'm not a queer and that we're not really sitting in the hospital waiting for good news of great joy, for in fact I'm sitting in my bedroom scrawling with a tooth-marked biro on this page and it's coming in a steady happy stream and I'll get it all down this evening if I'm not summoned from the room to take part in the family prayers, which would, of course, have to take priority over a little metafictional tale concerning the interaction of three clichés. And, in reality, she is no older than the pair of us, him and me I mean and not me and you, though she's no older than you and I either and she's so strong that we homage her. No! (Ulster says) I can say damage but not homage – I have to pay homage singular and if necessary only pay damages plural.

Perhaps you have the perverse idea that someone like me would have no interest in the company of a young woman, or that she would have no interest in me and him, indeed I fear, policeman, that you would be sickened if I tried to explain to you that the reason we are both here, me and him that is and not you and me, is that we don't know which of us is the father of the child. One of us is going to be disappointed, but, on the other hand, the good news will delight us and he that is not the natural father will be the godfather.

I don't suppose you've ever seen a bed as big as ours.

And then suddenly the door –

And, of course, you expect the doctor, or someone else wearing a white coat to come out and announce 'congratulations, it's a bouncing baby boy' but to tell the truth that would be another cliché and even the relative realists – wasn't it Ó Faoláin himself who said it – believe that the title is most important.

So, in reality nothing happens because all that was going to happen has already happened and you can stop pretending that you're a policeman, really, especially if you're reading this story in the Gaelic. Now you're one of my mates listening to me reading this out in the pub off some tatty pages I've pulled from the pocket of my big coat, or maybe you're the vexed editor of a magazine, or of this very book, or maybe you could actually be a reader, an ordinary reader, sitting on the bus or in your armchair beside the fire, or even, and don't blame me for this, the unfortunate student trying to make sense of something as disorganised as metafiction using something as formal and structured as an essay or an exam answer – wow!

And then of course I'm not really a queer, and him and her on the other side of the door can go on with their lives and as soon as we leave, the doctor will come out with the good news. And as far as you and I are concerned I have just written and you have just read the latest story from the tooth-marked pen of Séamas Mac Annaidh (26) of Enniskillen – though I guess you've guessed that already.

And what happens after this is up to you, for you know better than I do what suits you best. And that's the way it goes. Honestly. Well then, that's it then.

Oh, and we never did say the rosary tonight.
OK then, you're free to go. Good luck so.

Translated by 'the other'.

HOW THE AUTHOR DIED

Fionntán de Brún

The more time you spend in a pub or a café the less you believe in time itself – after a few hours clocks and watches cease to have any use. Having spent most of the day in a café in Montparnasse, I realised that I would need to leave if I were to get the last train. All that remained of the day's customers were two couples who, having nothing left to say, sat rigidly staring ahead, in a timeless stupor. This was encouragement enough to face the outside and then to cross the street without looking for traffic, wondering all the while about the one great timetable to which every city submits. Hurrying along the pavement, I took care to skip over the black slush that would fill my canvas shoes with the iciest of cold water. Under the brass arch of the métro station I stopped and listened for the sounds below, letting the final groans become a death rattle and then a vast silence.

Perhaps I had no part in it, perhaps I missed the train because of an internal clock in all of us that governs even the time spent in pubs, constantly turning over, recording and directing us according to its desire. I had returned to the same café at any rate, a little busier and with no sign of the couples. The crowd that had come in were night workers, people who wanted to postpone the long night ahead just a little bit. Of course they paid no attention to me, knowing that I belonged to a different 'frequency' and that we would have little in common. One person, however, did speak to me. Firstly, it was to ask for a cigarette. Then he stood with me for a while, intending, as I presumed, to give me a cigarette's worth of conversation in return. But he wanted more cigarettes, one after the other. Eventually I had to pretend that I didn't have a second packet in my coat pocket.

'I'm sorry. Perhaps one of your friends has a cigarette?'

'Friends?'

I realised then that he was alone, like myself. I opened the packet and gave him a cigarette, warning him that his death would be on my conscience if he smoked too many of them.

'I don't think you'll be with me when that happens,' he replied, 'besides, I might never get any of the diseases, they don't strike everyone down.'

He must have noticed my becoming impatient with the conversation. I was certainly doing my best to ignore him, hoping that I might be left with even one or two cigarettes. The only thing left to do was to will the café and all of its customers into a time-trough and escape it for a while. But *he* was there all the while, smoking my cigarettes and shifting from one foot to the other, remaining always a yard or two from me or right up beside me. Then, without warning, he sidled up as though about to kiss me.

'Do you know – *could you tell*,' he whispered, 'that I am a murderer?'

He filled his throat with smoke and started to cough. His eyes were full of tears and his head turned away slightly with the coughing, yet he kept one eye on me expecting some sort of answer.

'Shocking, don't you think?'

'I don't know. There are murderers and those who have murdered. Which are you?'

'Perhaps I should say that I am a "literary murderer", in that I killed a writer.'

'Do you mind if I ask who, or is that part confidential?'

'Not at all. I killed a man whose work is held in libraries all over the world, a man who was a hero to thousands, millions perhaps. He has been my hero ever since.'

He stopped momentarily as his voice began to catch.

'I am the man who killed Roland Barthes.'

'Roland Barthes?' I repeated, laughing incredulously. 'I thought Barthes was run over by a van of some sort.'

'He was,' he answered. 'I was driving the van.'

There was a look in his eyes that demanded pity rather than mockery and so, as though handling a holy shroud, he took out his wallet and carefully revealed a newspaper cutting from within its folds. It was brown with age and had been reduced to four precariously thin squares. He gave me time to read it, staring intently at me all the while, before showing me his driving licence for further proof.

'Well, what do you think?' he asked.

'I'm surprised you're still allowed the licence,' I replied.

He didn't respond but turned to order us two glasses of beer. Now it was my turn to be beholden to him, not having the money to pay for the drinks.

'I'm sure I don't envy you,' I started, 'I don't have a car but if I knocked someone down I'd say I'd ...'

'I couldn't get it out of my head,' he said slowly, interrupting. 'The noise his body made against the van. It was sudden, vulgar ... oafish even. All of the things the great man was not.'

'Did you know him?' I asked.

'No … no, up until then I had never laid eyes on him. But I have got to know him very well through his books since then.'

With that, he raised his glass in his honour.

'I don't know why he crossed my path like that, but all I know is that it was the equivalent of the *big bang*, if you don't mind, in my life. When I stepped out of that van to look at him it was like stepping into another world, a world in which I was a complete stranger.

'My marriage was the first thing to go. That awful noise never left my ears for months afterwards – I couldn't sleep with it. I just couldn't lie at peace in bed. I understood entirely when my wife threw me out – she really had no option. The biggest thing any couple have to do is sleep together. Eight hours lying together every single night! Thinking about it now, I don't know how people do it. But once you start to disrupt a couple's sleep, it's only a matter of time … She has a man now who sleeps like a baby. My job in the laundry was the next thing to go, but I wasn't fired. I left the laundry of my own volition. It was after reading an article by the great man – about washing powder – that I understood I was merely wasting my time in the place.

'Every word of his that I read was a revelation. Of course, it wasn't easy reading to begin with, what with me never having really read anything before that. But I gradually started to realise that this society we live in is founded on myths and illusions and that we are like sleepwalkers who may never wake up. After that, I couldn't see the world as I'd seen it before – everything I saw was passed through the filter that I had been granted by the great man. Wrestling! Those men you see on television, roaring and brawling like mad children – it was only when I read an article the great man had written, that I understood that these wrestlers are really gods, the key that opens our nature to separate good from evil to reveal to us the purity of justice. Imagine explaining that to your friends! Me that had always been one of the lads, here I was spouting philosophy and morality. It wasn't long before they started to avoid me.

'Bad as the loneliness was, I soon got used to it, and anyway, no one is ever really lonely in a city, provided their mind is switched on. The people that go about their lives in a sleepwalk, these are the people who are truly lonely. They exist only to sustain myths and lies, filling their minds and bodies with useless crap. I don't subscribe to any of it – insurance, savings accounts, digital television, mobile phones, leather settees and foreign holidays. The leeches that run people's lives use that stuff to make them believe there's nothing else. I understand their deceptions better than they do, believe me.

'I got my freedom the day of the accident – there can be no question about it – I'd still be driving about Paris blind to the world if it weren't for the accident. I mean, I still drive around Paris, but at least I know why I do it – to bear witness to this great modern mess, to deconstruct and confound it ... All the same, it was the accident that set me on the right path and I've been a long time waiting for another one – obviously the same accident can't happen again. It's just that I don't know sometimes if I'm spending my time wastefully or not.'

'Wouldn't the answer to that question be in one of Barthes' books?' I asked.

'Yes, of course. If only I could decipher it. Perhaps he would have shed more light on my dilemma, if I had left him more time. Perhaps his mind was on it as he lay in a hospital bed in Pitié-Salpetrière, unable to breathe for himself with the injuries he had received in the accident. Perhaps that was the topic of conversation he had with Mitterand and Foucault when they had dinner together that evening. He was hurrying from them when he headed towards rue des Écoles

... plenty of wine in his veins and a nice cigar just smoked, no doubt. He was hurrying to his mother's house, like a good and loyal son, for he was always good to her. Perhaps he had the answer to some question that had been perplexing him, who knows. I always imagine there was a fresh breeze in his face and that he felt like he was walking up some heavenly corridor. I was hurrying as well – around the corner. I bent forward to light a cigarette and *bang*.'

I pulled myself out of the café, lest it should fall into another time-trough. Outside, an emerald-coloured lorry was sweeping the litter from the edges of the streets with a couple of men following to pick up what it had missed. There was no way home now, but to get the *noctambus*, an irregular service that collected the final stragglers from the streets before meandering off in a haze towards the end of the night.

Translated by the author.

THERE IS SOMEONE ELSE LIVING HERE

Dáithí Sproule

First Story

A snowy night in the month of November in Minneapolis, Minnesota. A snug wooden house in a quiet street. A young man and his wife sitting on a great pillow watching *Quincy*. The man has a glass of wine in his hand; the woman is considering going downstairs to get a glass for herself.

Eoin is sick of the television: he has work to do, but he can't bring himself to get up. Eithne has a special liking for the programme, and this gives Eoin an excuse to remain sitting in front of the little colour television.

Eoin raises his head suddenly as if to listen for something. This startles Eithne – she hasn't heard anything – she doesn't know what is bothering him. 'What's wrong?' she says. Eoin doesn't answer; he's listening. With that, they both hear a knock at the door.

'Scott and Kathy, maybe?' says Eoin, rising stiffly and walking towards the staircase. Eithne looks nervously out the window.

'That's odd,' she says. 'There's a police car on the far side of the street.'

Eoin goes downstairs. He opens the wooden door, then the metal door, the screen door. The street is white, and the snow is falling heavily.

'You called?' says the small fat man who is standing on the doorstep, his uniform speckled with snowflakes. A policeman, a doubtful, kind expression on his face.

Eoin frowns; Eithne is behind him, looking out anxiously.

'No, we didn't call ...' says Eoin.

The policeman glances around, then looks up at the number that is written above the door. 'Thirty-two fifteen ... well, that's the right number.'

Eoin shrugs his shoulders. 'Well, it certainly wasn't us who called.'

'It must be some mistake, I suppose.' He turns and takes a couple of steps. He stops on the sidewalk, raises a small radio to his lips, and says something. Eoin sees the gun at his side, black against the snow.

Two hours after that, the couple go to bed and make love. They have completely forgotten the policeman by then: they are cosy and comfortable under the eiderdown quilt. The house is warm inside, and outside the world is cold and white.

There is a basement – an underground floor – in the house, as there is in every dwelling house in the city: a shelter from the summer tornadoes, a place for the washing machine and for the drier, a place where things are left aside.

About half past one, the mice in the basement hear an unusual sound, as if a stone door is being opened, in a place where there is no door. Some being is moving slowly and carefully in the darkness of the underground room. A light is turned on.

There's a man standing in the middle of the floor, having just pulled the cord that turns on the basement light. He squints and puts a dirty thin hand above his eyes. He stands like that for a minute until he becomes accustomed to the light. He lowers his hand then and looks round impatiently with red bloodshot eyes.

A tall thin man, wearing an old blue suit, dirty and tattered, his grey hair rumpled. A bent-shouldered man, his drawn, unshaven face ashen-pale. He makes for the basement's wooden stairway; he gives only a glance at the two cotton dresses that are hanging above the dryer.

He walks slowly upstairs and turns on the light in the back hall. He enters the kitchen as quietly as he can.

He becomes excited when he sees the refrigerator. He opens the door quickly and takes out bread and cheese. He glances around; there is a knife lying on a cupboard beside the butter. He spreads butter on a piece of bread, places a slice of cheese on that, and gulps it down greedily. He eats a second piece, and he is about to take a third one when he is smitten by doubt; he pauses for a minute. With that he wraps the paper round the bread again and places the bread and the cheese back in the fridge, just as he found them.

His eyes light up again when he notices three eggs on a shelf in the refrigerator; he takes two of them, he thinks for a while again this time too, and he puts one of the eggs back. He stands in front of the stove, the perfect white egg in his filthy wrinkled hand. He wears a sad, lonely expression. He closes his mouth tightly, breaks the egg, then sucks the yolk and the white out of it. He rubs his hand across his mouth and throws the wet broken shell in the rubbish bin beside the sink.

He begins to look more relaxed. He goes into the sitting room, a small, comfortable room. He sits on the couch, stretches, and sighs.

He hears a sound; someone is moving in the bed upstairs. The man looks hard at the staircase. It becomes quiet again. He looks around the room – it is filled with books; most are cook books and law books. There's a good-quality tape recorder, and a mandolin hangs on the wall.

He examines the walls of the room closely and stops in front of a colour photograph. He shakes his head; the old people in the picture are not the ones living in this house.

The man is startled to hear the sound of a car outside. He crouches down so that he won't be visible from the outside. The car passes by without stopping.

He stands up straight and notices the two pairs of boots at the door where they were left to dry when the people of the house came in. He decides to go upstairs.

There is only one room up there, the bedroom. There is light coming in the window from a street lamp: the ragged grey-haired man stands at the edge of the bed and gazes down at the couple. The man's face is clearly to be seen, a soft American face. The woman is turned so that her face is not visible, but the beauty of her auburn hair makes his heart leap.

The woman moves, and the husband stretches slightly, but they do not awake. The man from the basement turns on his heel and tiptoes down the stairs. He enters the kitchen. He makes certain that he has left no trace of his presence. He is about to go down to the basement, when he sees a couple of cans of beer on the floor in the back hall. He lifts one of them – it will not be missed – and heads downstairs.

He turns out the basement light. But he does not move. His breath is to be heard in the quiet of the night; his breath comes more quickly, more roughly.

He turns on the light again. Some strong emotion can be seen on his face. He sees the two cotton dresses: one blue and one pink. He lays a dirty hand on one of them and then lifts his hand off: he has left a print on the cloth. He grabs the dress firmly, pulls it down, and tears it. He makes a ball of it and throws it to the ground.

A moment after that, the basement is dark again. There is the sound of a stone door being opened and gently shut – a door not visible to the people of the house.

The snow shower has ended – Eoin will have to shovel the walk in the morning. For now, however, Eoin and Eithne are dreaming in the cosy wooden house, and the world is at peace.

Second Story

Sean McMahon had been married to an American girl for about a year, and he was very happy with the life he had with her. They had a grand small house rented cheaply, and he liked Minneapolis. She had a good teaching job, and he had part-time proofing work, and they had no shortage of money. Both of them were interested in Irish music, and they would go to concerts together when a traditional band was in town, and to the weekly sessions that took place in a pub in Saint Paul, a city that lies side by side with Minneapolis.

Only one thing was bothering Sean. A couple of years beforehand, after he had spent a good while working full-time for a publishing company in Dublin, he had concluded that that way of life did not suit him, that he needed a livelihood that would provide him with creative satisfaction. When he was at school he used to write little stories, and it occurred to him now that the best thing for him to do would be to make a serious effort at the writing.

He liked what he was writing, and as time went by and with practice he was of the opinion that he was improving at the craft. Since he had settled in America, however, he had not succeeded in getting any stories published, and he was losing hope.

It occurred to him that he wasn't producing the right kind of stories, that he was aiming too high and too fancy. He had been trying to describe people's emotional life in such a way that it would bring comfort to others – you could say that he was trying to write literature. Apparently, magazines were not interested in the kind of material he was writing, and there was a good chance, said Sean to himself, that he didn't have true literary ability.

He was sitting downstairs at his typewriter one snowy day at the beginning of winter and thinking about those things. He felt as if his mind was paralyzed.

Suddenly a thought was coming to him: a simple little idea, the slightest suggestion of the plot of a story. He couldn't say what was attractive or interesting about the story growing in his mind. It wasn't really a story, but a strange inexplicable incident.

What did it mean? He could interpret it as a fable, but maybe it wasn't the story that was most important, but the peculiar feeling it awoke in him.

He set to putting the bare bones of the story on paper: a couple living in a small comfortable house in Minneapolis, they go to bed, a man comes out of the wall in the basement, a hungry ragged man, he goes upstairs, he eats a little of the food that is in the refrigerator, but doesn't eat too much of it – he doesn't want to let the people of the house know that he is there – he is curious about the couple, in the end his curiosity overcomes his caution and he goes upstairs to look at them. Is he going to attack them? No; he goes downstairs again to the place where he hides, and that is the end of the story.

Sean's wife, Peggy, was in a bad mood when she arrived back from work, so they decided to go out to a Chinese restaurant for dinner and to bring a bottle of wine home with them. Dinner was lovely, so they were both in a good mood coming home. They were upstairs watching the television when they heard the knock at the door – it was the policeman – and that's the incident Sean put in the story just as it happened.

Before starting to write the next day, Sean went down to the basement to see if any ideas would come to him that he could use in the story. That was when he saw the two cotton dresses above the dryer, on which he was able to base the end of the story.

Sean wrote a draft of the story that morning and was very happy with it. He put a copy in an envelope and wrote the address of one of the big New York magazines on it; he went straight out to put it in the post.

After dinner the next day, Sean was in the sitting room playing the mandolin when Peggy came in to him in tears. She reached out towards him, her hand was holding the dirty torn dress.

Sean's face went white, and his heart started to pound as if it was about to break. He rose shakily to his feet. 'What's this?' he said.

'My dress ... my new dress ... this is how I found it in the basement,' she said through her tears. Sean put his arm around her. 'What happened to it?' she asked, sobbing.

That's the question, of course, that was exploding in the mind of her husband; but what he said to her was, 'It must have been the mice that did it ... or a squirrel that got into the basement.' That seemed plausible, since once before a squirrel had somehow got into the basement and made a mess of the kitchen.

But Sean himself could not believe in such a coincidence, that there was no connection between the story and the tearing of the dress – he had said nothing about the plot of the story to Peggy. When she had pulled herself together somewhat, Sean went slowly and nervously down to the basement. He turned on the light.

Everything was just as it had been the day before, except that there was only one dress hanging above the dryer. It was difficult for him to believe it, and he didn't want to believe it, but he himself must have been the one who had torn the dress. He had done the damage. But when? How could he not remember doing it?

He thought back to the previous night – had he been drinking? But he hadn't been. The dress had been all right yesterday and it was ruined today, just as it had happened in the story. There was only one solution to the problem: he had done it in his sleep. He must have been thinking so much about the story that he had risen from his bed in the middle of the night – in his sleep – and had gone down to the basement. It was a terrifying thought, that he would do such a thing in his sleep, that he would do something like that to Peggy.

He was turning to go back upstairs when he noticed the beer can. It was lying by the wall. He lifted it and threw it into the rubbish bin beside the washing machine.

Sean did not sleep too well that night or the night after either: it was difficult to fall asleep when he was scared that he would go walking in his sleep.

The first night he had a horrible dream that he had woken in the night and had seen himself standing beside the bed with a can of beer in his hand.

But the morning after the second night he was in better form. It was a sunny morning and he had to go into the city centre to do some proofing in a publisher's office. The short journey on the bus lifted his spirits and the work cleared the worry out of his head for a while.

He felt much better. That is, until Peggy went to the fridge that afternoon looking for eggs and said, 'You must be eating a lot of eggs these days.' His heart fell. 'I bought a dozen the other day and there are only four left.' She smiled at Sean and was startled to see his frightened expression. She took his hand: 'Poor Sean, I wasn't complaining!' He tried to smile, but he couldn't speak. He had no memory of eating any eggs for several days before.

It was three o'clock in the morning. Peggy was sound asleep, but Sean was awake, tormented with fear, fear that there was something wrong with his mind, fear that he would do something bad in his sleep again.

He would have to tell Peggy about the story, and go to the doctor – he did not relish imagining that interview. What would the doctor think at all?

It was five minutes past three when Sean heard footsteps down below, a cupboard opening, silence. It was a small house – he couldn't be mistaken: there was someone downstairs.

Sean lay there, afraid to take a breath, listening to someone walking into the sitting room. Silence again.

The reader can understand the thoughts that were running through his head. The worst thought of all: is it possible that he is coming up?

He heard the footsteps again, footsteps on the stairs, coming up slowly. What would he do when he saw the man? What would the man do? In a second the dark shadow of the man, the shadow of the man from the basement, would be visible at the top of the stairs.

There he was: a dark shape standing a couple of yards from him. The man began to approach the bed.

A piercing horrible scream. Sean leapt up: Peggy was sitting up, screaming at the top of her lungs. The man turned and hurried down – Sean heard a sound as if the man had slipped on one of the stairs.

Peggy threw her arms round her husband crying. He tried to quieten her: footsteps in the sitting room, in the kitchen, in the back hall, on the basement stairs.

Sean had no alternative: he had to find out if the man was still in the basement. He went down to the kitchen and got a hammer and a large knife from a drawer. He paused with his foot on the top step of the basement stairs. The hall bulb was casting a little light down, but the basement light was off. He went back and got a torch in the kitchen.

Down he went step by step, pointing the torch here and there all the time. Which would be worse, for the man to be there before him or for the man not to be there? He succeeded in reaching the middle of the basement without fainting, and he turned on the light. There was no trace of the man to be seen.

Sean and Peggy did not get a wink of sleep after that. He told her the story, knowing all the time that the man was still there somewhere, that he could come out again any time he wanted. He considered calling the police, but they would have an unbelievable story to tell and no evidence to back it up.

When the sun rose, they searched the house from top to bottom, searching for the stranger's hiding place. But they found nothing.

Was he a ghost? What connection was there between the man and the story? The only thing that comforted Sean was that he was not crazy after all.

Neither of them went to work. It was half past nine when something occurred to Peggy and she asked Sean to get his copy of the story. She wouldn't take it from him, but she said, 'No matter how strange or how silly it is to say it, the man came out of the story; maybe if we destroyed the manuscript, he would leave.'

It was a silly thought certainly – it was a child's logic, the logic of a primitive. But what logic was there in their situation?

Sean tore the paper into tiny pieces. He took matches with him out to the garden and burnt the paper on the snow.

But the magazine publishers had a copy too. He phoned them up and was put on to one of the editors: 'Yes, we have read the story, we have indeed. And I have good news for you, and I'm glad to be able to tell you personally. We are accepting the story – we will have it in the February issue.'

'Hold on a minute,' said Sean. 'Peggy, they're accepting the story. They are going to publish it.'

She took a firm hold of his hand: 'But, Sean, if it is put in print – I couldn't stand it – I know it's your big chance. But if one story is accepted, another one will be too. Please, Sean ...'

He told the editor that he couldn't allow them to print the story, and he asked them to tear it up immediately. It took him some time to convince the editor that he was serious, but he finally agreed to do as he was asked.

They did their best to keep their hopes throughout that day. They stayed awake for much of the night, but they didn't hear a sound, and nothing was taken from the fridge that night.

Three days and three nights went by peacefully. They were still in bed on Saturday morning when they heard a sound: there was someone in the kitchen.

Peggy whispered to Sean, 'We have no choice: we must go down and speak to him. Whatever his connection with your story, he's a human being, or he wouldn't need food, and he hasn't done any harm to us up to this.'

'But he'll leave if he hears us coming,' said Sean.

'We'll call down to him,' said Peggy. Sean sighed heavily – at least it was daylight. They got out of bed quietly and made for the stairs. They were halfway down when they heard the footsteps in the kitchen. Peggy called out, 'Wait a minute – we want to talk to you! We won't do anything to you!' They rushed down.

The man was standing in the middle of the room in his torn blue suit, just as Sean had described in the story. He had a piece of bread in his hand. He had a scared, suspicious look on his hungry face.

Sean couldn't bring out a word; it was Peggy who spoke. 'Look, this is our house. We have a right to find out who you are and what you're doing here ...' The stranger said nothing. 'And to ask you to go and leave us in peace.'

Then Sean found his speech: 'If you need food or money, we will give them to you. Take whatever you like from the fridge.' The stranger backed towards the fridge; he opened it and took out bread and a couple of eggs.

But Sean moved till he was in his way, standing at the end of the hall. The man from the basement had no escape route. 'You're not going back down there,' said Sean. 'I won't let you. You'll have to leave now or we'll call the police.'

The fear could be seen in the eyes of the stranger. He threw the food in Sean's face and pushed him aside. But Sean was after him; he grabbed his arm at the top of the basement stairs. They struggled for a second – Sean smelt the sour smell of the stranger's breath. Then the man fell tumbling down the wooden stairway and fell with a thud on the stone floor of the basement.

Sean went down after him. He was lying in a motionless heap. He was dead.

They called the police. Sean had just left down the phone when it rang. 'Hello,' he said.

'Hello, I'm the editor you were talking to a while ago about one of your stories. I thought I should call you again and ask you are you serious about tearing up the story – maybe you've changed your mind ...'

'Didn't you do it?' screamed Sean. 'Well, destroy the bloody thing now! I want to hear you tearing it up!'

'All right, if you're sure. Here it is.'

Sean put the phone down and looked at Peggy. Was there any chance that the dreadful body was gone with the story?

They went back to the basement stairs and looked down. The body was still there.

They heard a knock at the door – how would they explain the situation to the police? Sean went out and opened the two doors, the wooden door and the screen door; the small fat policeman was standing on the doorstep. 'You called?' he said.

'Yes, Officer, we called. Come in.'

Addendum

When I have written that last page, I rise from the typewriter and go to the kitchen for another cup of coffee. I put my new record on the turntable, a recording of harp music that the musicians themselves gave to me last night, a gorgeous light-hearted record. I stand at the window. The snow is old now, a little bit grubby, but it is bright white on the roofs of the houses. My wife, Anne, will be home soon from work. Isn't it a wonderful life we have here in this cosy little wooden house? I go upstairs to write an addendum.

Translated by the author.

THE JUDGEMENT

Alan Titley

Adam heard the music first. I thought it was a ghetto blaster or some music store trying to flog their latest wares.

'Listen!' said Adam. 'I think he's out of tune.'

'Bloody sure he's not bloody Eddie Calvert,' said I, plucking a name out of the past. 'He wouldn't get a job with a bloody bad brass band.'

I had to admit I didn't feel that well since early morning. A shiver down my backbone and a quiver up my thighbone told me it wasn't going to be a lucky or a sunshiny day. The alarm clock failed to go off, Docila slept through, the children were late for school and a molar started acting up. The last time I felt as lousy as this the boss called me in and gave me a rise. This only went to prove I couldn't believe either my hunches or my bones.

Adam and myself were hoping to have a quiet lunch in the restaurant on the corner of the street, but when he heard the music he gave me a dig in the ribs. There were others who noticed it also. Some grinned, some grimaced, all turned around looking for the music. I saw two guys starting to dance on the street, but the rhythm screwed them up and they shagged off. I saw an old fellow scrunching the butt of a fag and hiding it under his coat despite the heat of the day.

Even though we were both starving we had to stop and listen. We thought the music was coming from the next street, but when we went looking for it we always discovered it was still just one street away.

'Listen to that,' said a stranger next to me. 'You'd think we had enough electioneering by now. Lies and promises, promises and lies! What more are they good for?'

'Election, my arse,' said someone else, 'stay where you are and you'll see the greatest show on earth. Didn't you hear that the circus is coming to town?'

'It's all one big circus anyway,' said Adam, not entirely seriously. He was like that when he wanted to. We gave as good as we got when we needed to, but for some reason I felt a big grey lump growing quietly in my gut.

White fluffs of cloud dabbed the sky, but they didn't cross the sun. I looked up to see two helicopters like fireflies racing above the city. I imagined by their frenzy that a bank had been robbed or terrorists had escaped from some prison and were now on the run. And then they vanished as if they had never fluttered above the roofs of the houses.

'Come on,' said Adam, grabbing me by the elbow. 'Let's split. We can't spend the day staring at the sky. Fuck 'em all. Let's stuff our guts and let them all piss off.'

I was a bit reluctant to leave as long as there was a hullabaloo in the streets, but hunger and convention won out. We sat down at the table where we had our lunch for nearly twenty years. We had a good view of the streets in case it was a *coup d'état* or the boys were back in town.

'Just imagine the tanks rolling by,' said Adam, his mouth watering while he enjoyed and took pleasure from the thought. 'I'd give anything for ten minutes of absolute power. Just ten minutes.'

'What would you do?' I asked, wondering about his grasp of the conditional mood.

'I have a little list,' he said, speaking in a conspiratorial hush in case anyone with big ears was listening. 'I have been compiling it for years. Every politician, every journalist, every sports commentator who has been a pain in the ass, they're all on the list.'

'It must be quite long so,' I said.

'As long as a wet day in County Mayo,' he said. 'I'd put them all into one big enormous tub. A huge transparent vat with a hole at the top just big enough for one person to go through, simultaneously and at the same time.'

'You have been thinking about this for a while,' I said, as if I didn't know. It was always interesting to see if he had another turn of the screw or if anybody had been added to the list.

'Do you see that crane?' he asked, pointing his spoon in the direction of the tall construct waving about above the City Hall like a scorpion's tail about to strike. 'I'd hang my specially designed state-of-the-art tub off the top of that and do the hippy-hippy shakes up and around and topsy-turvy and head over heels, so that just one of my chosen list would fall out, one at the time. That is the circus that I want. Just ten minutes.'

'Well, bully for you,' I said, thinking of my own list, 'but I'm afraid that whenever the *coup* comes neither you nor I will have much to do with it.'

'Speak for yourself,' he said, calling the waiter for something or other. 'I have military training just as well as you. You can't put that one over on me.'

'Five weeks in the FCA twenty years ago! I know of some petty dictators who still wouldn't have us. When the tanks roll up, I'm going to stay sitting here smoking my cigar.'

If this was bullshit we were under the illusion it was good bullshit, and anyway if we couldn't pass muster we could at least pass the time. We all got whanged by life's vicissitudes, but we still had our middle-aged dreams to keep us warm. Our ship would come in, or we would find the crock of gold at the end of the garden, or we would fall in love with a rich Jewish princess. Or at any rate we could keep talking as long as we had no other choice and there was no other thing to do nor any other place to go. Oh, yes, we had our complaints, but it was better to curse the darkness than light a penny candle on a star.

'You'd better stuff yourself with that apple tart,' I said to Adam, having nothing better to say, 'you won't get anything as good as it until tomorrow. There's nothing worse than pangs of hunger in the smack-bang-middle of the high afternoon.'

He would do that anyway without any encouragement from me, but that didn't mean we were in any great hurry to pack up and go. To be on duty was not the same thing as to be in work. We still had time to gabble about the ex-President's mistress, the humour of the financial pages, ecological holidays in Greenland, the etymological derivation of the exclamation mark, the man who died of a broken fart which was great gas, and the pimp who thought everything was great crack. We paid a fortune for our lunch in order to help the economy as we did every day and we wearily wended our way back to the office.

Out on the street everyone was on the move. They all looked as if they were going in the same direction. There was a look in their eyes which had never been there before. You knew that even if you had never seen them until now. I tried to talk to one young fellow but he stared at me from out of eyes that welled up in tears.

Adam tried to chat up one woman, but she laughed at him with a nervous highly-strung laugh.

I grabbed one old wrinkly by the elbow, but he shook me off with a viciousness which I scarcely thought he could have.

Adam spoke to a child, but no wisdom came forth from his mouth.

'Has the government fallen?' I shouted to the crowd.

'Fallen, my arse,' said one guy with a wart on his nose, who vanished in the great wash.

'Has the stock market collapsed?' Adam pleaded, because he could be quite sensitive about these moneyed things when he had to be.

'Fuck the stock,' said another guy who looked to be about a thousand years old and never enjoyed a day in his life.

'Have the Brits attacked?' I shouted, falling back on the old enemy in time of necessity, but I only got an emphatic 'Not at this time' from a woman who was sucking her thumb.

'He's over there!' screamed a man between horrors and hosannas who had a rosary beads or a knuckle-duster wrapped around his fist, and pointed us with his whole body to the corner of the road where we thought we had first heard the music.

'Who is it?' we both asked in unison and together, scarlet butterflies rising in our stomachs.

'This is the day I have been waiting for since the beginning of time,' the man said, and then grabbed us by the dirty scruff of our necks and shoved us forward to where the crowd was gawping up at the building.

'This is it now,' said your man, as happy as a kid going in to see Santa Claus, 'you're all fucked, you shower of fucking fuckers. Thanks be to God!'

'Who is he?' I asked, even plaintively, about the guy standing on the corner of the upper window who looked as if he was about to jump. 'Why doesn't somebody get the ambulance or the Gardaí? If he falls he'll make an awful mess.'

'Shut your face, you fool,' said your man again, a smile like a flea's arse flitting across his face. 'There's no chance of him falling. Don't you see his wings?'

He was, unfortunately, right. I had been paying attention to the trumpet in his right hand and to his unusual get-up and hadn't noticed the two golden wings sticking out behind his back.

'Jaysus, I know who it is,' said Adam, nearly licking my ear, 'it's fucking Goldie Horn.'

I suppressed a chuckle as nobody else was chuckling, and anyway, this was real serious public shit rather than simple private angst.

'Or maybe it's Icarus,' I retorted. 'He's probably forgotten that we have aeroplanes for the last hundred years.'

'Judas Icarius,' said Adam, 'give him enough rope to hang himself.'

'It is written also,' said your man 'that thou shalt not go free because this is the day of accounting.'

'We had those accountants in last week,' said Adam, 'and they were some accuntants.'

Just then Willie Wings on the window let a great blast from his trumpet and everybody jumped back in horror. He laid down his trumpet and did produce a big red book from within his breast and commenced to read.

'Districts seven and eight,' he proclaimed, in a voice that had a certain eastern accent to it, 'that is to say, Cabra, Phibsboro, Arbour Hill, Stoneybatter, Inchicore, the Coombe, the South Circular Road and adjacent areas, Section A;

Districts three and nine, Clontarf, Ballybough, Clonliffe, Drumcondra, Whitehall, Santry and Griffith Avenue, Section B; Districts five and thirteen, Coolock, Artane, Raheny, Bayside, Barrytown, Sutton, Donaghmede and Baldoyle, Section C; Districts one and six, Ranelagh, Rathmines, Rathgar, Terenure and Harold's Cross, Section D; District four, Donnybrook, Ballsbridge, Sandymount, Sandycove and Ringsend, Section E; Districts ten and eleven, Ballyfermot and Blanchardstown, Section F; District eighteen, Cabinteely, Foxrock, Cornelscourt ...'

People began moving away as their districts were called out, some obviously despondent, others proud and haughty, but nobody was saying very much. Whatever sounds there were came from the buzz of the announcements and the shuffle of feet beginning to move into the distance.

'Where are you?'

'Section E, I think. I hear we'll get our entry cards at the gates.'

'What about the wife and kids?'

'It's everyone for himself now. That's the rule. Anyway they will have heard by now.'

'I don't know if I'm suitably dressed. My mother always told me to have clean underwear on me in case of an accident, or unforeseen circumstances. Maybe this is what she was warning me about.'

I turned around when I heard the newsboy shouting about the evening papers. The first edition was out earlier than usual because of the news.

'*Herald* or *Press*,' he roared, his voice reaching new heights of excitement. 'End of the world news! End of the world this afternoon! Official statement from heaven! Last judgement in the Phoenix Park!'

I shoved him the price of the paper and Adam looked in over my shoulder. According to their religious correspondent angels were landing in different locations all over the country since midday proclaiming the news. Judgement had already been given in most other European countries. The heavenly host was moving with the sun and wouldn't reach America until early in the morning Irish time. I suppose there was no such thing any more as Irish time, but it was difficult to get rid of the old metaphors. There was no hard data as yet available from the rest of the European Union, because all the fax lines were clogged up and the Internet was acting funny. There was a small diagram at the bottom of the second page which purported to show unconfirmed figures for the number of saved and the number of damned in each country so far. It gave us some satisfaction to see that good Catholic countries like Spain and Portugal and even Italy had the highest saved rate. But Adam said that they also were the biggest producers of red wine, and that was the real reason. Against that there was a very high damnation rate in awful Protestant countries like Germany, Denmark and Finland, but England was the worst of all.

'Eighty-four per cent!' said Adam, in wonder and not a little satisfaction. 'That won't leave much room for us, thanks be to Jaysus.'

'Any mention of Purgatory?' I mentioned, scanning the page up and down, 'or the likes of Limbo?'

There wasn't, but there was more than enough speculation about whom amongst the great and mighty and the eminent greasies of the country would go up and who would go down. The journalists were very kind to themselves, but more than nasty to politicians whom they didn't like. They weren't too sure about the Cardinal as he had criticised the press the week before, but they did admit that if the Pope was saved then he had a very good chance also. I supposed this was an attempt to be fair now that the end was nigh. There was a full page of the detailed arrangements: the various routes to the Park, parking lots, the sites of the different pens into which people were to go, the tents of the Red Cross, fish and chip stalls, beer tables, bookies stands, photographers, toilets.

'They all seem to be walking anyway,' I said, as we had failed to hail a taxi, 'let's go.'

We hit the road and joined the throng making its way to the Phoenix Park. Most of the people were quiet and reflective, although there was the occasional murmur of prayer and the jangle of a rosary beads. Dublin Bus was providing a special cheap knock-down one-way fare, but most people seemed to want to walk. I suppose it gave them a chance to stop and think every so often and to examine the state of their souls. Others were going back over the course of their lives trying to put it all together. The humour improved as we went on, however. We heard an occasional nervous laugh as if people were practising confessions on one another.

'Do you remember?' Adam asked me reflectively, 'do you remember you asked me once what would I do if I knew the end of the world was coming? Remember that?'

'I was talking about the Third World War then,' I said. We were passing by Phibsboro at this time and the road was getting congested at the major junction. 'We all thought it would happen that way. But I suppose since the Russians and Americans decided against frying us all, God decided he'd have his pound of flesh anyway.'

'It's just as the poet said: "This is the way the world will end, this is the way the world will end, this is the way the world will end, not with a bang but with a wimpey".'

'And you said you'd go mad around the streets rubbing and robbing and plundering and whoring and fucking and blinding and doing all those things that only crawl under the skin of civilization. And I said I'd blow my head off with a gun. Funny that we don't want to do any of those things now.'

'Life must go on,' he said wearily, 'that's the way it is – so it goes.'

'Last few ices, last few ices,' a vendor shouted, 'anyone now for the last few ice-creams.' He pushed his way through the crowd with skilled and sharp elbows.

There was a small bunch of angels standing guard outside Glasnevin Cemetery as we were going by. They had their golden swords drawn and had their backs to us. We thought this was a bit unusual until we saw them holding back the crowd inside. A motley collection of emaciated corpses, rotting bodies, skeletons, stiffs, cadavers and carcasses jostled at the gates trying to get out. It must have been that they were looking for a second chance. I have to say that they were not suitably attired to join the likes of us on our way to the general judgement.

'Do you see de Valera?' shouted one woman, pointing out a lanky tall skeleton peering longingly through the bars of the gates.

'He hasn't changed much, anyway,' said another.

'Except that he's a bit straighter now than he ever was,' said a third.

'So much for the Treaty,' somebody mumbled.

'Who called him a traitor?'

There might have been a row only somebody joked that he could hardly be called the devil incarnate now, which drew the reply that he was at least the devil of Éire.

There were others who swore that they saw Roger Casement who would certainly know his way to the Phoenix Park; and yet others who said that it had to be Daniel

O'Connell arguing with the angels with big rhetorical flourishes in the hope that he might be let out. Maybe he thought he had one more big speech in him before a captive audience.

We didn't have time to follow the discussion as we were swept along in the tide of people, away from the tide of history. It might have been interesting to have them along. They could have told us all that stuff the biographers never dug up. Ah well.

'Isn't it enough for any one of us to be living in the present for none of us can be living forever and we must be satisfied,' said Adam, taking the words out of my mind. But he said many other things also which are not the matter of this story but which might be worth telling by somebody else some other time.

When we reached the gates of the Phoenix Park the crowds were as thick as flies on a summer eve. They were coming from every direction, some on their own, some with their families, some with their second families, some others uncertainly with their present partners of similar gender or bent. Life was still ours but the future which beckoned was short. Guardian angels were posted every few yards giving directions and orders as required. We were all given identification cards on the other side of the Zoological Gardens. It would certainly be tragic if anyone was sent to hell as a result of mistaken identity.

The great blue sky was awash with music as we approached the centre of the park. Those cherubim and seraphim must have been practising for aeons and aeons just for this one day. I couldn't quite see them yet, but could hear the brass and the boom and the hosannas and hallelujahs. I was lucky to be still with Adam although I must admit that Docila and the children did fleetingly cross my mind. If I didn't see them this side of the judgement, it was unlikely I would see them on the other.

We had red cards and we followed all the directions until we got to our pen. We were made sit on long wooden benches and told to wait until we were called. The odd vendor had sneaked in and was attempting to sell Coke or orange juice because it was a hot day. The angels didn't seem to bother too much about them. I think they were more worried about the ones who were trying to duck back in the queue and were giving bribes to people with holier faces. They were also trying to ensure that we kept our eyes glued on the giant movie screens that were posted around us showing different pictures. I was hoping to get a glimpse of the Judge and the throne and what was happening in the centre of the action, but that didn't seem to be coming up yet. To tell you the truth they were quite interesting. We had a choice of about seven different screens, but could only concentrate on one at a time.

The one I was looking at was a kind of horror movie. For a moment I thought it was a video of what was going on in another part of the park. There were angels in it, I remember. Seven of them if I recall correctly. They had trumpets and were preparing to blow them. When the sound of the first trumpet was heard, I did see a beast coming up out of the sea, having seven heads and ten horns, and upon its head ten diadems and curses spewing out of the mouths of the seven heads. And then another one blew his trumpet and I saw it as a sea of glass mingled with fire and the fire was licking the rims of the mountains and the people were climbing up the mountains to escape from the fire. And when the third angel blew his trumpet the mountain rose up and crashed down into the sea and the sea became blood and swallowed up all the boats and the fish. This was like unto *Krakatoa, East of Java*, only better! Then a star fell from heaven to earth and opened up a bottomless pit, and the pit belched up smoke that threw up poisonous scorpions and hydra-headed monsters and cookie zombies with *papier mâché* make-up that wouldn't convince anyone. Grand if you like that kind of stuff but I felt it had all been done before. The producer of this movie wasn't very subtle, and anyway I don't think it scared anybody.

I suppose the idea was that it would pass the time and divert our attention from the moving queues going past us to the place of judgement. We tried to stand up every so often in order to stretch our limbs, but we were really trying to get a glimpse of the bench.

'Did you see him yet?' Adam asked me, after I did a little hop and a jump.

'I don't think so,' I said, 'he appears to be entirely surrounded by the Deitorium Guards. I think he's tall, slender, blonde, bearded and blue-eyed.'

'He has no beard,' a wise-looking guy next to me said, speaking as if he really knew something that the rest of us didn't. 'He's as bald as a baby's bum, as well-dressed and groomed as any chief executive of a big company.'

'I heard that,' said a red-headed man courteously, 'and I beg to oppose. I saw him a few moments ago and he was big, fat and hairy. Quite like the Pope actually, apart from his fine head of hair.'

'Ye're all wrong ye ignorant slobs!' A woman was standing on a seat wringing her hands and mouthing at us in a brassy voice. 'She's a woman I'm telling ye! A big strong power-dressed woman with glasses! I saw her.'

'Yes, and I suppose she is black too, and wears a "Save the Whales" button, and is eating a macrobiotic sandwich,' I said, but I don't think anyone heard me. They were too busy holding forth about what God looked like, but I think in the end we had to agree that nobody had really seen him. A few people might have got clocked if it wasn't for the angelic police keeping a close eye on us. Adam said he was a bit pissed off with all this theology stuff, although he did admit he was getting excited at the prospect of meeting Him. If it was only that He was the biggest cheese of all in the history of the world and that he wanted to satisfy his own curiosity.

When we saw the people in the pen next to us getting up and being organised into queues we knew our time was not long off. They were moving along so briskly that it dawned on me there could have been more than one judge, or else he had a few assistants like Santa Claus at Christmas. Or else again that you didn't get much chance to plead your case. Maybe it was all written down in the Big Book of Judgement and your fate was sealed ever before you got to the bench.

A strange quietness came upon us and the banter died away as we were told to stand up and be ready. This was the day and the hour of which we didn't know. I gritted my teeth and a weird tingle went down my spine when we were ordered into our queue for the long walk along the beaten track of the green, green grass to where our home would be decided. Now was the time for examining our conscience for the last time and weighing up the good with the bad. I remembered all my vices with some affection – pride, covetousness, lust, gluttony, anger, envy and sloth – but I couldn't say I was particularly good at any one of them. I also had many virtues, but it would be a vice to enumerate them. If there was sometimes evil in my heart there was also charity. I had no machine with which to weigh them against one another, however. How could you measure cigarettes and whiskey and wild, wild women against doing your duty and saying your prayers and voting for the government? Anyway, I'd soon know the answer. The same questions must have been bugging Adam because he had got very quiet. Or maybe he had just remembered some big bad sin that had escaped him until now.

The queue stretched out as far as my eyes could see, yea, nearly unto the ends of the park. There seemed to be still millions packed into the pens on each side of us, and needless to say they weren't green with envy. We got prodded with batons every so often to keep us moving, and I even saw one guy getting thumped by an angel for dawdling. After a while the judgement area began to become clearer but we were still too far away to guess what was happening. I was amazed how quickly we were moving, almost like a Sunday afternoon stroll.

'Make way! Make way!' a guard shouted at us and pushed us to one side rather roughly. A huge lorry was making its way along the track and was being driven by two angels. Its siren went through our ears like glass cutting through bone. It swept past us in a swirl of dust and we were allowed crawl back into the centre of the passageway.

'What was that all about?' I heard one guy ask impatiently.

'Did you not see what was on the back of the lorry?'

'Skins,' said somebody or other, 'I saw another few lorries just like that when I was coming in a few hours ago. One of the angels told me they were sheep- and goatskins. We are all given one or the other of them after sentence has been passed – depending on where we are going.'

'It was mostly goatskins so on that last load.' This much was spoken by a large lugubrious mountain of a man for whom any kind of a fitting would have been a professional challenge for the heavenly tailors. 'They must be in great demand.' This much spoken resignedly.

I should have been surprised by the petty conversation going on all around me but I wasn't. Life was too important to be left to the philosophers. I overheard one woman asking her friend if she thought God would be as good-looking or as sexy as Brad Pitt, but then she suddenly remembered she had forgotten to hang out the wash. What looked to me like a fancy rugger-bugger was discussing his golf handicap with another guy who was only interested in car upholstery. A priest ahead of us spent his time looking into a pocket mirror and combing his hair. There were, of course, others whose faces were ashen and drawn as if they knew that the wages of sin were about to be paid. On the other hand there wasn't much point in throwing yourself on the ground with wailing and gnashing of teeth.

'Would you mind if I went first, I mean go ahead of you?' Adam asked me as we began to approach the judgement throne.

'Would I mind?' I said incredulously. 'Of course you can. Those few seconds might make all the difference between everlasting torment and an eternity of celestial bliss. Go ahead!'

By this time we could get a good look at the judgement throne and at God himself. There was a huge angel standing on his right-hand side. He was wearing formal evening clothes with a green carnation in the lapel. A big leather-bound volume was open before him. There were a few other angels lolling about the throne also, but they were obviously getting bored with everything. Two lines stretched out on both sides behind the throne, but it was clear that the one to the left with the people wearing the goatskins was much longer than the other. The angel giving out the sheepskins was more or less redundant.

Our ears were pricked up the closer we got to the interrogation. It was difficult to follow every word at first but I soon began to get the gist of it. It appeared that God would say something, and then the angel would ask a question and the person would be whisked away after that. I found myself hiding behind Adam, but I knew that I couldn't get away with that for long.

'I see you're not wearing a tie,' I heard the angel say to a teenager just a little bit ahead of us, 'go to hell!'

'In the hoond of the cakes, purples or aflamed with cloaks,' I heard God say to the next guy, 'foreplicate that forum, O Muckle.'

'God says that you're all right,' the angel said stretching out a hand towards the heap of sheepskins, 'I'm told you went to the right school.'

'Oily zounds!' God said, looking at the nice young woman who was next, 'bydeboils alanna buddy hast a vein twinpeekaboozies and whale clonking doanlast didgiridoo. Dattbee a through ghostspill, you bedda boleweevil me!'

'Bye-bye, farewell, *auf Wiedersehen*, goodnight,' said Muckle the angel to her, 'he didn't like your clothes. Next!'

The next up was an elderly man who looked scholarly and pious. He took off his hat and curtsied politely.

'Who the fofo costuree me?' said God, 'a burden in the bosh wotnot joice addlerup pound for pound. Amon aye right? "Botchito ergo sum" samizdat I pray tallways.'

'Put on your goatskin,' said Muckle, 'you ain't got no ticket for heaven. You should have bought it when you had the chance. It's too late now.'

'Whoroo the lustie dabbie plunking the plushty?' God asked the next young girl, who had obviously put on her very best dress for the occasion. 'Or oroo the chickybiddy whang woofs the woost waddie joke buzzer? Whorov the squidge and squish ovdat hah!'

'He has just asked you if you know the third law of thermodynamics,' said Muckle interpreting for her, 'but as it is perfectly plain that you haven't the least clue you better fuck off down to hell.'

I was looking very carefully at the priest because if anyone had a passport he surely did. He stood up directly and made a brief humble bow before turning his head ever so slightly towards the judgement throne. God looked kindly down on him and smiled widely from ear to ear showing a perfectly formed row of golden teeth.

'I om the Ram of Gob,' he said, 'and thee pissed a balls prophet. The dimple tooth you buggerup and you bekim alloy for alloy. As furry high cough earned ukan shakov. Jew dearme?'

'But I spread your word, I preached the gospel,' the priest protested, as he didn't really need a translation, 'I kept all the commandments, I followed the truth ...'

'The truth?' Muckle snorted, turning towards God with a query on his brow, 'what is this truth thing of which he speaks?'

'Oh, snot dafflechut to hobble that,' said God, 'the tooth is sumpty this, and sumpty that and sumpty sumpty else.'

'He says that you were consistent,' smiled Muckle handing him a goatskin, 'and that the truth is sometimes this, and sometimes that and sometimes the other. But you were too tied down to see that. Off you go!'

The next guy didn't have any identity card, the woman who came after him didn't have enough money, and the man after her again didn't have the right measurements. They were all damned. A quiet woman just ahead of us was given the benefit of the doubt, because she had nice curly hair and was a distant relation of a nun. She skipped away happily and Adam took three steps up to his judgement.

'Come closer,' grunted Muckle, as Adam seemed a little reluctant and not too surprisingly. I was afraid I'd soil my pants when I came next, or else no words would come out of my tongue. My mouth was dry and my lips were cracked and my knees were weak. Adam didn't appear to me to be so frightened, but he never was one to let the big occasion get him down. I could see everything perfectly clearly now. The big stream of the damned going off to the left and vanishing down a hole in the ground; the small trickle going off to the right and ascending a shining escalator which appeared to vanish in the blue of the sky. I could also see the face of God and it was clear that he was enjoying every minute of this. There was a permanent smile glued to his face as of somebody wielding power that had never been wielded before. He would take off his glasses every so often but it didn't change the serenity of the smile. If it wasn't this particular day and this particular afternoon that would never come again even the most gloomy person would have to enjoy the balmy sun and the easy warmth.

'Fot is the fie or the fairfore ovoo?' God asked gently, 'or waywho war wore rootings, whore poor ants?'

'He is asking you what you have ever done for the environment?' said Muckle, a bit grudgingly.

'I have to admit that I have done nothing at all,' said Adam in a kind of a pally way. I thought this was quite inappropriate. 'I mean really nothing. And come to think of it I have done nothing either for my neighbours. Or for the state, or for the church, or for the poor, or for the third world. In fact, every single thing I have ever done has been for myself alone. Just me. That's me in a nutshell.'

'Well that's it so,' said Muckle. 'Take yourself off to hell. We have no time here for liars. I know that you once gave a penny to charity when you were a little boy and you could have spent it on sweets. You lied, you bastard! You're not as bad as you make yourself out to be. So fuck off out of my sight.' He handed him a mangy-looking goatskin on which there was a large brown stain.

Adam took it from him quietly and was just turning away when I heard the bang. I spun round and saw two holes in

God's chest with his life's grace pouring out of them where he had been plugged. I saw the gun in Adam's hand and Muckle drawing the sword from his scabbard. I saw another hole blown in Muckle's skull as he flopped to the ground. I saw the other guards coming with their swords at the ready but they were no match for an automatic pistol. I heard the death rattle in God's throat as if he was trying to say something to the world as he was leaving it. I wasn't really able to understand them as he never was a very clear speaker. I thought it was something like 'Dally the Llama, it is spaghettini' but I couldn't be sure.

'Now that God is dead,' Adam said to the world the following day, 'we may as well begin all over again. And this time there will be logic and order and justice and peace.'

We gave God a good funeral and made sure there was a respectable crowd there. I couldn't attend myself as I was too busy making sense of our new world and was beginning to enjoy the power.

Translated by the author.

ADAM'S STORY

Alan Titley

When Adam was nine hundred and twenty years of age, or thereabouts, it dawned on him that his eyes were growing weaker, his voice was failing, his bones were creaking and arthritis was setting in to his joints. He began to notice that the birds of the air died, and the beasts of the field, and every living thing that walked upon the earth. And he thought that such a death might come his way also.

His children often came to visit him, and their children, and their children's children, and their seed and breed and generations. There was nothing he enjoyed more than telling them stories, because stories at that time were young and new and had not been heard before.

'The one about the snake, tell us that one,' said Tufit, who was a bit of a hard man, 'I always liked that one.'

'No. Something more personal,' said Ruthy, 'like the way you met your wife, how it was for you, the first time ever, and that kind of stuff. I have to hear this again.'

'Forget it,' said Harum, 'the one about the apple. I want the apple!'

'It wasn't an apple anyway, you twit. It was a pear.'

'An orange!'

'A fig!'

'A pomegranate!'

Adam had forgotten the details by now it was such a long time ago, and he nearly believed his own version. But there was one thing he hadn't forgotten and it welled up in him like a lump in his throat. He had to get it off his chest to set the record straight.

'Look,' he said, 'it was like this. There was no apple. In fact, there was no fruit at all. Well, of course, there were olives and cherries and berries and lemons and grapefruit and plums and nuts and bananas and growths for which we have no name yet. But none of them were forbidden. There was no forbidden fruit. We could eat them all ...'

There was a great silence that was only broken by a groan from far off which was like unto a myth slowly dying.

'And the tree in the middle of the garden?' asked somebody tentatively.

'There were many trees in the middle of the garden, wherever that was.'

'And the snake?' someone else tried.

'No snake either. Or if there was it was just as friendly as every other animal.'

'And God?'

'He never chucked us out of the Garden. We left ourselves voluntarily.'

Some of the older offspring began to get a little angry, not just because they had had to swallow this stuff for hundreds of years, but because they had to earn their bread by the sweat of their brow. They looked down at their calloused hands, and at the scars and cracks and warts and weals, and they felt more deeply the pain in their lower backs.

'OK, let's get this straight, once and for all,' said

Aleymbibic, who appeared already to have the makings of a good committee chairman. 'Do I take it that what you are saying is that yourself and our great-great-great-great-great etc grandmother were living together in this fabulous garden, that you had sweet fanny adam to do except to frolic beneath the trees, no stroke of work to do, food and sweet sustenance dripping from the trees, the beasts of the world as your slaves and servants – and then one fine day you just upped and fucked off out of Paradise leaving it all behind you?'

'That's about it in one go,' said Adam, with a certain relief now that the truth was out.

'And why were you so dumb-assed stupid, to leave the Garden of Paradise, to leave all that behind you?' asked most of them in chorus.

'Because it was boring, of course,' said Adam, 'boring, boring, boring.'

Translated by the author.

CHAOS THEORY

Alan Titley

The woman lived in the big city with her lovely family and devoted husband. She was very religious and lit the brightly-coloured candles and prayed at the correct shrines. She paid her dues and lowered her eyes and covered her head. Her faith was as deep as the earth and as firm as the foundations on which the city was built.

Some charlatans who had often predicted the end of the world also predicted the earthquake. In the former they were so far wrong, but in the latter they were absolutely correct.

The city was devastated in seven seconds flat. Bridges buckled and buildings collapsed without warning. The earth opened and swallowed up thousands. Thousands more were crushed under flats and offices and houses. Thousands more again just vanished, never to be heard of by the few who remained.

By some fortune or happenstance the good woman survived under two beams of wood which marked an X over her head. Her lovely family and devoted husband were not so lucky, meeting various sticky and gruesome ends which are too awful to recount.

It wasn't then that her faith was crushed just like her lovely family and devoted husband, or that it vanished like the thousands who were swallowed up in the cracks of the earth. It was more that it was shaken like the foundations of the city which a few seconds before seemed so secure. And it being shaken she required answers.

She betook herself to her religious advisor and sought from him the final and ultimate answer as to why her city had been destroyed and her family killed. He told her it was the will of God. 'Who knows,' he said, 'maybe something worse would have happened if it had not been for this.'

She was puzzled at these words, being a simple but good woman, as she didn't know how God could have willed the destruction of her lovely family and devoted husband, and even more so it puzzled her that anything worse could have happened than the earthquake which devastated her city. So she went on her way perplexed and dismayed.

She then went to her ministering priest who told her it was a punishment for all of their sins. But she was puzzled at these words because she knew she hadn't sinned since she knew the meaning of the word and likewise she knew her family and friends to be righteous and proper and good-living and God-fearing. So she continued on her way still perplexed and dismayed.

She then met a guru with a long beard who had studied the latest physics at the cuboid glass-covered state-of-the-art university (now demolished) at the edge of the city.

'You want to know the reason for this earthquake?' he asked, 'The real and ultimate reason and not something about faults in the earth's plates?'

'Yes,' she said, 'I want to know why.'

'The reason for the earthquake which demolished our city,' he said, 'is because an ant farted in Tierra del Fuego.'

Translated by the author.

JESUS WEPT

Alan Titley

And it came to pass in those days that Jesus was born in Bethlehem of Judea, to Mary and to Joseph, the woodworker. And after he was born she placed him in swaddling clothes because it was cold and she laid him in the manger. And she rejoiced in her motherhood, and commenced to hum to him, and to sing, and to chant lullabies to put him to sleep. And she gave him sustenance and comfort and spent much of the day and most of the night hugging him and minding him, because he was her first-born. And the child looked back at her, and hummed, and sang, and made small gurgling childish noises. And she rejoiced even the more that he did not whinge and cry and cry his guts out as most children do. And Joseph rejoiced even more again, because Joseph was a man, and would not be expected to put up with the whinging and mewling and puking and screaming of babies.

And some short time after that, when King Herod discovered that the so-called wise men from the East had fooled him, and had gone their own way without informing him of where the infant Jesus lay, he ordered and decreed that every male child under two years of age in the vicinity of Bethlehem be put to death. And the soldiers zapped through the town and ripped the children from their mothers' arms, or swept them from where they slept, or from where they played, and they hacked the heads off some of them, and chopped the legs off others, and extracted the nails from the fingers of yet more just for the fun of it, although the more humane of them drove their stakes through the children's hearts so as to get it over with quickly. They did this because they were soldiers of the emperor, and they were just obeying orders as soldiers of the emperor do, and just because there was a lot of big fat money going on the corpse of every child, no matter what weight they were.

But by this time the baby Jesus and his mother and Joseph were safe and sound in Egypt. It hadn't been that difficult for them to escape, since Jesus was always a good child and had never cried nor bawled nor whinged.

But when the souls of the dead innocent babies left their bodies, they sailed through the air to whatever place the souls of dead innocent babies go who have been murdered without mercy. But as they floated through the air one of them looked down on the infant Jesus, and showed him his smashed skull, and his bloodied hands, and his extracted nails, and his little soul that had never been allowed to grow, and his pure undefiled body that had never had the opportunity to contemplate sin, and his spirit cried aloud to Jesus, 'This is all your fault!'

And the infant Jesus looked up at him from the straw in his manger and his eyes filled up with tears.

That was the very first time that Jesus wept.

Translated by the author.

ANGELA BOURKE writes in Irish and English. Her books include *The Burning of Bridget Cleary: A True Story* (1999); *Maeve Brennan: Homesick at the New Yorker* (2004); *By Salt Water* (1996), and, as Angela Partridge, *Caoineadh na dTrí Muire: Téama na Páise i bhFilíocht Bhéil na Gaeilge* (1983). She is one of the eight editors of *The Field Day Anthology of Irish Writing, Vols 4 & 5: Irish Women's Writing and Traditions* (2002). Now emeritus professor at the UCD School of Irish, Celtic Studies, Irish Folklore and Linguistics, she lives in Dublin.

DEIRDRE BRENNAN is a bilingual writer of poetry, short stories and drama. She has eight collections of poetry, the last being *Swimming with Pelicans / Ag Eitilt fara Condair* (2007) and a collection of short stories, *An Banana Bean Sí* (2009). She has contributed to *The Great Book of Ireland* and is the recipient of many prizes including a Poetry Ireland Choice of the Year, *The SHOp* poetry translation prize, Oireachtas awards for poetry and radio drama, and a Listowel Writers' Week short story award. Her stories in English have been broadcast on national radio.

FIONNTÁN DE BRÚN is a writer and lecturer in Irish at the University of Ulster, Coleraine. His collection of short stories *Litir ó mo Mháthair agus Scéalta Eile* (2005) was awarded the Bord na Leabhar Gaeilge Oireachtas prize. His other published work includes *Seosamh Mac Grianna: an Mhéin Rúin* (2002), a critical study of the work of the renowned Donegal writer, and an edited collection of essays on the history of the Irish language in his native city, *Belfast and the Irish Language* (2006). He is currently working on a novel in Irish.

SÉAMAS MAC ANNAIDH is the author of six novels and two collections of short stories in Irish as well as a number of Irish and local history books in English. He has been writer-in-residence at Queen's University, the University of Ulster and most recently at NUI Galway. He lives in Belcoo, County Fermanagh with his wife and daughter. His interests include genealogy, travel and cooking. As an Irish-language writer he has been keen to explore new forms and subject matter – his most recent novels have been set in Turkey and France.

SEÁN MACMATHÚNA is from Kerry. He writes in both Irish and English. His short story collection *The Atheist* (1987) was nominated by the Arts Council for the European Prize in Literature. His play 'The Winter Thief' was produced by the Abbey Theatre, and two novels in Irish are still floating around out there.

ÉILÍS NÍ DHUIBHNE writes novels, short stories, books for children, plays and non-fiction, in both Irish and English. Her short story collections include *Blood and Water* (1988), *Eating Women is Not Recommended* (1991), *The Inland Ice* (1997) and *The Pale Gold of Alaska* (2000). Among her literary awards are the Bisto Book of the Year Award, the Readers' Association of Ireland Award, the Stewart Parker Award, the Butler Award and Oireachtas awards. The novel *The Dancers Dancing* (1999) was shortlisted for the Orange Prize for Fiction. Her latest novel for young people, *Dordán*, was published in 2010, and her new collection of short stories, *The Shelter of Neighbours*, in 2011.

As a creative writer from the Aran Islands, DARA Ó CONAOLA displays a deep understanding of the cultural inheritance of his people, drawing from that rich source in his writing. Among his books are *An Gaiscíoch Beag* (1979), *Mo Chathair*

Ghríobháin (1981), *Night Ructions* (1990), *Sea Mission/Misiún ar Muir* (1992) – a bilingual fantasy staged by Na Fánaithe at the Galway Arts Festival and Expo 1992 in Seville – and *Ag Caint le Synge/Talking to Synge*. Noted for his distinctive style of writing, humorous, imaginative, and full of mystery, he has also written stories and plays for children.

BRIAN Ó CONCHUBHAIR is Associate Professor of Irish Language and Literature at the University of Notre Dame. His monograph on the intellectual history of the Gaelic Revival, *Fin de Siècle na Gaeilge: Darwin, An Athbheochan agus Smaointeoireacht na hEorpa* (2009), received the Oireachtas na Gaeilge non-fiction award and the ACIS award. He has edited *Gearrscéalta Ár Linne* (2006) and *Why Irish? Irish Language and Literature in Academia* (2008) and is Series Editor of *Kerry's Fighting Story 1916–1921*, *Rebel Cork's Fighting Story 1916–1921*, *Limerick's Fighting Story 1916–1921*, and *Dublin's Fighting Story 1916–1921* (all published in 2009).

MICHEÁL Ó CONGHAILE was born in Conamara, County Galway. He has published poetry, short stories, a novel, plays, a novella and translations. Among his awards are the Butler Literary Award; the Hennessy New Irish Writer of the Year Award; the Stewart Parker/BBC Ulster Award; multiple Oireachtas Awards and a Writers' Week/Listowel Award. His books include *An Fear a Phléasc* (1997), *Sna Fir* (1999), *An Fear nach nDéanann Gáire* (2003), *Cúigear Chonamara* (2003) and *The Connemara Five* (2006). His works have been translated into various languages, including Romanian, Croatian, Albanian, Slovenian, German, Polish, Macedonian and English. He established the publishing company Cló Iar-Chonnacht in 1985.

DAITHÍ Ó MUIRÍ's first short story was published in *Lá* in 1993. His first collection of short stories, *Seacht Lá na Díleann*, was published in 1998. This was followed by *Cogaí* in 2002, *Uaigheanna agus Scéalta Eile* the same year, and *Ceolta* in 2006. He is a native of County Monaghan and lived for a number of years in Dublin, but since 1990 has lived in Indreabhán, County Galway.

MÍCHEÁL Ó RUAIRC was born in Brandon in west Kerry. He is the author of three collections of poetry and of ten novels in the Irish language. He has also published one collection of poetry in English, *Humane Killing* (1992). His poems have been published in various anthologies, including anthologies for Junior Certificate and Leaving Certificate. He has won numerous Oireachtas prizes for his writing through the years, and his first collection of short stories for adults, *Daoine a Itheann Daoine*, was published by Cló Iar-Chonnacht in 2010. He has started working on a collection of short stories in English.

GABRIEL ROSENSTOCK is the author/translator of over 150 books, mostly in Irish. He is a member of Aosdána. Among his awards is the Tamgha I Kidmat medal for services to literature. Books in English include *Haiku Enlightenment* and *Haiku, the Gentle Art of Disappearing* (2009), the anthology *A Treasury of Irish Love* (1998), and his début volume of poems in English, *Uttering Her Name* (2009). His vast output includes radio plays, work for TV, novels and short stories, and among the anthologies in which he is represented is *Best European Fiction 2012*, published by Dalkey Archive Press.

DÁITHÍ SPROULE is a native of Derry City. After ten years in Dublin, where he obtained his master's degree in Celtic Studies at UCD and worked as an editor at Folens Publishers, he moved to Minnesota, which has been his base ever since.

He is a singer and guitarist, and has toured and recorded extensively with Skara Brae, Altan, Trian and many other traditional muscians. He has also taught courses in Old Irish and Celtic culture at UCD, and at the University of Minnesota and the University of Saint Thomas in Saint Paul. His book of short stories, *An Taobh Eile*, was published in 1987.

ALAN TITLEY is the author of five novels, four collections of stories, several plays, some film scripts, a few poems and works of scholarship. Much of his literary work has been translated into other languages, and has received numerous literary prizes. He writes a weekly column on current and cultural affairs for *The Irish Times*. He is Professor of Modern Irish in University College Cork.

COLM TÓIBÍN is author of many books including the novels, *The South* (1990); *The Heather Blazing* (1992); *The Story of the Night* (1996); *The Blackwater Lightship* (1999), shortlisted for the Booker Prize; *The Master* (2004) shortlisted for the Booker Prize; and *Brooklyn* (2009). His short fiction collections are *Mothers and Sons* (2006) and *The Empty Family* (2010). In 2006, he won the International IMPAC Dublin Literary Award, the world's largest literary prize for a single work of fiction, for *The Master*. He is Professor of Creative Writing at the University of Manchester.

Angela Bourke's 'The Dark Island' first appeared in its original Irish, 'Iníon Rí an Oileáin Dhorcha', in *The Field Day Anthology of Irish Writing, Vol. 5: Irish Women's Writing and Traditions* (2002).

Deirdre Brennan's 'The Banana Banshee' first appeared in its original Irish, 'An Banana Bean Sí', in the newspaper *Foinse* in 2004 and in the collection *Nuascéalta,* Seán Ó Mainnín, ed., in 2005. It later appeared in the author's *An Banana Bean Sí agus Scéalta Eile*, (2009).

Fionntán de Brún's 'How the Author Died' first appeared in its original Irish, 'Mar a Fuair an tÚdar Bás', in *Litir ó mo Mháthair Altrama agus Scéalta Eile* (2005).

Séamas Mac Annaidh's 'The Three Clichés' first appeared in its original Irish, 'Na Trí Chliché', in *Féirín, Scéalta agus Eile* (1992).

Seán MacMathúna's 'The Queen of Killiney', 'The Atheist' and 'The Doomsday Club' first appeared in their original Irish, 'Iníon Léinín', 'Págánaigh' and '"Habann Tú Banana"', in *Banana* (1999). 'The Quizmasters' first appeared in its original Irish, 'Na Quizmháistrí', in *Ding agus Scéalta Eile* (1983). The stories were first collected in English in *The Atheist* (1987).

Éilís Ní Dhuibhne's 'Rushes' first appeared in its original Irish, 'Luachra', in *Scéalta San Aer,* Cathal Poirtéir, ed. (2000).

Dara Ó Conaola's 'Sorely Pressed' first appeared in its original Irish, 'I nGleic', in *Comhar* in February, 1979.

Micheál Ó Conghaile's 'Whatever I Liked' and 'The Word Cemetery' first appeared in their original Irish, 'Mo Rogha Rud a Dhéanamh' and 'Reilig na bhFocla', in *An Fear nach nDéanann Gáire* (2003). 'The Stolen Answer Bag' and 'The Closeted Pensioner' first appeared in their original Irish, 'An Mála Freagraí a Goideadh' and 'Ar Pinsean sa Leithreas', in *An Fear a Phléasc* (1997).

Daithí Ó Muirí's 'Great and Small' first appeared in its original Irish, 'Beag agus Mór', in *Seacht Lá na Díleann* (1998).

Mícheál Ó Ruairc's 'Cannibals' first appeared in its original Irish, 'Daoine a Itheann Daoine', in *Daoine a Itheann Daoine* (2010).

Gabriel Rosenstock's 'The Khrushchev Shoe' first appeared in its original Irish, 'Bróg Khruschev', in *Bróg Khruschev agus Scéalta Eile* (1998).

Dáithí Sproule's 'There is Somebody Else Living Here' first appeared in its original Irish, 'Tá Duine Eile Ina Chónaí Anseo', in *An Taobh Eile agus Scéalta Eile* (1987).

Alan Titley's 'The Judgement' first appeared in its original Irish, 'An Tríú Scéal Déag', in *Eiriceachtaí agus Scéalta Eile* (1987) and in English in *Fourfront* (1998). 'Adam's Story', 'Jesus Wept' and 'Chaos Theory', first appeared in their original Irish, 'Faoistin Ádhaimh', 'Íosa ag Gol' and 'Chaos Theory', in *Leabhar Nóra Ní Anluain* (1998) and in English versions in *Parabolas: Stories & Fables* (2005).